THE LOST
EL DORADO

W. Michael Gazdar, DC

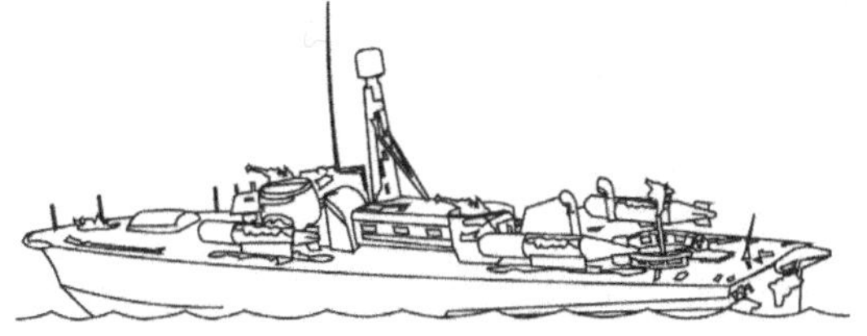

Copyright © 2002, 2007, 2023 All rights reserved.
W. MICHAEL GAZDAR, D.C.
Walnut Creek, California

Second Edition

Published and distributed by:

JMCC
2021 Ygnacio Valley Road, Suite C-204
Walnut Creek, California 94598
Phone: (925) 939-2225
Fax: (925) 939-8017
Email: michael@gazdar.com
Web: www.michaelgazdar.com
      www.gazdar.com

This book is a work of fiction. Names, characters, places and incidents are products of the author's imagination, or are used factitiously. Any resemblance to actual events or locals, or persons living or dead is entirely coincidental. No part of this book may be reproduced without the author's written permission.

Cover design by Emily's World of Design
Back cover photo by CBJ Gazdar
Layout by Courtenay Design Group
Formatting update by Jen Henderson of Wild Words Formatting

Publishing Assistance: Eric Van Der Hope

Cover Art Assistance: Courtesy of PT Boats, Inc. Museum and Archives, Germantown, TN, USA. Alyce Guthrie, Exec VP

Library of Congress Control Number: 2023900514
Gazdar, Michael

THE LOST EL DORADO

ISBN 979-8-9875183-0-4 Trade Paper Edition

Printed in the United States of America

Dedicated to my wife, Teri and our children, Christian, Brandon and Jonathan. Thanks for giving Daddy love, support and belief. Your happiness and laughter got me through the hard times more than you will ever know.

ACKNOWLEDGEMENTS:

No one writes a book alone. I would like to take this opportunity to thank my friend and original editor, Rob Cook. He has constantly been there to make timely literary suggestions and corrections to the original manuscript. I would also like to thank retired Captain Jeff Bailey, Tish Gallegos and Martin Rollinson. I also need to thank the people at PT Boats Incorporated for their assistance in helping me keep it real.

THE AMAZON JUNGLE, 1495

THE DRUMS BEAT SLOWLY, enchantingly, mixing their steady beat with the wet, steamy jungle heat. Midnight would soon be here, and with it, the new moon would be full overhead. The Chibcha Indians controlled this entire valley - in this case a valley in the clouds. This tributary river, in the mountains of Colombia, emptied itself into another river, which finally flowed, many miles later, into the mighty Amazon.

The Indians swayed to the beat. They numbered over two thousand and were actually split into two major tribes. The larger tribe was the more violent and aggressive of the two. They controlled the gold taken out of the mountains and rivers and were sworn to protect it. They made sacrifices to the gods of the river and to the gold. They were fierce warriors who hunted and fished.

The smaller of the tribes, were more intellectual and labored growing food, coffee and, of course the coca-leaf. Many years later cocoa would prove to be this area's richest export, even greater than gold or rubber. They also were the architects and main builders of the fabled City of Gold, The El Dorado. They did not participate in the rituals to the river, not because they were unbelievers in the gods - they worshipped them too in a more peaceful manner, but rather because they were frightened of their more fervent cousins. They did not believe in sacrificing their young women to the demons of the river the others had bred.

Just as one large bull can become the dominant species on a ranch over time, the larger tribe bred the deadly piranhas to become gigantic. They started many centuries before - this was now 1495 A.D. At first the Chibcha interbred the piranhas with the much larger, but peaceful pacu fish. Then, as their offspring got larger and larger, they inbred them with the much larger pirarucu, which grew over 12 feet in length. These fish retained the deadly traits of the piranha and fed on anything which entered the water. They still hunted and attacked in packs, just like their small, gold colored cousins, who were also kept as pets. However, when there was a shortage of food, they were known to turn on each other. Then only the largest and fiercest, would survive to attack again.

The keepers of the fish, were regarded with respect only second to the King and the Medicine Man. While the giant piranhas never became emotionally attached to their keepers, it was whispered that before one could become a keeper, he had to swim unharmed across the river in the middle of the fish. Because of this, many perished and only a few survived.

The natives stood in a ring formation surrounding four young Indian girls. All were virgins and were approximately sixteen years of age. The men and women around them began chanting a sacred text, paying homage to the river. As they stood near the water's edge, they could see and hear the splashing and bubbling sounds the giant piranhas made, even though they were over a hundred yards away.

The girls, with their backs to each other, moved in a counterclockwise direction, while all the others around them moved clockwise. As the drums beat faster and faster, all the dancers shifted their rhythm to keep time. The four young girls, naked except for small loin cloths, began to spin, even as they still moved in a circle, within the larger circle.

Thousands of Indians outside the circle, and stationed in the trees of the jungle, looked on. Suddenly the drums stopped. Everyone froze. The Chief, easily seven feet tall and over four hundred pounds stepped inside the circle. He moved over to the four girls, who were frozen with their arms above their heads. He took coca leaves out of his pouch and placed several leaves inside the mouths of the girls. His action was unnecessary. They had been given leaves to chew constantly since early dawn and scarcely knew where they were. The cocaine had completely numbed their minds to their intended fate.

The drums began to beat again slowly, and the circle parted. The chief led them down to the river. Each had a male attendant to lead them, as they could barely walk. The surging and bubbling water had moved within a few yards of the procession. Suddenly the Chief raised his hands above his head and clapped twice. Without notice the girls were thrown in the water. There was no noise except the mad churning and thrashing of the water. It was over in less than four seconds. When the water returned to its calm state again, the full moon broke through the clouds and flooded the valley with golden light. A sign, it was said, that the river gods were happy again.

******

CHAPTER I

BEGINNINGS

PROFESSOR JOHN WAALES pushed his chair back from the computer screen and rubbed his eyes. He'd studied this same satellite map for over three hours without a break. There had to be a clue here somewhere. Between the satellite photos, with their low resolution, and the various old and new maps he had in his possession, he should be able to crack this mystery. It was already three in the morning on Sunday. He had been at it since 11:00 the morning before, almost without any breaks for food or rest. One particular map, had occupied his mind for the last 30 years.

When he was 14 years old, he became inflamed with the story of the El Dorado and its lure of lost gold. The treasure was reputed to be millions of pounds of pure 24 karat gold. It wasn't just about the gold, however. As a professional archaeologist, he was lured to a greater extent by the promise of a lost civilization - a civilization which existed long before the black gold of rubber which had been taken out in the late 1800's and the "white gold" of cocaine of the late 20th

Century. Both brought ruin to the honest, hard-working people of the region, not to mention what cocaine did to the world as a whole. This ancient civilization may have existed before the time of Christ. He had to find the answer – his professional reputation depended on it.

John Waales was a striking man of over six feet, possessing brown hair, peppered with grey and a distinguished looking face. He had a body which would make men half his age proud. He kept in shape playing racquetball and working out at the gym at the University of California, Berkeley, where he was a professor. He also played golf twice a week at the Olympic Club in San Francisco. He had been a member since he was a child and was a past club and junior champion.

He thought about the inherent dangers of a safari in the Amazon Basin. There were the snakes, alligators, caiman, poisonous bugs and of course the piranhas. There was a legend that the old kings of the region bred the meat-eating piranhas - already fierce in their own right - with that of their more docile, but much larger vegetarian cousins the pacu. Not content with their size and ferocity, they then cross-bred them with the giant river fish the pirarucu. This produced a fish, which weighed over 500 pounds and was easily two feet thick and over twelve feet long with razor sharp teeth and a penchant for eating intruders of all kinds. Fortunately, it was just a legend. Literally millions of people had gone down the Amazon and its tributaries without ever seeing one. He rubbed the stubble over his face. Of course, no one had ever found the Lost City or its fabulous cache of gold either.

He stood up and replaced the cap on his fifth bottle of

Anchor Steam Beer. It was still half full and he decided he'd had enough. He had to get some sleep before the sun came up. His daughter Kimmiko would be expecting him to get up early - she wanted to go to church. This was a new thing for her, but, as with everything else since her 18th birthday, it took on a major sense of urgency. They would be attending services at Northbrae Community Church, a local nondenominational church at the top of Solano Avenue in Albany, the quaint, bedroom community next to Berkeley.

He took one last look at the map before shutting down the computer. There was one spot which didn't match up with the satellite photos he had obtained. Somewhere there was an access off the river, which led to the promised land.

He decided to turn in. Once the lines on the map started to wiggle on their own, it was time to get some sleep. As his head hit the pillow, his last thought was of Kimmiko. She had grown up so fast - and, for the past six years, without her mother. He often asked himself whether anything was worth living for after Lindsay had died. If it wasn't for Kimmiko, and his responsibilities at the university, he might have taken a few too many of his prescribed sleeping pills a long time ago. He had heard it said that you should be afraid to die until you have contributed something significant to the world. And, since all of his previous escapades had been failures, he should not be ready to die. He looked over at Kimmiko's and Lindsay's pictures together on the wall. If only they could spend one more night together playing The Game of Life, like in the old days - The Game of Life, now there was some irony there. His mind blended into the shadows as he drifted off to sleep in his bed.

****

Kimmiko Waales looked at her watch. It was already half past three in the morning - as best as she could read the clock by the dim light from the dwindling fire in Billy Johnson's fireplace. His home overlooked the entire Bay Area. It was a new residence, built on the spot occupied previously by a house, that had died a nasty death in the Oakland Hills firestorm of 1991. Billy was the hotshot Quarterback for Cal and was given this 4,000 square foot home on the hill for the enormous sum of $100 per month - just for being able to throw a pass 75 yards straight and lead his team to a Rose Bowl spot. Who said the alumni weren't generous?

She quietly pushed the covers back. They were both still naked. Like most guys she had slept with, once it was over, they fell asleep immediately. The good ones at least kissed you first - but not Billy. He was simply out to catch the new freshman, or in this case the new fresh-girl, on the block. She looked at him as he slept. He was a good lover. He had a nice body and told her he had a secret weakness for Asian girls. Even though Kimmiko was only half Japanese, she looked more Asian than Caucasian.

As she stood up, she caught a glimpse of herself in the mirror on the wall. In spite of her tender years, she was quite striking to look at. She had a really great body - thanks to all those years in high school, of taking out her aggressions in the weight room and on the track. She went to the bathroom, and, more by feel than sight, found a towel and cleaned herself up. She stepped out into the bedroom, and, by the dying embers of the fireplace, quickly got dressed in its fading light. She glanced over at the sleeping Billy. For a moment, she thought about her dad and her dead mother, feeling very sad and lonely. She shouldn't be looking for love in all the wrong places, or so some song went. She knew Billy wouldn't wake up for several hours, because of all the beer he went through and her dad would be asleep, thinking she was already in bed at home - he never checked.

It was time to leave. She slipped out the back door and into her small Honda Civic. As the motor started up, her radio instantly came on. She pulled out and down the hill to the sounds of Neil Young's *Cinnamon Girl.*

****

With a sigh, Dr. Jack Paris unzipped his white smock and tossed it on the guest chair in his private office. He had been working virtually nonstop on patients since before 6:30 this morning and it was now well past 8:30 in the evening. He glanced over at his desk by the telephone. There were at least 30 messages written on those little white and blue message slips all lined up in a row starting from early this morning. Some were from the East Coast - three hours earlier than he started out here in the West. His chiropractic assistant, Denise, had lined up the messages and call-backs in their proper order of importance - which meant that the messages from his wife Lisa - there were seven - were on top. Denise had told him to stop several times and call her, but there were always insurance adjusters, attorneys, patients and other doctors to call.

Somehow Lisa always seemed to be underneath the pile of priorities. No wonder she never wanted to be underneath him anymore he thought sarcastically.

He sighed heavily. His wife, son and daughter were slipping away from him. He wondered if any profession had a higher divorce rate outside of Hollywood. He glanced at the other messages. They would wait. He grabbed his black leather jacket, eschewing the black sport coat which complimented his gray slacks. It was late February and still cold in the San Francisco Bay Area city of Walnut Creek. He decided to call home from his car phone. He jumped into his red Porsche – 14-hour work days had some advantages - and jammed out of the parking lot. For someone who had just turned forty-three, he was still in great physical shape. His wife, Lisa, had been a bodybuilder and they both worked out five days a week in their home gym and also at the Olympic Club in San Francisco, where they were members. He speed-dialed the home number and Lisa picked it up on the first ring.

"Are you just starting with a new patient or are you finally on your way home?" she asked without bothering to say hello or ask who was on the line.

"How do you know this is me and not your boyfriend?" Jack asked laughing.

"Because my boyfriend always rings twice - oops, I guess I picked it up too soon, Honey!"

"I'll tell you what. I'll let you pretend it is your boyfriend tonight after we turn off the lights, if you forgive me for being lost in my work again."

"Okay," she said, "but he lets me keep the light on." She

realized she was taking the joke too far. "Come home quick. I've been alone all day."

"See you in about ten minutes," Jack said. He hung up. They were still able to banter, even though there was an element of strain in their relationship with his long hours and her feelings of despondency since the kids went away to junior high school. While they were in grammar school, she had been instructing them at home in a formal homeschool program through their school district. They had been safe from the stupid schoolyard shootings, unprofessional teachers and all the problems which plague schools, both public and private.

Lisa had suggested a marriage counselor and they had decided that they should reexamine their priorities. The office, as stimulating as it was intellectually, and as grateful as the patients were, would not substitute for the solace attained by a stable and happy home life.

Jack sighed. Another night of feeling guilty and hoping there would be some love and closeness tonight. Life had changed when the HMO's arrived. They never saved the employers or health subscribers one dime, but they helped to rob the doctors of their legitimate fees and the patients of their right to decent health care. The 1990's and early 2000's would forever be known as the decades which tried to stop the rise in price of health care, but only resulted in the preservation of the bottom line for the insurance companies and the HMO's. Ten times the stress and work for one third of the fees. Always stress and dilemmas. His son was 14 and his daughter was 12. All this, and teenagers to boot. His last thought as he pulled into his driveway on the quite street in Walnut Creek, was the old saying, "That which does not kill you, will surely make you stronger."

******

The overhead fan in the strip bar turned slowly, vainly trying to stir up a breeze against the jungle heat. It was real heat - wet and sultry. There was an element of evil, which came with it. Bill Treese slumped over the small table, which served as the break between him and the dark brown girl on stage. He was oblivious to her. The young Peruvian with the hard body danced her dance without emotion for the fifth time that night. First the top came off and then the bottom, night after night. The only way she made any real money was later after the dance had ended. Usually, the customers were nice...

Bill snored soundly. He was on his seventh double Jack Daniels tonight and would soon awaken to down a few more. In spite of the heavy drinking, he was still the best riverboat captain on the Continent. This small place was his hangout and generally his home. He would sleep for awhile, drink whiskey, possibly eat the greasy mess they served up here, and finally go to sleep in one of the back bedrooms – ones usually reserved for more strenuous activities.

Fortunately for Bill, he had always shared his money with the local owner and the working girls. He didn't even ask for return favors. It was one of those unusual relationships like sharks have with remoras - symbiosis - each living with the other in harmony and cooperation. He gave his money with free will and they took care of his needs, whatever they were.

Everyone was happy... .

Bill jolted awake with a scream on his lips. He was dreaming about Vietnam again. In 1970 he was the captain of a Patrol Boat, River, also known as a PBR, Mark II gun boat in the Mekong Delta. A little over 31 feet long and around seven tons, a PBR could get up and move at over 40 knots, with some modifications. Bill won the Navy Cross for bravery in action and even the Purple Heart, which got him a trip back to the U.S. and ended his career. Unfortunately, typical of many vets of his generation, he returned home to a country divided, a broken marriage and a wrecked career. Over time, for some unknown reason, the jungles of Southeast Asia, had become his home. After three years of trying to restart his life in the United States, he pulled up stakes and fled to the jungles of South America. There he became a riverboat captain and a tour guide, while fighting a new enemy, the U.S. Government, for his pension, service awards, fuel, ammunition for his boats and everything else. He also fought against the local government until he found a way to make peace with them, usually through bribes and long term, regular payments. Although, he thought on many occasions, it was really the same enemy all along. Politics never changed, only the faces of those in power changed.

His dream was always the same. The boat pulled up slowly to the dock. The village was peaceful. Bill went below decks to attend to the Captain's Log while the first officer made fast the moorings. Bill looked up from his writing through the porthole, to see several Vietnamese teenage boys and girls approaching the boat singing. They were all dressed in common Vietnamese attire, carrying small bundles of vegetables and fish in their arms. This scene was peaceful and had been played out a thousand times at a hundred different ports on this river. Suddenly, the children parted to reveal a beautiful woman / child, naked to the waist, long, long flowing jet-black hair partially covering her front, carrying a large covered basket in front of her. She came forward to the boat and offered it up to the deck. Bill, looking at her from below deck could not see whom she was handing it to, but assumed it was the deck officer. His gaze tarried for a moment on her young body. The heat made the scene seem surreal. She stepped back and turned to the other boys and girls, bowing low - then spun back around and crossed herself while dropping to her knees. The teenagers broke for the village. Everything became very clear in a moment for Bill. His heart leapt to his throat and he turned to move up the ladder to the deck. His scream of warning was drowned out by the tremendous blast of a detonating C4. Everyone on the deck was killed instantly. He was spared from death by the heavy steel bulkhead over the ladder. It took the Navy welders over 30 hours to reach him and another 12 hours to cut him free from the wreckage. His dream was always the same after that - he had just cleared the bulkhead before the blast came and was met by his crew - all dead and glad he came to join them... .

Bill's eyes came into focus as they usually did, in spite of the smoke, dimness and loud music. He saw Roxanna dancing lewdly in front of four underage kids from the local town. They were in obvious lust as she ground her pelvis toward them. He was grateful that he wasn't dead and not at the mercy of his crew, whom he felt he'd failed. He was, however, almost just as depressed to be here, in the jungles of Brazil, alone and virtually without friends or hope.

******

Thomas Reichen looked at his watch. The drop was late. He looked up and out toward the tops of the trees. The jungle here in Colombia near the Amazon River, was thick, but he was on the edge of a small clearing. This spot was well known to the local drug smugglers, but not many in local law enforcement knew of its whereabouts. That made him smile. Many of the local police were also paid informants.

A light rain began to fall and the wind moaned softly down through the trees. He listened intently. There was only the wind and the occasional screech of a monkey deep in the jungle. He wanted a cigarette, but didn't dare light one. He had learned his discipline a long time ago while in the Central Intelligence Agency. His fellow agents always knew he was a cool customer, who could carry out even the most horrendous duty without remorse. Not that he was a bad person back then, but somebody had to clean up the crap of the world and he excelled at it. A master of kung fu and ju-jitsu, he was athletic and strong. He wouldn't back down from a fight, preferring to meet it head on and kill or be killed.

Of course, that was when he wasn't a bad person. Now he was. He was an assassin, a killer and a drug smuggler. He lied, slept with informants, cheated on drug deliveries and had made this little part of the world his to command - even if his dictatorship was rather silent to the rest of the world.

He didn't hear the noise behind him, but rather felt a presence. By habit he had his left hand inside his rain jacket next to his 9 mm Baretta. In the sleeve of his right hand was a small, concealed, spring loaded sword. It only had a pointed tip; it didn't need an edge. He looked upwards again and quietly gauged the striking distance. If there were one or two, he would use the sword. If there were more, he would start firing. Time stood still as he listened and looked upwards. He glanced down at his feet and saw a blurred, cloud enhanced shadow. Had he been facing five degrees to his left he never would have seen it.

Suddenly, he spun 180 degrees, dropped into a fencer's stance, triggered the sword and stabbed at the first target. The tip of his sword hit the surprised native drug runner between his fifth and sixth rib on the left next to his sternum - a fatal blow. The assassin dropped his Uzi machine gun with a loud grunt. Without hesitation, Thomas moved his shoulders slightly to the left and hit the next target, a native about six feet tall, with the exact same blow. This one had a sawed off shot gun and tried to get off a shot, but he fell to his knees and collapsed without a sound. Not more than one and a half seconds had passed.

Thomas dropped into a crouch, pulled out his pistol and aimed it at belt level. He spun around in a 360-degree circle-twice quickly to assess any possible nearby targets, then twice more at a much slower rate to check the larger area for any back-ups. There was nothing but the moaning of the wind and the light patter of raindrops that were beginning to fall harder. He looked over at the two dead men. He pushed them over with his boot, mindful of their weapons, which he kicked away.

They were both of South American descent, probably in their early twenties or late teens. Such a waste he thought. He knew that they had been told he was an easy mark and they would take his money and keep their cocaine for themselves. They would then split it with whichever Cartel member who was behind the heist. Had they survived, they would have hoped for a better assignment - perhaps guarding the drug king's family members.

Thomas noticed there was indeed a briefcase on the ground - it had hit a mango tree root and broken open when its owner had stumbled in his appointment of death. He flipped it over with his boot- this required much more dexterity than moving the men. There still might be a booby trap inside. These guys liked to make a drop and line the inside with explosives just for kicks just to eliminate the competition. He opened it carefully. The case was empty except for one kilo bag of white powder. He reached inside carefully. The deal had been for 10 keys and he knew he was about to be ripped off. Plus, the drop was supposed to be from a helicopter specially outfitted for near silent flying. He stuck one fingernail into the bag and sampled the powder. It was cocaine, and very good quality. These two had either snatched the other nine keys or had never been given it in the first place. It made him laugh to think about when he was so interested in finding the lost gold rumored to be high up in the mountains around Bogota - the El Dorado! He spat on the ground. He lifted up the kilo bag of cocaine. This was real gold! Pure, white and worth more per ounce than platinum. To hell with the stuff you mined.

He picked up the dope and his own briefcase filled with

cash - this was supposed to have been a legitimate deal - and backed slowly out of the clearing towards the tributary stream, which held his small outboard boat. Perhaps he would find their boat too and relieve them of the rest of the coke, if there were any. He glanced at the two lifeless bodies grinning up at the darkness. They wouldn't need it he thought.

******

Robin Quigley pushed away the heavy volume into the pile of other books on the library desk. He pushed it hard enough to stir up the deeper layers of dust in the creases of the leather covers. He slumped in the heavy wooden chair and crossed his arms over his face in exhaustion. His sigh reflected a mixture of relief and disgust. He had been sitting in this library at U.C. Berkeley since 7:00 a.m. and it was now 8:30 p.m. They would close soon. There were five floors of books and desks above the main floor, where the checkout was. He had eaten little, subsisting on three slices of Blondies Pizza and several Cokes. He had rested even less, working while he ate. The payoff was he now finally had the answers he needed.

Robin was 24 years old, good looking, intelligent and in great physical shape. He had graduated from Stanford across the San Francisco Bay and was finishing his Master's Degree in Anthropology at U.C. Berkeley. He was actually in the Ph.D. program and had earned his Master's as a matter of course. He had an interest in archaeology, but he was no Indiana Jones. He was much more interested in cash rewards and long, lost bounty, not the quest for knowledge. He had been inspired by stories of finding fabulous wealth in exotic places, not digging for elusive bits of data for days on end in dusty libraries.

However, he had found a couple of fringe benefits in the last few months, however. One was his bosses', Dr. Waales cute daughter Kimmiko. He had noticed her when she was only 16 and knew she would develop into a beauty. He was looking to get into her mind and her body very soon. She was 18 now and very available. Also, he had been getting private offers of profitable ventures via email transmissions from a very wealthy gent who was interested in archaeology which paid excessively- much more to Robin's liking. The problem with Dr. Waales was, he was just too damn interested in pure historical knowledge, whether it was profitable or not.

****

The song blared on the cheap juke box - all the words were in some Middle Eastern dialect, but he knew them well enough. It was Robert Palmer's song, *Money for Nothing*. Leon Scarborough noted with a grim laugh that he was looking for that same concept - money for nothing. He, however, would have to work for it for a change. It wasn't like he didn't have enough; he was a millionaire many times over. But he wanted to be a billionaire, and he didn't want to wait for his old man to kick the proverbial bucket. He never believed in the practice of working for money - it was his to wield and command. In fact, if Pops would just die a little quicker, it was his plan to take over a major computer company, or more likely an internet company, with the family fortune. It never occurred to him which one, and, in fact, he didn't even like computers, but he did like money.

In spite of his relative youth, he was only 25, he had already turned to the fat of middle age. He detested exercise and hated sports. His only true talent was, he was that he was a genius on the computer and had helped his father build up their computer company since he was eight years old. His talent was legendary in the industry, but after working for his dad for over fifteen years, he was burned out on his daily toil. Much to his father's dismay, he now only took amusement in collecting royalty money and blowing it on sex, drugs and rock and roll. Because of his looks and his porcine size, he generally had to flash an equally substantial roll of cash at the local bars he frequented in order to ensure some company. Two of his favorite places to pick up young coeds near the Berkeley campus were Larry Blake's, a blues club and also Henry's, an upscale bar on Durant Avenue one block south.

He sat back and took in the scene. The two hit men drank their tea slowly. He did not know their exact nationality, but he knew they were from the Middle East somewhere. It didn't matter. They were not working for one country, but rather a group of religious extremists from several Middle Eastern countries. Their hatred for the Infidel Americans translated across political, religious and geographical boarders.

Leon knew he was in charge of this operation, but a deeper part of him conceded that these men would just as soon cut his throat, dump him in the desert and return to their tea without even a moment's thought. He may have had the money, but they had the power. The strange thing was that he knew that they knew, that he was relatively helpless, but they acted as though he was totally in control. They showed him complete courtesy and respect, and did as he directed them. For all his posturing as the head of a wealthy business, they could smell his weakness. He was fearful and cocky at the same time. His bravery was financed by his wealth and his arrogance was defined by his luck. He never knew that these people knew who he really was - the son of an American billionaire.

Leon had been quietly following the findings of a certain professor of archaeology at U.C. Berkeley. This Cal professor, Dr. John Waales, was hot on the path of the famed El Dorado and its reputed city of pure gold, located in the heart of the Andean Mountains near Bogota. All of the world - at least as far as the scientific community was concerned - knew that Professor Waales, had a new theory that proved that the city was really located up a small tributary of the Amazon Basin. This location, if it really existed, would serve as the perfect site of a satellite relay and a new type of laser weapon, give or take a few square miles. If he could become a part of that safari, he would be in position to set up the site and, if gold were found, bring back a nice healthy bonus and get well paid by the terrorists. They needed his knowledge of computers to enable them to set up the relay and a properly integrated defense system.

The plan was to move into the jungles of Brazil, down the Amazon River into Colombia and find the lost city of the El Dorado. There they would appear to take out a fortune in gold, but their real mission was to set up an undetectable satellite link and jamming system, coupled with a laser defense system. This would serve as a strategic point to stop America's defense capabilities with the development and deployment of Star Wars, the program started by president Ronald Regan in the 1980's and seemingly abandoned. However, companies within the U.S. continued the development and the deployment of a of a Star Wars-like system, also known affectionately as Star-Track. Although an obvious play on words, Star-Track had the capacity to catalogue and follow all forms of ballistic insults - from missiles to bullets-throughout the world. Research on this project continued through the 1990's and into the new Millennium without the knowledge of the American people. In fact, the entire scandal of the Chinese Government's theft of knowledge related to the U. S. nuclear research program - which rocked the Clinton Administration - was played up by those wishing to continue funding Star Wars. The subsequent revitalization of the Star Wars prequel movies provided fuel and fascination for Americans and for official funding of the once defunct project.

Once the new Bush Administration came into being in 2001, there was an immediate increase in the cry for an end of the 1972 Anti-Ballistic Missile Treaty, created by Richard Nixon and Henry Kissinger with the then Soviet Union. Since the new millennium, at least eight nations had acquired nuclear missile capabilities, making the U.S and her allies vulnerable to attack. The terrorist attacks on American soil, the resulting war against terrorism and then the war in Iraq, simply heightened tensions throughout the world. There was now a need for a new defense system.

Whatever the means, it was effective. Star Wars was now a covert reality and Muslim fanatics and certain right-wing officials - who existed separately from the official Middle Eastern governments - wanted a strategic footing in their own defense system. This small position in the Amazon basin would provide a silent base for American defeat. Once this occurred, they would align with the Chinese and the Godless Communists. Although they cited that their mission was to spread Islam, the real reason was the eventual dominance of the world. Working with the Chinese at first, their goal was to bring all of the countries of the Middle East, Europe and the Americas under their control. They would work to establish the obvious supremacy of their faith and eventually give the world two choices - Communism or Islam. They believed the world would eventually choose God over Communism and they would then overthrow the Chinese. Their powers desired absolute control, first in the Arabic world and secondly in the entire world.

Leon had also been in touch with a certain Thomas Reichen, a man who was on the inside in the Amazon Basin. Reichen had valuable assets and knew important people. He also knew about discretionary warfare. Here was a man who knew the area, the drug trade and the people who could help Leon get his foothold in the exact location he needed with little fuss.

Leon, in his pitiful vision, simply saw himself as the richest man in the word - with his billions guarded by his newfound friends. He sat back and relaxed as the tea he'd spiked with his hidden liquor, forbidden in this part of the world, warmed his stomach and fogged his mind.

******

The screeching of several monkeys in their cage on the Amazon River dock caused Aleta to spin around suddenly. She looked sadly into the cages, which held over 100 of the animals. Even though she was only twelve years old, she thought more like an adult every day. Her mother had noted that since her father had left them last June, she had grown more and more sensitive to the suffering of others. Even with the pain of her daddy not even saying good-by to them, she found the courage to feel for other's who suffered, putting aside her own grief to help an orphaned puppy or a kitten now and then.

Her mom, Gwendolyn, sat their bags down on the dock. They would soon be leaving this place and going back to her homeland of Colombia. She was sad that her husband, Santiago, had left them for some *putah*, but she had to admit, she had seen the signs coming. She had been reluctant to tend to his manly needs ever since Aleta had been born. At first, she used this as an excuse, but after two years had passed, even her gynecologist had said that it was unnatural for her to not desire some sort of sexual relations with her husband. For her part, she couldn't understand why the thought of him on top of her seemed so utterly undesirable. Perhaps it was because they never talked and he never seemed to care for her beyond the normal comforts. The last time he brought her flowers was on their wedding day. He never wanted to kiss her and showed her affection only when he wanted to have sex. Perhaps, after more than ten years, this was why she no longer desired him. So, unavoidably, he sought pleasures elsewhere.

She sighed. Her daughter was beautiful, inside and out. Even now, she placed some of her water from a plastic bottle into the small opening in the cage of the screaming monkeys. They surged forward, as they fought for the liquid and lapped it up greedily. It was very hot on the docks. They would soon board their boat and leave for the villages and countries up river. She shivered in spite of the hot sun. She could hardly wait to get away from this place and start their new life.

****

As she hung her head over the sink in the small lavatory of the Brazilian dock, Marianna Andolino was sure she was about to lose her breakfast. If only it were morning sickness again and her now deceased husband holding her head, she knew the world would be in its right place. Unfortunately, her husband was gone and she was no longer pregnant. Miscarriages often happened to first time moms. But the loss of the two month old baby inside her paled in comparison to the loss of her husband. She was simply retching from the fact that she was now alone and was about to leave the life she had known for the past seven years. She held onto the sink tightly for a few seconds until she regained her balance. Then she washed her hands, gathered her things and, smoothing her hair in the tiny cracked and dirty mirror, stepped gingerly out onto the deck.

She looked out at the peaceful river, quiet and dark at the early morning hour of 7:00 o'clock. In stark contrast, there was chaos all around her on the dock. People were moving in every direction. Boats were lined up and it seemed as though everyone had something to sell. The din of the voices was almost too much for her ears. She moved quickly down the dock until she spotted the steamboat, The Aleutian. It stood over three stories tall and had another deck below the water line. Painted white a long time ago, the river had ravaged it to a dull gray and brown.

She thought back to her life in New York seven years before. She was a native New Yorker and had lived there all her life. Still a very young looking thirty-two years of age, she had the dark skin of her Sicilian father and the angelic face of her Chinese mother. She had fallen in love with Dave, who was an executive in her firm, from the first moment she had seen him. They had five perfect years together, before he had succumbed to leukemia. She never thought it would happen to her, but it had. At first, they thought they had beaten the disease, but it spread faster and farther than even the doctors imagined. He quietly passed away in the hospital two years ago while she held him in her arms. She had never known such sadness and loneliness. Even in the two years that had passed, the pain was still unbearable.

Her company had been great. They had given her a choice of any assignment. She decided on the Amazon Project and had taken over a year to study and map it out. After relaying her report to the Board, the company decided on a location deep inside Colombia. There was a tributary to a tributary to the Amazon, which could be a good spot. The only problem was that there was no solid mapping or photo recon of the area to give them reason to believe this spot would be a good satellite relay station. They were proceeding on topography, latitude and longitude alone. It was her job to find and secure the spot. The intense planning and thought process she had to do on this project helped to keep her mind off her loneliness. But she never forgot Dave. Not for a single second of her life.

She shivered, in spite of the early morning heat and humidity. Picking up her bags, she smiled sweetly at a native porter. He bowed graciously and a little too gallantly.

"Por favor, senorita, may I be of assistance?"

She smiled. "That one over there, she said gesturing with her chin, "May I tip you *senior?"*

"It is up to you, *señorita,* but *mi esposa y mi niños* would be *mucho contento.*

She smiled again. As she led him toward the boat, she pulled out what she hoped would be a very good tip.

****

The morning shadows broke across the strong face of Mondo Salvaci'on. In his first instinct of wakefulness, he feigned sleep, keeping his eyes shut. He motionlessly sensed his surroundings. He felt his wife, Cornelia beside him, and between them, the very tiny body of their new baby, Damien. Their older children were scattered about them, wrapped in brightly patterned blankets, on the soft dirt floor of the hut. He cracked his eyes open slightly. Instincts told him it was about two hours before sunrise, but the early morning light played tricks within his hut. Their hut was larger than most, as befitting those who were leaders. He thought about their lives here in the jungle. They had the right to be leaders in the City of the El Dorado, but they had been banished. He led those who were the new, young breed, who wanted to learn about the outside world. They wanted more opportunities for their children, which had been denied to them as they grew up. Occasionally they would find a magazine from the outside, which would be inspected carefully by every member of their tribe. In the past, they were sacred warriors of the Chibcha Tribe of the upper Amazon. Now they were simply enemies of the bad Chibcha's who ruled The City and the gold.

He felt Damien move ever so slightly and suddenly felt Cornelia, awake from deep sleep in that rapid way mothers always do. She turned over with her hand on his back. She listened intently for a few seconds, decided everything was all right and then turned over and went instantly back to sleep.

Mondo smiled. He doubted she even woke up, but her instincts were so extraordinary, that she didn't even need to. The baby, along with their other six children, was completely safe. So was he, he imagined and decided to close his eyes for just a few more minutes. When dawn came, he would be moving quickly. It was time to hunt the pacu fish. He shuddered at the thought of the giant piranhas. He was glad he, his family and the others had left the evil tribe and their devilfish. No one was safe from his father-in-law and brother-in-law. Somehow, he thought, in his last seconds of wakefulness, there had to be a way to reunite the tribe and get rid of them both. They were the bad ones standing in the way of everyone's happiness and prosperity.

****

Chief Sanek Omagua sat on his royal throne in the Temple of Worship and looked down at the fish. They were indeed large. Every once in a while, one would come up to the surface as if in greeting and show a huge toothy grin. It was as if they were thanking him for the sacrifices, yet inviting him in at the same time. He shuddered slightly. Only his son, Prince Sajava, could handle these monsters. He had raised his sons to be good to the fish and to carry on the tradition. Sajava would, of course, lead the way after he, the Chief, was gone. He sighed. He had no idea what would become of his other son Damien. Named, of course, by his dead wife. He looked like her and acted like her. So much so, that he seemed to be the twin of his older sister, Cornelia, who had betrayed them all. He had no desire to kill or exile his son, like he had done to his daughter, but he hoped that there would be others who would do it for him. He felt, in his old age, he would not have the heart to do it, but he hoped his culture would be preserved.

The Chief looked out at the fish and his son, Prince Sajava tending to them. He was waist high in the water as they swam around him, jumping out of the water to take food from him by hand. It was almost surreal, thought the Chief. They never even bit him, but would play with him all day or all night, if they could. One constant remained the same, however, Sajava would never enter the water if the fish were ravenous. For even they, could not control their beastly appetites. They had to be fed regularly and fully, or else no one was safe. They were truly carnivorous, but were smart and would feed when and where they wanted. They could not be tamed and could not be persuaded to do their tricks for them, but like other relationships in the jungle, which form over many years or many centuries, they would respond to attacking enemies, as long as they were sufficiently hungry.

The Chief's eyes blinked rapidly as he looked over the message, which had been sent to him via their contacts down the river. There were white men coming who wished to purchase gold and, more importantly, the coca plant, which they used in the same fashion, as did the Chibchas, as a relaxing tonic. While the Chibchas, simply mixed the leaves with lime and chewed it all day long, the *Americanos,* mixed it with gasoline and other bad things and sniffed it up their very noses. He shuddered again. They were so *stupido,* he thought. It didn't matter. His tribe would get what they wanted in guns, medicine and supplies and the *gringos* would get some trinkets to make them happy. And, if they protested, they would become fish food, he thought with a smile, as he watched a large fifteen footer leap out of the water to grasp meat out of his son's hand.

****

Like his brother-in-law many miles away, Prince Damien also lay next to his wife, Patricia', and their newborn daughter. The baby's name was Cornelia, oddly, enough that they had named their children after each other, as they had not seen each other in over fifteen years and did not know, at least on a conscious level, if either was still alive. He moved closer to his wife and baby. Cornelia was their first child. Damien, barely twenty years old, still had his mother's passion for life and love. He could read and did so with great gusto. Somehow, his mother had found books for him, written in both Spanish and English. Through his father, he had limited association with outsiders, but he was fluent in both languishes - an extraordinary accomplishment. Damien was devastated when his mother died ten years ago. She could laugh and make everyone else around her laugh. He always felt, though that she died of a broken heart, as her husband, his father the Chief, would never let their daughter, Cornelia come back to the tribe. He had threatened her husband Mondo with death, and that meant he would be fed to the fish after the Chief and his witch doctor had their fun with him.

He shuddered. Why was he thinking such horrible thoughts, so early in the morning, he wondered? Life was joyous now. He loved his wife and he loved his baby girl. He snuggled close to them and inhaled deep her baby soft smells of innocence. His brother and father may despise him, but these two loved him and from them he would draw his strength.

****

The late morning sun beamed through the green window slats in the back room of the bar. Their fiery streaks scraped across the raw eyelids of Captain Bill. In the first instant of wakefulness, he instinctually threw his forearms up across his eyes for *protection. In this, he found a moment of peaceful darkness.* He may have slipped gracefully back into the arms of another Jack Daniel's induced sleep-hangover, but there was a sudden loud knocking at the door.

"Capitán Bill! Capitán Bill!" He recognized the young voice of his friend Manolo Santos, who cleaned up the bar in the morning and readied it for the noontime crowd, seeking relief from both heat and thirst. "There is a phone call for you from California." Bill did not answer. "The *United States!*" he added for emphasis, as though this fact alone would rouse his sleeping *amigo.*

"Okay, okay Manolo," mumbled Bill, "Just let me get my clothes on.

He threw back the covers and with a slow hip thrust, rolled out of bed onto the mud floor. He reached out instinctively for his pants and shirt lying at the end of the bed. He didn't bother with underwear, it was too hot and, besides, he liked being naked most of the time when no one was around, unless you counted the House Girls, and they obviously didn't care. He did put on shorts when he was on board his boat, a habit left over from being in Country, otherwise known as Vietnam. His uniform then was not exactly spit and polish, but then, neither was that damn war.

He slid into his deck boots and walked out the door into the main barroom. It was already hot and steamy, just like the jungle, he thought wearily. The phone was off the hook, on the bar top. Manolo was already back at work stocking the shelves of liquor. He smiled at *Capitán* Bill.

With both his parents working two jobs and with Manolo's money from this job, they had a roof over their head and were able to feed the other five younger children. Bill smiled back. He knew Manolo worked hard for the bar, but he also helped the girls in the back with whatever they needed to help them get ready for the day. They paid him separately of course in their own friendly way.

Bill picked up the receiver. "Yeah?" he grunted.

"Hey you drunk!" came the happy familiar voice of Professor Waales, "Whatcha doin'?"

Bill groaned loudly. "Hello John," he said, "how's life in the real world?"

"Couldn't be better buddy. How's that boat of yours doing? I could maybe use a bit of a transport and you were the first charter I called."

"Sure," said Bill, "I'm the only charter you called because I'm the only captain dumb enough to take you into places you shouldn't go." He reflected a minute, "Your always there when you need me though."

Professor John Waales chuckled. He looked out over the peaceful San Francisco Bay from his living room in the Berkeley Hills. He imagined what it was like in Bill's part of the world, an entire continent away. "You still driving that McHale's Navy boat of yours, or have you gone modern on me?"

"Well, that depends," answered Bill.

"On what?"

"When you come down of course. It seems the military here and several private citizens up your way would like to own a genuine World War II Patrol Torpedo Boat, especially one that still fires all its original weapons. I've been keeping them off my back with my medals and," he cleared his throat loudly, "my political connections and all, but it seems the price is going up and I'm still in hock to that loan shark I told you about the last time we spoke." He paused and added sadly, "I don't know about this time old buddy. I might finally lose her."

John grew quiet for a moment. He knew Bill had bought the rotting hull and broken engines for a song and spent the next dozen years fixing, restoring and re-outfitting her. That boat was Bill's last possession in his life and, in fact, it was his life. When he was not driving tourists up and down the Amazon in one of the U.S. Navy's original PT boats, he was ferrying scientists and adventurers up into parts of the Amazon and its tributaries most people would never see. Those journeys were usually fraught with danger - either from the local animals and reptiles or from the natives, sometimes both. Here, they rarely took prisoners, but the sound of a .50 caliber gun was usually enough to get their attention and send them packing. Even the drug runners, as powerful and organized as they were, avoided Bill.

"Listen buddy," John said, "I've finally got a good line on some hard data. I really need you for this trip and I can't take some damn party boat. You tell me what it's going to take to get you and the 109 and I'll get it to you."

Now it was Bill's turn to think. He really liked John and loved his daughter Kimmiko as though she were his own. In fact, he had introduced John to Kimmi's mother, Keiko over 20 years ago at a Viet Nam Navy five-year reunion reception. They had been smitten with each other and fallen deeply in love.

"Look, Bro," Bill began, "you're the last person I would turn to, to fix my problems." He scraped his painful, raw eyelids with the back of his forearm. The hangover was very bad now that he was standing upright and thinking about his problems, and confessing them like some feeble altar boy. It was grating on his nerves. "I mean, just do the charter like we always do and that will be okay," he said trying to regain some dignity.

John would not be put off. "Bill, this is hard for me too, okay. I need you to go a long way up the river - a very long way up. Are you listening? I need all your skills as a captain and as a navigator. I also may need your skills as a marksman," he added quietly.

Bill was getting the message. The word marksman between them could only mean one thing - assassin. It was their code word for the possibility of serious trouble on the river. Neither one of them were killers, but they had been forced to do their duty in-country, and the rivers around the Amazon Basin were literally like those in Southeast Asia. Dangerous and unforgiving.

"It's the El Dorado again, isn't it?" Bill asked.

"I could tell you, but then I'd have to kill you," John joked. Both men laughed. It broke the tension. "How much do you need right now and how much do you need to complete the miss…, I mean the expedition?" John asked.

Bill didn't hesitate. "Ten thousand right now would help me out of a big hole and if you could get me five to ten after, that would be great, uh, how many days are we talkin'? Guess I should find that out before I go shootin' off my mouth."

"Seven to fourteen days, tops, hopefully. In and out just like the old days, eh? But I would like to sweeten the deal though. I'll wire you twenty-five thousand today and also an extra ten for your friends in high places. I don't want any questions when we land. I'll give them my passport and the passports of my people, whoever they are, but that's it. I want someone you trust to bring us to your boat. Once you start making preparations for as much as four weeks on the water, I don't want you to leave the boat, *comprende?* I want this to be very safe and quick, just like going through the express line at the supermarket. No one looks at my equipment and I want all papers, documents, travel destinations, security clearances made out in advance with the destination left blank. We'll fill it in when we get there. At the end of the trip, I will pay you another twenty-five thousand dollars, or twenty percent of what we find, whichever is greater. In fact, I will put the twenty-five thousand in your account with a post-dated check one month from today, guarantee issue. Is it a deal?"

Bill was 100% sober now, but he still had the headache. "John, it's a deal, but why the formality? We're friends, right? I can make all that happen. Don't worry," he said with a slight scowl.

John was not fazed at all. "Listen, buddy. I love you, okay? We go back a long way. Most people in life don't know what it's like to live, fight and die together. We do. Right now, I'm playing for very big stakes. Not just financially for me and my daughter. It's for my professional reputation and maybe I'm just a little bitter that all this work and sacrifice in the world of academia hasn't paid all that well. This job could be life or death for us both. You know the people where we're going like to play rough." His tone softened a little. "Please forgive me, but I know you have had some problems there. This has nothing to do with how I feel about you. But on a more personal note, I might be bringing Kimmi along and I can't take any chances. I don't want her to come. It's too dangerous, but she has her mother's stubbornness, and she's become my right hand in my research." He paused, "And she's got my sense of adventure of course. Again, please forgive me, but I have to make absolutely certain that you know you will be well paid, and mostly in full before we depart. I really need that extra ten thousand to get into the right hands. I need to trust you, Bill - you're my only hope."

Neither man said anything for the next several seconds. Finally, Bill said, "It will be great to see both of you together again. Does she still look like her mom?"

"Spittin' image." John relaxed. The job would be done according to plan. Captain Bill had his faults, but treachery wasn't one of them. He would never let anything happen to Kimmiko, and he would die fighting to protect her.

"Still have the same bank account?"

"Still the same. I'll look for two deposits of twenty-five and one of ten thousand and I will make sure the *El Presedente* and *Capitán* of the Guards is given your respects. Is there anyone else I have forgotten?"

"You would know best *amigo*. Just remember that if you need any extra right now for outfitting, I can get to you, but tell me now."

Bill thought a moment. "Could you send and extra five thousand? I may need some extra ordinance for this mission."

"Yes," John replied, "Oh, and I almost forgot. Do those old depth charges and torpedoes work?"

"Sure, as long as I do the prep work. What are you going to do, nuke some poor village and extract gold from the people's teeth?"

John grimaced at the analogy. He had just watched the DVD version of *Schindler's List*. "No, but I may want to be prepared if we see any of your river friends up that way."

"John, the giant piranhas are just a myth. No one has ever seen them in recent times and I know some pretty weird old dudes from up country here. They all say it's just a myth."

"Well, good buddy, you know how I feel about little piranha and the caimans and snakes and red bellied frogs and gar fish and pirarucu and…," they both were laughing, "tarantulas. So, get me some weapons, okay?!"

"Okay, John, I'll call you in a couple of days and they we can figure out a hard target date for all this to happen. Good-by!" He hung up the phone and looked down at his worn deck boots. He was no longer laughing

****

The one nice thing about first class flying, thought Leon Scarborough, was that you got to eat and drink as much as you wanted, for as long as you wanted. His family was rich, but his father was still too cheap to spring for a Lear Jet. Maybe after this little adventure he was on, they might have enough for at least a small Citation Jet.

As usual, he was the first in line to disembark. He always got the closest seat to the hatchway leading out of the aircraft. Sometimes on the overnight flight, he could induce a young female passenger or a lonely flight attendant (they were more reserved these days), to keep him company when the lights were out. He sighed. Not this trip. Because of shortages, he had had very little liquor and no female companionship since he'd left the Middle East four days ago. However, now he had some useful information to give his father, but he had to meet this guy Thomas first. He sighed again. Always complications. Thomas was supposed to be a real professional assassin, but he had no idea how to get in touch with him. His contacts he had just left, assured him that he would be met in New York upon landing.

The 747 hit the runway and taxied to the international terminal without incident. He had to go through Customs, a process he hated, but this should be simple, as he had very little baggage and no souvenirs. The plane taxied in, halted and he disembarked. An hour later, he was picking up his one checked in bag when a hand reached out and touched his arm. Stifling a scream, Leon whipped around and found himself staring at a large, light brown-haired man. He was smiling and looked completely at ease.

"Jeeze, you startled me," Leon whined to the big man, who had stuck out his other hand in greeting.

"Thomas Reichen, at your service!" He grinned and looked down at the frightened, smaller young man.

Leon shook his hand guardedly. "Can we go somewhere private to talk?"

"Of course," Thomas replied, "I have a car waiting and we'll be in the back alone. No one will hear our conversation." It was a lie. Thomas had his car set up to record everything.

He had played this game many times. Once you delivered the goods, the rich, the powerful and the druggies had a very short memory of how much they had promised you in the beginning. In this case, it was unnecessary, as Leon's father and the people from the Middle East had already paid him very well, plus more to follow. In fact, this job was so lucrative, he could stop all his other little investment games and ride this one into retirement. He smiled inwardly. This tape was just a precaution, just like everything else.

He and Leon stood at the curb. A black stretch limo pulled up and, with a gesture from Thomas, they got inside.

"Have a drink," Thomas said good-naturedly. I'm having one!" He poured Old Bushmills Black Bush Irish whiskey into a large glass filled with ice. He handed it to Leon and then promptly filled another for himself. Thomas could drink great quantities of alcohol and not get so much as a buzz. This had also served him well over the years as he extracted more and more information from people, especially those he seduced sexually. The game was fun, no doubt.

As they toured the streets of Manhattan, Thomas and Leon had a nice chat about how Leon would be in charge and how they would split the profits 70% to Leon and 30% to Thomas. Leon excitedly laid out his plan for gaining the local native's cooperation, which Thomas had secretly done over six months before. They stopped in Brooklyn for Italian food at a place Leon knew. He loved playing the host in New York City. After a couple of bottles of rich red wine, he even got Thomas laughing hysterically at his mimic of a New York Gay, Jewish, Italian man by the name of Jewseppi. Leon, of course, had no way of knowing that Thomas' mother was of Italian Jewish descent from Brooklyn and that Thomas had had lovers, both male and female. Thomas knew from the start that Leon would not last long in the jungles and swamps of the Amazon. His dilemma was how to get rid of him and keep his father's money and capital flowing. He smiled as Leon became louder and bolder with his comments, causing the other guests in the restaurant to turn and whisper at his obvious rudeness.

****

Kimmiko couldn't sleep. She finally gave up around four a.m. and got up to make coffee. It wasn't her tryst with Billy that was keeping her up—she figured he wouldn't even acknowledge her on campus after their first date—but he had. He'd invited her to share a mocha with him and his friends at the Café Roma on Durant Avenue, and he'd said that he really wanted to see her again. No, the problem was with her father.

He'd told her last Sunday after church that he was heading back into the Amazon. She'd become immediately upset. He had tried to calm her down, but her memories of the jungle and the dangers that lurked hidden there, including what happened the last time, really wound her up. They'd gone to lunch at nearby Zachary's Pizza where the garlic and clam deep dish pizza, plus a straw-berry Italian soda softened her up a little. Distracted and somewhat distraught with his only daughter, John helped himself to a couple of Anchor Steam beers on tap.

They talked earnestly for over two hours—the late lunch crowd had long since departed. The Professor and his eighteen-year-old daughter remained until the early dinner crowd began showing up.

Unfortunately, they didn't settle a thing.

John Waales was adamant that Kimmiko could not go to the Amazon Basin and Kimmiko Waales was adamant that she could. There was no gray area here. They each put their foot down in their own way. At one point, Kimmi's small face looked up at him, only inches away, and did not flinch as she proclaimed, "You took Mom along when it was dangerous and she did the same damn thing I have been doing for you, and yet you think I am too small and weak to defend myself. You always said that!

"Mom and I were the only two people you could trust completely with your work, but now you want to shut me out. Why?"

Unfortunately, the Professor, in spite of his PhD., advanced Science and Letters Degrees and long history of discovered and published antiquities, could not think of an answer for his baby girl.

Now, at 4 AM, as Kimmiko made her way to the kitchen in their comfortable home in the Berkeley Hills, she was surprised to see her dad sitting at the kitchen table with two mugs of steaming coffee in front of him. He smiled as she pulled her robe tightly around her and sat at the small oak kitchen table opposite him.

"I've been waiting here every night for the past three nights, expecting you," he smiled. "What took you so long?"

Kimmiko smiled and looked down at the hot coffee in front of her. She took a sip. "Peet's Arabian Mocha Java! When did they get it in?" she inquired. "They've been out of it for two weeks."

John smiled. "They flew it in special, because I promised them a new blend from the Amazon.

"As soon as I find it," he added hastily.

Kimmi nodded and drank the hot blend. Dad never put in enough sugar, she mused silently. Still worried about my teeth and immune system. She smiled.

"So, Dad, let's cut to the chase. There is no middle ground here. Am I going, or not?

John Waales couldn't look her in the eye. He got up and drained his cup. He began washing it in the sink, his back to her. "The jungle is a dangerous place, but I have the edge this time. I have maps, photos and I am getting Uncle Bill to help out again. It is a quick in and out." He turned around and smiled. He spread out his arms in an expansive way. "See honey, there is no need for you to even go."

She looked him hard in his eyes—she never wavered. "So, if it is a quick in and out, then there is no real danger and no real problem for me to be there. If, on the other hand, there is danger and, neither you or Uncle Bill can protect me, there is a greater probability of success if there are more people you can trust on board. Isn't that why Mom always went with you?

And remember what happened last time? You guys barely made it out alive. You needed more hands, and I'll be damned if I'm going to sit quietly on my ass in Biology 101 for two weeks while you risk your life and the life of my uncle for this cursed treasure!" Her voice was rising. She had had enough, and she wasn't going to cry like some lost little girl. "It's either with me or not at all. I can make my own way down there, you know! Ever since Mom died, I've typed up your research, preserved all your artifacts and helped you weave your data together. I deserve this, and I'm going to go!

He paused for a brief moment, then softly said, "Okay, you can go."

The suddenness of her victory caught Kimmi completely off guard. "What did you say?"

"I said, you can go. I will probably need you in spite of my concerns. I know it's dangerous, but in truth, the success of the mission could depend partly on you. You know the work and you know what we're looking for. Your mother knew it too."

"Yes, Dad, it was your obsession. Mom knew it. That's why she helped you until her last days." She hung her head. Sometimes thinking about her mom was still just too painful.

John Waales walked over to her. He put his hands on her shoulders. "Mom was always proud of you. She told me a long time ago that you and I were two peas in a pod. She said that your drive and stubbornness would take you a long way." He paused, "She also said that one day, you would be the greatest asset to my work. She was always right." He sighed.

Kimmiko reached up and took one of her father's strong brown hands. She leaned her head into it. "Oh Daddy...," she trailed.

Suddenly she straightened up. She turned and looked at her dad. "Is Robin coming?" she asked.

****

"Jack, John, is on the phone," Lisa Paris called up the stairs at her husband. The kids were both asleep and she was trying not to be too loud. She and Jack had made up for their earlier strains on the phone. In fact, Jack thought, they had made up for a lot of things in the past two hours.

Jack grabbed the phone, "Yo babe!" he chided. It was late and he wanted John to know it.

"Sorry it's so late," John apologized. "I was wondering if I could request your presence at the dawning of a new era!" he said grandly.

Jack replied in a flat voice, "Let's see, you've found another lost map and you want to take another run at the El Dorado again, but this time you want some company, to help share your good fortune, or else to hold you up if it's a total bust?" Jack giggled good-naturedly, just to show he was not being mean.

John responded in kind, "I don't know what you mean about 'a total bust'. I have no plans to fail this time, and I can guarantee you a first-class, round trip airfare to the Amazon River, plus first-class accommodations to our destination. Then the gold will be ours for the taking. Interested?"

Jack could almost hear him smiling over the phone. "So, what's the deal, *amigo?*"

"You know. You said if I ever went to South America again, you wanted to go. So, what do you need, an engraved invitation?"

Jacked looked up at Lisa, who had joined him in the library. She was now sitting on his lap, facing him and had both hands on his shoulders. She was wearing a very tiny tank top, which didn't cover her at all well. Even at 38, and after two kids, she still looked great. She was kissing his neck affectionately. She paused and looked up at him. She nodded. "Yeah, buddy, I was just talking it over with Lisa." who had gone back to kissing his neck, making conversation somewhat difficult, "She and the kids are going back to see her parents in Davenport, Iowa. So, I guess, if I don't want to see the birthplace of chiropractic for the five hundredth time, I guess I am free for the next couple of weeks."

"Neat, Buddy!" John exclaimed. I'll e-mail over the itinerary to you. "You current on your shots?" They both laughed. Jack never consented to any vaccinations, ever, unless they were absolutely necessary for international travel and were also from the most pure, pharmaceutical lots, usually those sent up to Canada, or else he simply used homeopathic vaccinations.

"Now, John, would you want me to poison my blood with the crap they make the American kids take? You know I won't put that junk in my body. I might make an exception, you know, if they would purify the stuff, or at least stop using mercury and formaldehyde as the mixers of choice. I though your research friends were going to expose those drug companies for what they really did?"

"Sorry, pal. Most colleges are heavily funded by these guys and you know how much money they sling around at the politicians. Hard to turn it down. Even the doctors never get all the inside information on the side effects of the stuff. Plus, there's the U. S. Government putting its stamp of approval on everything and there you go!"

"Yeah, yeah, at least I can still get my homeopath to vaccinate me and sign me off. But I might get a malaria shot. I hear it's a nasty death," he chuckled.

"So, is that a yes?' John queried.

"Absolutely, I'll just make sure Lisa is okay with it," he paused as she was now making him feel excited all over again, "and I will call you tomorrow to get all the arrangements."

"Cool, my man, you won't be sorry. I have already arranged it with our river boat captain and my assistant Robin. Kimmi is going also."

Jack smiled. "Looks like we'll be having a wild time, *amigo!*" He hung up the phone and pulled Lisa to him. They kissed passionately. He wanted to have a long happy night with her.

CHAPTER II

THE AMAZON

THE JUNGLE WAS WET AND HOT, which set up some strong thermal updrafts for the approaching 727. The pilot, a young, but experienced left-seater, began his approach slightly hot, meaning he kept a little extra airspeed and didn't start extending his flaps at the normal position. Since this airstrip in the jungles of Brazil was usually unattended by tower personnel, depending on the local state of the government of course, the pilot began to execute his approach at a 45 degree entrance on the downwind leg approach. This put him parallel to the runway he was to land on, but going in the opposite direction. Next, he would then turn to his base leg course, or 90 degrees to the landing strip and approximately one mile outbound. When he reached a position in line with the airstrip, he would turn to his final approach, which was directly into the wind. In order to slow his decent into the airport and thus ensure a "soft" landing, a pilot used his flaps, which acted as a strong drag and also caused a loss of altitude without dropping the nose down. The objective, was a slow, gentle descent-

avoiding a stall of the aircraft - which would result in a smoother landing.

Unfortunately, with the intense thermals caused by the rising hot air, the pilot had to descend faster than normal. He delayed setting the normal 10 degrees of flaps. He lowered the nose of the airplane with the elevator even more and reduced the throttles control slightly, both working in harmony.

The pilot picked out a spot on the horizon approximately five miles ahead and parallel with the runway. The heat was causing his plane to rise and he purposely pushed the yoke stick forward, dropping his nose down even further in order to pick up additional airspeed.

Back in the cabin, John Waales, his daughter Kimmiko, Jack Paris, and Dr. Waales' research assistant Robin Quigley, noticed the increase in airspeed and the sudden drop of the nose of the aircraft. Kimmiko looked across the aisle to her dad and said, "Daddy, are we making a water landing on purpose or are they doing this just to impress me?

Dr. Waales looked over at his daughter and just shrugged. He then pulled his seatbelt tighter and pressed his back into his seat a little harder.

The pilot turned to his base course and then, with his airspeed still at about 180 knots, began to ease back on the throttles. Almost immediately it was time turn to final approach.

The microphone crackled to life, "Fox-Trot Alpha niner niner niner, we have you on final approach one mile out, do you have the numbers?" This meant that the field was controlled by tower personnel, and there were people watching his approach. They wanted to know if the pilot had the current information on the altimeter settings, the wind direction and the correct runway in use, as planes had to land and take off into the wind.

The pilot looked at the copilot with a grimace, "Roger that! We're sorry sir, we were told that this field was currently uncontrolled."

"Roger sir. We just came to work, but have been monitoring your approach. Set your altimeter to 2-9-9-2, winds are at 2-7-5 at 2-0 knots, with heat thermals. Runway two niner zero is in use. There have been a few gusts, but no wind shears. Please set controls and turn on your landing lights, sir!"

"Roger that," said the pilot. He looked at the copilot, "Damn it," he whispered. He was upset that the NOTAMS, (Notices to Airmen), had not informed him that this was now a controlled field. It made him look bad, in spite of the understanding kindness of the tower control officer. The first officer reset the altimeter and began preparations for landing.

"Sir," said the tower control, "we have you coming in very hot at a high airspeed. Please state your intentions, now!"

"Roger," said the pilot as he eased back on the throttle and dropped the flap 20 degrees. "Nose down, 20 degrees of flaps and reduced airspeed. Engage landing gear. Noted, no wind shears, altimeter set to 2-9-9-2 and thermal updrafts accounted for. I've done this before, sir," he noted dryly. "I'm coming in a little hot due to the thermals, but I have great brakes. Don't worry," he added quietly.

"Roger that." The air traffic controller, a balls-to-the wall, no-B.S. kind of man, noted the change in airspeed, attitude of the aircraft and descent pattern. This was a good pilot he thought. He was a native to the region and had seen good pilots come and go, but they all appreciated his help.

The plane hit the numbers on the runway at precisely 145 knots, a perfect landing. In the back, the passengers felt only the "thud" of another landing, which they likely would not remember as their thoughts moved forward to their luggage, transportation from the airport and getting to their homes or hotels as soon as possible.

As the plane pulled into the landing dock and stopped, the passengers all got out of their seats and started pulling their luggage out of the overhead compartments.

****

Bill Treese set his grip down on the deck of the PT 109, in this case, a symbolic number, as the original PT 109 was John F. Kennedy's boat, which was rammed by the Japanese Destroyer Amagiri at approximately 02:33 hours on August 2, 1943 in the Blackett Strait of the Solomon Islands during W.W.II. He had salvaged this newer PT boat from the Navy and saved it from the scrap yard. It was an 80 foot Elco, built in Bayonne, New Jersey. Its number had been scrapped off by the time he bought it. But he loved JFK and wanted to honor his memory. He then sailed it from Baltimore, through the Caribbean and finally to the mouth of the Amazon. He then proceeded up the river until he came to his home port. Since that day, he had managed his life by giving rides to tourists fascinated by the opportunity to travel one of the most wild and possibly dangerous stretches of the Amazon River by an original PT boat from W.W.II. He even had working torpedoes, depth charges, two twin .50 caliber Browning machine guns and the original 20mm Oerlikon gun mounted to the stern.

Bill went below to check his supplies. He could easily stay out of touch with civilization with five passengers over a month and still eat well. He checked his rifle mounted to the bridge armor shield, a Winchester .50 -110. This was a lone survivor also from another time. The Winchester Repeating Rifle, the "Rifle That Won the West" was manufactured in several different calibers. The .50 -110 was the largest and had the most fire-power. There was one more special feature to this rifle. He had the lever specially modified so that it was tied to the trigger. When you pumped the first shell into the chamber and squeezed the lever, the pin depressed and hit the primer, firing the bullet. Squeezing the trigger was unnecessary. He had seen this on the old western show, *The Rifleman*. Chuck Conners was another hero of his and he had modified his rifle to fire exactly like the T.V. show rifle. It was still no comparison to the Uzi machine guns the drug traffickers carried, but he was a marksman, and the extra fraction of a second between rounds allowed him to aim better. He had only had to use this rifle a few times against the bad guys, but it had performed well, with deadly accuracy.

Bill knew in this part of the world, the dead were simply tossed into the jungle or the river - the thinking was, if they were moving drugs and got into a firefight, then they either deserved to die, or simply disappear. Of course, he always had the two mounted .50 caliber machine guns, the starboard one even with the bridge and the one on the port side mounted just aft of the main cabin. If all else failed, he also had the 20 mm Oerlikon gun on the stern, which would just rip the livin' crap out of any drug running boat which might try to get cute with his cargo or charter. They were also aware that he had armed and active torpedoes on board - a further deterrent. It was a general consensus up and down the Amazon that it was just best to steer clear of PT 109.

He heard the distant roar of the military truck approaching the dock. He looked left and right. There were people out of sight he knew, armed and watching him. The money sent by Professor Waales had eased the tension somewhat between Bill and the loan shark. He knew if he paid the man off, he could keep his boat. But if he faulted on the loan, he would lose the boat. These people were friendly to him now, but could be turned by the right amount of money, real or promised.

The truck was an old one and pulled up next to the dock with a metallic scream of protest as the brakes bit into the metal of the rotors. The back was covered in camouflage green, and the cab was a dusty brown. Bill looked at his watch. If it was Professor Waales, et al., then he was a day early.

The windows were covered with the dust from the road. The passenger door opened first and a young girl dressed in a halter and shorts jumped out. "Uncle Bill!" she screamed, running toward him with her arms outstretched.

Bill smiled. It had been at least five years since he had seen Kimmiko. She was still a little girl to him. "Hi ya honey!" he cried hugging her tight, "My but you've grown!"

She jumped out of his arms laughing. "You're just saying that," she giggled.

Bill stepped back and looked her up and down. "What happened to my little girl?" he asked.

"Sorry Uncle, had to grow up sometime!"

He looked deep into her eyes and touched her upturned chin. Yeah, too soon after her mom died, he thought.

She looked back at her favorite "uncle" and the years seemed to melt away. She remembered the birthdays, the trips, the parties and all the good times they had all shared before her mom passed away. Uncle Bill always made the trip up north for her birthdays and Christmas. Everything seemed to melt together and get mushy all at once. The memories escaped suddenly at the corners of her eyes. She stopped smiling. "I missed you a lot, you know. Just because mom...," her voice trailed off and she had to look away quickly. Her eyes darted over the dock, the people and all the noise. She stared off. "I wish you had called more. I miss all of us together."

Now it was Bill's turn to rub his eyes quickly. Out of all the emotions he thought he might experience this was not one of them.

"Sorry, baby," he said, "I don't know what happened to all the years." He grabbed her shoulder playfully like he used to. "I still love my favorite niece, though."

"I'm your only niece, you know!" She smiled again, grateful that her tears left as quickly as they had started.

The remaining doors on the truck opened with a metallic shudder, thankfully, thought Bill. John Waales, Jack Paris and Robin Quigley all got out and jumped the remaining three feet onto the dirt road.

"Damn, it's hot!" exclaimed Professor Waales. "Bill, how

the hell are you?" He stuck out his hand to the big man, who grabbed him in a bear hug similar to the one he just gave Kimmiko.

"Yeah, too bad it's not raining a little," observed Robin, "then we might get a little relief from the heat."

Bill put John Waales down and eyed the other two. The young man was about 20, light skinned and on the smaller side. The other guy who was just looking around, looked to be about forty, dark hair and skin, some sort of Italian or Indian, and fairly short also, but with a much better build. He didn't say a lot, but it looked to Bill that he was pretty sharp and nothing much escaped his eye.

John Waales made the introductions. "Robin is my assistant at the University and Dr. Paris is my good friend and chiropractor."

Bill extended his hand. "What's a chiropractor?" he asked.

Jack said, "I'm a doctor, but I don't use drugs or surgery to help people get well. I just use my hands to adjust their backs and they get well."

"Hey," Bill said suddenly excited, "like in that movie *Jacob's Ladder*! That guy, uh, uh, Danny, what's-his-name? He was Jacob's chiropractor and he dragged him out of that hospital when he was injured and up in traction over to his office and fixed him up just like that!" He smiled. "I don't know about all of that stuff, but if you're John's friend, you're all right with me."

Jack smiled. He looked past Bill towards the boat. "Is that a real PT boat?" he asked excitedly.

Bill nodded with some amusement at his immediate

enthusiasm. It happened a lot when people who watched war movies saw a real combat boat. Serve on one of these, he thought, for a few weeks against the Japanese in the South Pacific or on the Mekong Delta with *Charley* shooting at you and you would wish for a nice big steel battleship to hunker down on.

"Yep, she's a real one. Saved her from the scrap heap."

"Cool!"

Robin Quigley was looking around with an annoyed look on his face. "Could we get some water and food, somewhere soon?" he asked. "I think I'm about to fall over from this heat and thirst." He added quietly, "Forget the water, just give me a beer in a bottle. I don't need the squats."

No problem, *amigo*," said Bill, step this way into my *Cantina* and I will show you a good time," he bowed low, doffing his cap towards his entourage. They walked up onto the dusty wooden porch and into the dark, cool bar.

****

In this part of the world, dawn comes swiftly and silently. The dark of the jungle, an evil inking, that forbids conversation or even movement when you feel you were being watched, thins suddenly as the first virginal rays of a new day begin. The sun cannot be seen because of the jungle, but its earliest whisperings turn into day without warning or sound. One minute it's completely dark, then misty and then, suddenly, the oppressive heat and light filled the river and jungle. Oh, and of course there were always the mosquitoes. They are present everywhere all the time. Even during the day, you are not safe from these vampires from hell. They live, bred and swarm in mass numbers, so that no one was safe. The Natives along the river simply got used to them and made them part of their culture. The Colombians and Peruvians either ignore them or go inside. It's the tourists who suffer.

In the back room of the *Cantina*, Kimmiko was the first awake. She looked up from her bed to see a young native standing and staring at her. She stifled a scream and, regaining her composure, smiled from under the sheets. He smiled back at her. The room was still bathed in a misty light. He was about 18, handsome and well built. He had on dirty white cotton pants and no shirt. It occurred to her that she had thrown off her halter and shorts during the night due to the heat and in spite of the mosquitoes. She realized that he could pretty much figure this out, as the sheets were very thin. The devil in her took over and she slowly got out of bed and stood up before him, wearing only a thin white thong, which stood out in stark contrast to her dark skin. He blinked quickly, stared at her for a few seconds and then looked away and flushed a deep purple color. Kimmiko smiled and reached for her shirt and shorts. It was still a little chilly in the gloom of the back room of the bar.

"Did you expect to find one of the working girls back here?" she asked innocently.

"No *señorita*," Manolo said shyly, "but," he added boldly, "you are *muy bonito* and would be welcome to share my *hacienda*. Who are you?"

"I'm Kimmiko Waales, Dr. John's daughter.

"*Mi Dios Mio!*", "My God Help me!" came the answer.

"Please don't tell my *padrone*, *Capitán* Bill I looked at you. *Pore favore!*" he pleaded.

Kimmiko suddenly felt bad. She walked over to Manolo and grabbed his shaking hands. "Sorry *amigo*," she said. "Sometimes I just like to play around with cute guys." "I won't do it again, ahh, *no mas,*" she added hastily.

She noted his sigh of relief. "I am Manolo. I help *Capitán* Bill and now I will help you. You would like some coffee, *si?*"

"Sure Manolo, that would be great."

"Hey Kimmi!" she heard from the other side of the hallway, "are you awake yet?" It was Bill. She heard the movement of the others from across the hall and realized the journey was beginning. She and Manolo looked at each once more and then he was gone to get coffee with a quick smile.

****

Bill, John and Jack sat at a table near the bar drinking coffee and eating fried bananas when Kimmiko entered the barroom. Jack stood up politely and offered her a chair. She giggled.

"You're so polite Uncle Jack!" she giggled again.

"Yeah, Uncle Jack," Bill mimicked her good-naturedly, "but she won't be a princess out on the river. On my boat everybody pulls their weight, even favorite nieces!"

Kimmiko gave him a pouty look and then suddenly brightened, "Hey, when do we pull out? I can't wait to get moving. This is going to be fun!"

The others smiled. Her dad spoke up, "We'll be leaving right after dinner this evening, just after sunset."

"Why so late?" asked Kimmiko looking puzzled. "We won't be able to see where we are going."

"Right," answered Bill, "and neither will anyone else. This mission..., uh, excuse me, this expedition is not without some danger." he looked around. "Everyone needs to know that there are some people upriver who like to play rough. But we have the advantage. I've sent people and money ahead of us to secure our right to pass." When no one said anything, he smiled. "Don't worry. We'll be fine. But I like to take precautions and everyone thinks we will be leaving tomorrow morning. You guys arrived early. This way we'll be ahead of anyone who might want to follow us."

"Or ambush us, right?" Everyone turned their heads to see Robin enter the room. He was wearing shorts, but no shirt or shoes. Fresh from a shower, he was towel drying his hair.

Bill looked at him squarely without expression. "There won't be any ambushes. I said I've taken care of all that." He paused, "Unless you know something we don't."

Robin stopped drying his hair. He tried to smile, but he felt suddenly naked in the room which had gotten chilly in spite of the early morning heat. "No, I don't," he said simply. "Can I have some coffee?" he said somewhat meekly.

Bill, amused that he had so easily caught him off guard, smiled and pointed at a prominent sign above the bar which read:

NO SHOES, NO SHIRT, NO SERVICE!
(THE ABOVE APPLIES TO MEN ONLY)

Robin smiled a thin smile and turned around to go get his shirt on.

John looked at Bill, "What was that all about?" he demanded.

Bill looked over at his best friend, "Cool your jets, big fella. I need to know the personality of everyone on my boat." He looked at the others. "Nothing personal," he said mostly to Jack, but I will be the supreme captain and commander on this little excursion and if anyone wants to back out, now's the time to do it. You can catch a plane back to the good 'ol U-S-of-A in about six hours."

They all shook their heads silently. Bill wasn't being mean they all realized, but this wasn't going to be a walk in the park either.

Jack spoke up, "I plan on taking a flight back, but in about a week, after I have seen the Lost City with my own eyes. And don't worry, I'll follow every one of your orders. I'll be right behind you..., hiding," he added. Everyone laughed and the tension in the room eased.

"Hey Robin," Bill yelled toward the hallway leading to the back bedrooms, "your coffee is ready, shirt or no shirt!"

******

The rest of the day was busy as Bill gave everyone an intimate tour of the workings of the PT boat. They went over the details of the trip, how to get out of the water safely if they were tossed overboard, what to do if they were attacked by men or beast, and how to signal or radio for help if something serious happened. The day was broken up by meals and restful naps. The bar's bedrooms were cooled by overhead fans, efficient devices, which kept much of the air circulating. The rooms were also dark, which was a further deterrent to the heat.

Robin had taken several long looks at Kimmiko. She looked great in her shorts and halter top. Manolo, in spite of his respect and fear of *Capitán* Bill, could not help looking either. He could not understand his feelings. He was surrounded by, and, if the truth be known, taken care of, by the working girls of the bar, who were also very young and pretty. Also, there had been several young female tourists on Bill's boat over the years and he had never acted like this before. But there was something exotic and tremendously exciting to his young manhood with this girl. He returned to his work with some reluctance. Again, this was new to him, as he had always done more than a man's day's work since he was a young boy. He did not like Robin. He supposed it was jealousy, as Manolo had seen her look at him, Robin, with a teasing look in her eyes. At this, Manolo squeezed the handle of the mop he was using to swab the deck of the PT boat, until his knuckles turned white beneath his brown skin. He decided to go below and check the supplies before he accidentally knocked Robin over the side. Manolo hoped he couldn't swim. He smiled in spite of himself.

****

The Amazon River begins as a small spring of fresh water, approximately 1600 feet high in the Chila Range Mountains of

Peru. Thus becomes the humble beginnings of the streams known as the Lloqueta and the Llactuema which form the Carhuasanta River. From there it flows into the Hornillos, which then goes to the river in the canyon of the Apurimac, then to the Ene River, to the Tambo River, then to the Ucayali River and finally forming the mighty Amazon which becomes over seven million cubic feet of water per second pouring into the Atlantic Ocean. *National Geographic* magazine, among others, had done several articles on the amazing Amazon over the years. The most powerful river in the world, it spans over 4,000 miles, three countries and almost an entire continent. With over five times greater discharge than the Mississippi River, the Amazon dumps 4.5 trillion gallons per day into the sea. No other river in the world even comes close.

People who live along its shores are known to be survivors. They have courage. Each day is a different adventure. They live their lives according to the river and its moods. Flooding along its banks is as natural as the sunrise and the sunset. The people are patient. Life moves slowly and predictably. Only in the cities are people spared the slow, monotonous grind of survival. In cities up the river from Brazil, into Colombia, life is more exciting - and cheap. Drug lords rule the area. The Colombian Cartel is alive and well, despite contrary official rumors. The government would sincerely try to control and contain the Cartel, but would then it too would wind up as victims in the struggle for life. The United States was of little help. They dammed the Colombians for producing the white powder, then became its best customer. The citizens cry for more border reinforcement and then scream when shortages force the price to go up. The Colombian Indians have used cocaine for centuries as a medicinal powder mixed with lime and also as a stimulant to live by. Certain rituals performed are as natural as life and are surrounded by the cocoa plant. While most Americans are appalled by the common use, they would likely ignore the daily habit of a martini followed by wine with dinner and a nightcap of brandy.

The river moves slowly and powerfully. Boats such as Bill Treese's, could be lost in either the mists, the mud or the tree trunks which flow daily down the river and impede movement up the river. But Bill's boat was an American W.W. II PT boat. It had seen and survived several battles with the Japanese Navy and also here on the Amazon. It was generally known to most of the savvy natives of the river, that Bill was not to be messed with. He was a congenial guy - friendly even for an American. He would give you a meal, a drink or even a fair fight. But, if you tried to catch him on his blind side, he would kill you. Even the drug runners, while not ever really afraid, realized there were easier pickings than the PT 109. The ordinance was real and Bill Treese was a crack shot. It was rumored that once, he observed a large drug deal going down on the river. Even though he turned his back and continued his run down the river, the unfortunate Colombians, thinking he was leaving to inform the police, followed him into the darkness. Shots rang out from the PT's .50 caliber machine guns and also the 20mm Oerlikon cannon. The drug runners' boat went up in flames and sank immediately, along with the money and the drugs.

The heat and the mosquitoes were as oppressive as ever, as the first day on the river began for the adventurers. Here, in

Brazil, the river was wide and moved slowly. Boredom was more prevalent than anxiety. It was after 0800, military time and Bill was at the helm. He had been driving the boat most of the night and knew the thick, wet heat, even this early, would be waking everyone up soon. Sure enough, as if on cue, Dr. John Waales started moving up the ladder from the cramped bunk in the stateroom aft of the bow to the bridge. The sun hit his eyes harshly and he quickly donned a pain of Ray Ban sunglasses. Bill greeted him with a grunt.

"How was your night, old man," Bill asked with absent curiosity.

"Sucked. Too damn hot and too much to think about," John replied. How long before we hit Colombia?"

"About two to three days. Say, what's with your young assistant? I mean, the doc seems okay and Kimmi is the same, but that kid, uh, Robin? He's a little strange. I get the feeling that he's watching and waiting for somethin' to happen."

"As usual, you are being paranoid. Robin's a good kid. I've been his mentor for over two years and, besides, I think he likes Kimmi." John thought a minute. "He's okay, just too intellectual sometimes for his own good. I have to admit, he's helped me with a lot of the research on the El Dorado and he has helped me figure out its true present location." "But," he added hastily, "they're still my theories and my leads. Robin has just helped fill in a few blanks."

Bill shrugged. "Whatever," he said, "I just feel you should watch your back." He glanced over at his Winchester rifle hanging just inside the cabin. "Don't worry, I'll watch my back and yours if I have to. By the way, just how sweet is he on Kimmi?"

John looked away quickly. There were so many times when he really wished his wife were still alive, and this was definitely one of them. "I don't know. I just get the feeling that they have been friends," he paused, "or more than friends, if you know what I mean."

Bill nodded. He looked at the river silently. Sometimes he was grateful he never had children, especially a daughter. God, he thought, was it a crime to shoot someone you thought was messing around with your baby girl? What could be more precious in life than your children?

******

Jack Paris started up the fore ladder towards the main deck. He had been sleeping in the cramped quarters of the bow, just ahead of the main bunks. On this PT boat, the berths were in the bow and slightly forward of the midship, which housed the fuel, the galley and a small cabin known as the "day room." The stern was the exclusive area of the three Packard engines which put out all the horsepower needed to attain over 45 knots, even in the rough head waters of the mighty Amazon.

Jack, like John, felt the heat immediately when he woke up. He was sleeping in the same forward area as Kimmiko. There were four small bunks, two on each side of the bow and the forward area immediately in the prow of the boat was a very small bathroom, known as the "head". John had set this up quietly, as he felt he could trust his married, best friend and the quarters were very tight. John slept just aft of the forward compartment, along with Robin, Manolo and on the port side of the boat in the

"Captain's Quarters", was Captain Bill. He had a private bathroom there, whimsically called the "Captain's head", but since there was a girl on board, he let the others use it too.

Jack hit the main deck and looked around. It was his first morning on the Amazon and he was excited. There were screaming birds, screeching monkeys and other boats all making their own special noise. This and the roar of the PT boat's engines was exciting, indeed! One surprise came when he realized he was being attacked by what seemed like thousands of killer mosquitoes.

"Holy shit!", he yelled as they bored into his skin. "What the hell are these damn things?"

"Here," Bill Treese came over with a large can of repellent. He sprayed Jack all over.

"Hold on," Jack said, as he took off his thin T-shirt. Bill sprayed him liberally.

"Much better," Jack said as he put his shirt back on.

"What about me?", Kimmiko shrieked as she emerged from below decks. She was wearing her usual short shorts and halter. The mosquitoes descended on her at once. Bill ran over and sprayed her all over. "Don't let the bed bugs bite," he laughed at her. His eyes twinkled. "Don't worry, sweetie, you'll get used to them. Kimmi looked over at Manolo in shorts and no shirt. "How do you do it," she yelled at him over the roar of the engines, Bill had hastily returned to the helm to power through a giant wave which had suddenly swelled up.

Manolo smiled, "I grew up with them!" he smiled.

Jack shook his head. The wind coming off the water in the face of the boat doing 20 knots, cooled their skin somewhat.

He looked at the jungles crouching like some wild beast on both sides of the Amazon. Although several thousand yards away on either side, he could see the treetops shrouded in a thick mist. Later, the mist would yield to rain. The heat was wet and oppressive. Even the breeze and the rain would not keep back the layers of the hot, wet jungle. You couldn't see two feet into the jungle, even if you were standing right in front of the vines descending down to the shore.

He shivered in spite of the heat. He thought about his family back home and wondered why he came along on this voyage. High Adventure, he smiled to himself, was desired simply when the little joys and thrills of a normal life ceased to have meaning, or bring the happiness they once did. He already missed being back home. He couldn't remember ever taking a vacation away from his family. Maybe this brief separation would help them all get closer. They needed that. He looked at the jungle again. It looked dark and sinister. He wondered what might be looking back at them as they drew closer to the Colombian border. Brazil was a paradise next to Colombia. The drug lords and runners ruled this part of the world. Jack remembered the *National Geographic* story which said that many who lived on this part of the river called it the "Black Hole." The feeling of being watched would never leave him while he was on the river.

Jack looked over to see John back behind the bridge, pouring coffee. He walked over and gratefully accepted a cup. "Good morning, Commander," Jack uttered around a mouthful of coffee.

John smiled at him, as though he knew what he had been

thinking. "It is a good morning my friend. A couple of days of smooth sailing and we'll find the city, take out the gold and be rich and famous."

"Lifestyles of the rich and notorious," Bill Treese chimed in. Now there's a concept. Do you think Robin Leach will feature my boat on T.V.?"

"Hard to say good buddy," John said, reposting with pleasure. "Maybe if we move you to a Caribbean Island brimming with royalty and celebrities. But," he said motioning to Bill's oil-stained shirt and cap, "you better get a uniform a little more like Captain Stubing on the 'Love Boat.'"

Bill grunted and turned back to look down the river. "See those black lumps in the water?" The men looked down river at the moving shapes, which caused the brown water to swirl around madly. "Logs, thousands of 'em. You never know when one might surface and rip out your bow. Worse than a damn floating mine." Some of the shapes had roots which descended down into the river. These were tree trunks. Bill slowed the boat and maneuvered expertly between the floating obstacles. "The river floods and the pressure of the water rips these guys out. They still clear-cut back the jungle and forests to graze enough cattle to make your Whopper Burgers and the land gets ruined. Runoff is the result. Even when the river is high and flooding, it's still brown.

"I thought it was the 'Color of the Sky'," Kimmiko said innocently, quoting the title of a book from a long time ago. She had wandered back from where she was standing at the helm with Bill. She poured herself a cup of coffee. "Is it Colombian?" she asked with a quick grimace. Like Navy coffee, Bill brewed it hot, strong and bitter.

"Sure," Bill yelled over the roar of the engines as he juked the boat around a particularly large log. "It's Colombia's finest. Use a little sugar and cream. That'll smooth it out some."

"*Red Sky at Morning,*" Jack said in response to her obvious quote to the classic book. "I remember reading it in high school. The title never really connected with the book. But I did connect with the story. I can't believe you read it, Kimmi."

"Part of my Advanced English Lit. class. We read all the classics. *Catcher in the Rye, Lord of the Flies,* tons of 'em. Even a bunch of Stephen King books. The teacher kept going on and on about how Mr. King was an English teacher first, and then he sold his first novel *Carrie,* and he never had to go back to teaching again. I think she was a little envious."

"Did you like the books, honey?" John asked her. He looked at his baby, who had suddenly grown up into a beautiful woman.

"Yeah, they were neat. But I don't like sad endings." Her words hung in the air for several seconds as everyone thought about her mother. Jack was the first to reach over and squeeze her shoulder.

John spoke up. "Hey Bill, how long will it take us to get to the tributary I showed you on the map?"

"About two and a half days. I have to cut speed at night for obvious reasons." The boat shuddered suddenly as a submerged log glanced off the port side of the bow. Bill slowed the boat a little more. I have a surprise for you John," he yelled without turning around.

"What, you already know where the Lost City is?" he asked hopefully.

Bill smiled. He reached into a large ammo box under the helm and took out a rolled up series of photographic prints, some as large as a painting. "Aerial photographs of the part of the Amazon you are interested in."

John felt the thrill of discovery course up his spine. He shivered in spite of the heat. "How did you...," he began, but Bill cut him off.

"Don't ask, don't tell," he said with a touch of pride. This was his mission too and he was pleased he could help his friend. It wasn't just pride, there was a lot of money involved here.

John started to unroll the photos and then suddenly stopped as he heard Robin, below start up the ladder. "Here Bill," he said handing him the photos. "Put them away." He ignored Bill's puzzled look as Robin appeared sleepily on the deck. In fact, as his cringed look gave way to a fake smile of greeting, he himself didn't understand what he was doing, just acting on instinct. He looked at Jack and Kimmi, but they were still engaged in a conversation about books they liked and didn't seem to notice what was happening. In any event, he couldn't wait to see what Bill had gotten for him. Aerial photos of the river could make all the difference. Not only for discovery, he told himself, but also for escape if need be. Robin was rubbing his eyes. "Coffee's forward on the bow, Robin," John said before grabbing the ammo box with the map in it and heading below to his berth.

******

Kimmi smiled at Robin, who had appeared on deck. Jack was in mid-sentence as he discussed how the ending of "Red Sky at Morning," was predictable, considering that the world was at war at the time and the hero's father joined the navy against all possible reason. "He was going off to be a hero," Jack was saying, "leaving his family behind to sit out the war. Then he gets himself killed and his family gets to pay for his idea of heroism...," he trailed off as Kimmi shifted her body subtly to allow Robin into the conversation. Jack continued, slightly annoyed at the interruption and also at himself for the position he seemed to be taking on this subject, "I know you have to fight for the country and all that, but you know, if he just stayed with his family and took care of them, he would still be a hero," he said plaintively. "You ask anyone who lost a son or daughter or a parent in a war, and they will tell you they are very proud of their kin, but they would give anything if they hadn't gone in harm's way."

"Hey doc," Robin began, "good morning. Uh, why are you guys talking so intellectually this early in the day?"

Kimmi smiled. "You dweeb! It's after eight o'clock in the morning," she squealed. "What time do you usually get up?"

Robin rubbed his eyes. "Not this damn early. I'm a graduate student, remember?" He suddenly felt the hungry mosquitoes which had discovered his soft, pale skin. "Christ!" he said slapping them away.

"No use, kid," Bill called over the bridge to him. "The little monsters are killers. Here, try this," he said handing over the can of repellent, which Robin grabbed quickly.

Kimmiko giggled as he sprayed himself liberally. "Cute

bod, even covered with yucky spray!"

Robin rolled his eyes. "I thought they only came out at night," he said ruefully.

Manolo, dutifully pouring coffee, smiled at the exchange. He knew this *gringo* was no match for Kimmi, but he couldn't understand the affection in her eyes. "*Capitán* Bill, I'm going to check the engines," he yelled as he went below deck.

The boat moved along, guided by the current and the logs. They made headway and knew that their adventure lay ahead in the mists covering the waters.

******

John Waales unrolled the map and the aerial photos of the river ahead of them, that Bill had given him. He used a magnifying glass to try to discern the smaller tributaries of the Amazon. Jack yelled down to him, "Can I come down for a sec?"

John flinched in spite of himself. He made a quick decision to trust one more person on this trip, he thought inwardly. Wasn't that why he brought Jack along? He hated the thought that he might be sacrificing his best friend for a few ounces of gold. The thought made him almost lose the bitter coffee he had just drunk. Jack would take care of himself he thought. He had balls and would give his life for Kimmi. In fact, they all would, except his greedy assistant Robin. Now why had he thought that? he wondered. Jack swung down the ladder into the small stateroom.

"Down ladder, make a hole!" Jack giggled as he swung into the room. "Damn these quarters are tight! Did you know that the crew of the PT boats were generally small, athletic men?"

"Yeah, like you, buddy." Bill moved to the side. "Look at this, *amigo*." They looked down at the heavy paper of the map and compared it to the photos.

Jack whistled softly. "You might just do it this time," he said. John tapped silently on a misty area lateral and upcountry to a major tributary to the Amazon.

"See, it corresponds to a spot which is not on the map," John continued, the excitement rising in his voice. "It is only indicated by this area denoted as 'Indian Territory' and covered by rain forest." His nail indented the thick paper of the map slightly.

Jack peered closely. "So what you're saying, is that this misty area and this rain forest are where the lost city is located?"

"Right, good buddy," John said proudly.

"Why are there so many small rivers around this area?" Jack asked.

John smiled. "I don't think you really want to know, but, if you are looking for adventure to spice up your dull life, you may have found it."

"What are you talking about?" The heat and the noise of the boat was starting to irritate Jack a little, but he did like a good mystery.

"Curse of the river, or curse of the gold, whichever way you want to look at it."

Jack looked confused. John continued. "Look, you don't just tend quietly to billions of dollars of gold," he whispered, barely audible over the engines which had begun to quiet down a little, "someone's going to want it. These natives knew they had to protect their treasure against people like Cortés, Pizarro, Sir Walter Raleigh and the rest of the invaders of Europe a long time ago. They took advantage of the rivers around the gold mines and began to interbreed the local fish."

"Right, right, the giant piranha!" Jack exclaimed.

"Not just any giant piranha. Killers! Man-eaters! They started breeding the piranhas with the larger and peaceful pacu fish, which resembled them. As they got larger and larger, some over three feet in length and over two hundred pounds, they began to introduce the much larger pirarucu fish. These puppies were over six feet long and growing. They weighed in at over a thousand pounds. Eventually, the natives of the area, known as Chibcha Indians, bred them to over fifteen feet in length, with all the aggression of the original piranha fish. The locals tell tales of when the Spanish Conquistadors ventured up the rivers in search of more of the plunder they received at the expense of the Aztecs, that they were met with spears and big teeth. Most of them didn't return."

Jack started to smile, and then thought better of it. "Just a rumor, right?" he said hopefully.

John shrugged. *"Quien sabe?"* Who knows?

Just then, the boat shuddered as the engines suddenly slowed, reversed and then sped forward. The men below were thrown backwards, almost into the Captain's Head.

John and Jack ran up the ladder onto the deck. Robin, Kimmiko and Bill huddled around the bridge, looking forward as they emerged topside.

"What happened?" yelled John, as the boat lurched forward and banked to the right.

Bill motioned with his chin to the right, towards a smaller boat, trying to keep up. It was a small boat, obviously built for speed and evasive action. It was also armed with what looked like a small caliber machine gun mounted to the bow.

"Drug runner!" Bill yelled. The boat turned left, moving swiftly toward Bill's boat. A man scrambled onto the bow and took aim at the much larger and faster PT boat.

"John," Bill yelled out, "take the port side machine gun!"

John seemed paralyzed. He suddenly realized they were in danger. He grabbed Kimmiko and shoved her down behind the steel bulkhead. He started to get up to go to the port gun which was mounted just behind, or aft of the cabin.

"Stay there!" Jack screamed. "Keep Kimmi down!" Jack went around the other side of the main cabin and dove over its top and down into the port turret of the twin .50 caliber Browning M2 machine guns. He came up quickly, his adrenaline rushing. He took aim at the boat which had closed the distance in what seemed like milliseconds and was now only two hundred yards off the port stern and closing. His hands closed around the dual triggers and squeezed. Nothing happened. "How do you fire this thing?!" he yelled to Bill, who had his own problems maneuvering the boat around the logs which were now coming at him quickly as he throttled up to 35 knots.

He yelled instructions as Jack pivoted the gun around to make up for the increase in speed. The hammer dropped and the gun, as if by magic, began to fire automatically. The jam-free belt bullet loader was designed so that it would always ensure smooth, continuous firing at over 1600 rounds per minute. Bill had secured several tracer bullets which were illuminated every tenth shell, allowing Jack to see and move his line of fire from the water in front of the drug runner's boat up into the hull, causing it to splinter and slow in the water. The man on the bow taking aim, never got a shot off as Jack's erratic firing went up the bow, crossing the gun mount and hit the main cabin. They could see him and the other men on board diving out of the way as Jack kept firing anywhere and everywhere. The boat turned on its side and, as if on a giant slingshot, whipped around in a 180 degree turn and sped off, obviously taking on water. Bill goosed the throttle and took his boat across the river towards the other shore.

"Whoa, whoa, easy there, Tex! Good shootin'!" Bill yelled at Jack, who was having trouble silencing his gun. He turned and grinned shamefacedly at Bill, who was laughing. "First time on a machine gun, buddy?"

Jack took a deep breath, "Somethin' like that, pal."

John's head popped up. He had been through this before, but not with his daughter on board. "You okay, honey? Anybody hit?" he yelled out. "Manolo!" He yelled back towards the engine compartment, "You okay?"

"*Si, amigo!*" he yelled, sticking his head out, "Those *cabrons* ran away!" he said laughingly.

"Everybody's okay," Bill said as he throttled back. "They never got a shot off. The only danger was from our doctor friend here," he laughed. "Hey, where's Robin?"

"Here, man," Robin said as he emerged from down below.

"Dangerous down there, son," Bill said somberly. "This heap is made of plywood. Navy's idea. Made the boats move faster through the water. Suicide boats they were called. Plywood coffins! Volunteer duty! Rounds go right through the hull!"

"The ones made later in 1945 had aluminum hulls," Jack added. He had climbed over the cabin and joined them in the cockpit. "Hope I didn't rattle anyone's cage," he gestured towards the disappearing boat, "except theirs."

"You did fine, doc," Bill added with good nature. "Thanks for stepping in. And your right about the hulls. I think I need some armor on this damn tub." He looked over at John. "Sorry buddy, I should have thought about Kimmi. Heat of battle, you know." He shrugged and smiled.

"Let me up, Daddy!" Kimmiko pushed her dad off her and stood up. "Who were they, Uncle Bill?"

Robin smiled at the absurd thought which instantly came to him of comparing this grizzled old sailor with clean-cut Uncle Bill of the TV show *Family Affair* he had seen on late night TV.

"Just the local talent. They know we don't have any drugs, money or gold, but if they can get ahold of my ordinance or my boat, then they could control this part of the river." Bill looked around and, finding the river now deserted, moved back into the main channel and throttled back up to twenty-five knots. "Anybody hungry?" he chuckled.

****

They had slept most of the afternoon, Bill's warning that they would be up much of the night looking for "critters", as he euphemistically put it, in the water as they moved up river, left little doubt that this was no pleasure cruise.

Jack's eyes opened and he stared at the ceiling. He was in that strange world somewhere between sleep and consciousness. He thought he felt his wife sleeping beside him, but it was only the proximity of the hull in the narrow bunk, lined with pillows. He glanced across the bow area to Kimmi sleeping peacefully. Climbing out of his bunk, he quietly made his way out of the small cabin, into the larger cabin and up the ladder past the other sleeping men.

He emerged on the deck, through the narrow hatchway in the bridge, to see Manolo steering the boat. He glanced at his watch, it was about 4:15 and the afternoon heat was giving way to the early gloom of the late afternoon.

Manolo smiled at him. "Good afternoon, doctor," he said in almost perfect English, obviously proud of his ability to overcome his accent. "Did you have a nice *siesta-* nap," he recovered quickly.

Jack smiled, "Yes, thank you. I was dreaming of back home." He looked up at the clouds. "Where's the sun?"

"Storm coming soon. It will probably hit us in the next couple of days. The waters may be a little rough up ahead."

"Will we stay on the river, or will we tie up on the shore?"

"*Quien sabe?* Whatever *Capitán* Bill decides. It also depends on the..." he struggled with the English, "natives. We are almost to Colombia and they may or may not be friendly."

"I thought Bill had always maintained friends on this part of the river?" Jack asked.

"*Si*, and everybody likes him. But..," he continued quietly, "the people change like the river. Someone may be paying them more to be friendly or not so friendly. Or, there may be threats. Then they may have their hands tied by those in power.

We must always be careful."

Jack nodded. "Where is Bill?"

"He is below, but asked not to be disturbed. He is looking over the map and photos with Professor John."

"I thought they were sleeping in the cabin."

Manolo hesitated. He liked this man, but he didn't know how much he could trust him. Trust meant life and death on this river. "They are below, but in a secret place. You must wait until they come back up. I'm sorry, *amigo*."

Jack smiled, "That's okay Manolo. I'm getting the picture that this is not exactly the 'Jungle Cruise' ride at Disneyland."

"Manolo looked at him blankly. "The what?"

Jack laughed, "Never mind. If we survive this, I'll take you there."

They heard the sound of someone coming up from below. Manolo said quickly to Jack, "*Senior*, can the other one, Robin, be trusted?"

It was Jack's turn to look unsure. "I don't know. I guess so. He's been with John for a while now. Why do you ask?"

The hatch opened and both Bill and John emerged.

"Hi guys," John said happily.

Bill grunted a hello. "Manolo," he said, can you go to the galley and start making supper?"

"*Si, Capitán* Bill!" Manolo, glanced at Jack as if to ask him not to say anything, and then started down the ladder.

The three men looked out at the Amazon. It continued to flow heavily and constantly against them as if they were insignificant ants which could be crushed instantly at their master's desire.

******

When Jack moved out of the forward cabin he shared with Kimmiko and walked past Robin Quigley, he thought he was being completely quiet. But Robin had been silently awake since Bill Treese had shaken Professor Waales awake and took him back to somewhere else in the boat. Since then, Robin had been lying awake, hoping the dumb chiropractor would leave Kimmi alone. It didn't take long.

Once Jack was topside, he climbed out of his bunk and, carefully arranging the pillows to look as though he was still sleeping, crept towards the forward compartment where Kimmi was sleeping. The sight of her on deck in her shorts and halter drove him crazy. He knew he should be focusing on his mission and trying to sack her was really stupid, but, what the hell, he thought. He could just put it down to a young man's lust.

His eyes were used to the gloom, but when he entered the forward cabin, the light was more abundant. Someone had left on the light in the head and the door was propped open.

Kimmi was sleeping under the sheet, but Robin could see her top and shorts lying on the deck beside her bunk. The thought of her this close to him excited him more than he could imagine. She was on her back with her arms over her head. Her hands blocked her eyes against the light.

Quietly Robin moved over to her. With a trembling hand he slowly pulled the sheet down past her stomach. She was more beautiful than he had imagined and for one moment he had second thoughts about endangering the mission. Kimmiko put her hands down at her side and looked up at him. "I was wondering if you were going to come in and join me," she said seductively, causing Robin to almost cry out in surprise. Kimmiko giggled. She reached up to him. "Stay for a little while."

With the blood roaring in his ears, Robin shed his clothes and jumped into the narrow bunk on top of her. Kissing her deeply, his hands moved expertly over her body, eliciting small squeals of delight from her. Her hands found his hips and she pulled him into her.

Manolo had gone below, hoping the doctor would not say anything about his fears concerning the young Robin. He did not even know why he didn't trust him, but his instincts had kept him alive on this river longer than many of his friends, and he had helped his family out with the money he earned. He hoped it wasn't jealously because he liked the Professor's daughter and he knew that she and Robin flirted openly. Jealously was one step away from death in this part of the world.

He glanced towards Robin's bunk and, noticing the misshapen pillows under the covers, instinctively knew he wasn't there. He had been slipping out of his house to work for *Capitán* Bill for years and this was his own trick, but his disguise always looked much more real than this. He heard familiar sounds from inside the forward cabin, like those he heard working in the backroom brothel at the bar. He moved to the closed bulkhead and listened quietly. He felt a surge of jealously and thought about opening it and confronting the two. As his hand reached out, he suddenly realized what he was doing. This would only cause problems and he had enough of those. He still needed his job to help feed his family and, besides, she wasn't his sister, or even really his friend yet. Better to keep an eye on this Robin and see what he's really up to. Sadly, he shook his head and moved away to start preparing the food for the evening meal.

******

CHAPTER III

THE FIRST BRANCH

THE PT BOAT'S ENGINES had been roaring upstream all night, as the current, seemingly the same, had actually increased. Bill looked toward the shore and, seeing the familiar landmark of the three broken trees lining the shore, now only 200 yards away, made his turn to start up the first tributary. It was about 3:00 A.M. on a cloud covered night. The moon peeked through for brief amounts of time, then was swallowed up again by the thick cumulonimbus clouds. He looked skyward and made the same determination that Manolo had earlier. These were storm clouds that would empty their mighty bellies full of water full of water sometime in the next 48 hours.

He had sent emissaries up river a few days ago with gifts and money, but he had not heard back from them - always a bad sign. He hoped the natives were still friendly. Sometimes the drug runners would stop them once they entered Colombia, which they were in now, or sometimes the friendly natives were now unfriendly, if they were being paid more by someone else.

He shuddered against the early morning chill. He still had contacts up here that could not be bought. There was still a measure of safety even up here. The only problem was that the farther you went upcountry, the less chances you had for protection. Life on this part of the river was never a guarantee. He glanced at his guns and torpedo tubes outlined against the dark sky. That's why you needed to take precautions. Bill, like one of his heroes, General George S. Patton, read his Bible every day. He, like Patton, also swore lustily and lived well. Even now, he couldn't help thinking about a blasphemous paraphrasing of the Bible which said, "Even though I walk through the valley of death, I shall fear no evil... because I am the meanest son-of-a-bitch in the valley." He smiled. He hoped God didn't mind too much. His faith and love of the Lord had gotten him through his life this far, and he didn't intend for this to be his last voyage. He had too much to live for.

As the boat began to turn, he could feel the current shift. There was always turbulence here and the boat began to rock and shake as the bow hit the two merging currents. Earlier at supper, they had been discussing what they could expect the next day. Bill had lectured them all sternly.

"You will probably see many of the locals coming down to the water to greet us. They will most likely be friendly and we will trade with them. Up here, trade means trade. Not like the other countries do with the U.S. Here, there is no trade deficit. We give them a dollar's worth of food and goods and they give us a dollar's worth of information and goods."

"What kind of 'goods' do you trade," Robin asked.

"Ammo, cheap jewels, machinery parts, candles and some raw materials they use. Their life is pretty simple up here, but there is always some danger from the locals in the cities.

"You mean the drug runners," John said quietly.

"Yeah," Bill replied, "there is always the danger from that. Unfortunately, it is a large part of the country's export, but they are trying to change that."

"Do you get involved," Robin asked.

Bill's voice went flat. "Watch yourself kid."

"Robin!" John said, "Watch what you say." The room had gone quiet.

"I didn't mean do you run drugs. I was just wondering if you are ever caught in the middle of the smugglers and the locals," Robin recovered quickly. The tension in the room lessened.

"Sorry, kid. I just get tired of the tourists on my boat asking me to get them a gram or two. I don't use drugs and I don't sell them. There are safer and better things you can do to make a living." He looked over at John, who was listening intently. "Even when I'm up to my neck in hock, I still can't bring myself to cross that line."

Nobody said anything for a few seconds. It was Jack who broke the ice. "This fish is good, what is it, Manolo?"

Manolo grinned, "Big piranha fish!" Jack, Robin and Kimmiko gagged and started to spit out their food.

"Relax, relax," Bill laughed, further easing the tension in the room, "Its pacu fish. They only resemble piranhas, but are in the same species." He added hastily, "Some weigh over 200 pounds, but they only eat vegetation, not meat."

"They are really good," Jack said around a mouthful of fish.

"My compliments to the chef!" Kimmiko added, looking towards Manolo and raising her wine glass towards him.

Manolo smiled, and looked away, *"Gracias, señorita."*

Kimmiko looked at him a little puzzled. She had talked a lot to Manolo that morning and found him to be warm and friendly. But while he was preparing dinner, she had tried to talk to him. He acted distant and, although still nice, would not add anything to their conversation.

She shrugged, *"De nada,"* she replied.

"So what about the real giant piranha, John's been telling me about for years?" Jack asked, "Is he full of it, or are there such things in these waters?"

Bill sat back in his chair and locked his hands behind his head. He looked up at the ceiling and paused, choosing his words carefully. "Yes and no," he began. "There are plenty of legends, but no actual proof. No one I know has ever seen them."

"So," John asked, "isn't that part of the legend, that no one who ever sees them lives long enough to tell the world?"

"That's convenient!" Robin chimed in.

Bill looked over at Robin. He didn't like or trust this guy at all. He glanced over at Manolo, who was staring intently back at him, trying to tell him something. Manolo had good instincts for a teenager. That's what living on this river did for you. He continued. "It's not just that, but you're right, that would be convenient. I know a lot of guys who do some pretty clandestine things up here and none of them have ever said anything about them. Sure, you have to worry about the smugglers, natives and the river, always the river. Most of the critters people fear around here are the caimans and the snakes. They are very dangerous and can kill quickly. The piranhas are of little concern, but you don't usually go into small, shallow streams where you know there are hungry fish. Explorers and traders, even though many of them are outsiders, never even mention it. Don't you think that if there were giant piranhas, someone would have at least seen some evidence? Even a washed up skeleton?

"Well, as Robin said," John added, "it's pretty convenient. Part of the legend says they are cannibalistic and they eat their own when one is sick or had died fighting."

"Okay," said Bill, "tell us what you know."

They all looked at John. "Well, the legend begins several centuries ago, up around the legendary Lost City of the El Dorado," he began. "They had decided that too many people knew about the location of the El Dorado, who was actually a chief. The local Indian tribe in that area, Lake Guatavita, near Bogotá Columbia, was known as the Chibchas. Some were good and others were very bad. Legend has it that they performed human sacrifices, to make their golden gods happy.

"Eventually, the Chiefs decided to move to an area down in a lower valley. An area equally rich in gold and surrounded by waters which eventually led to the Amazon River. There was a problem, however. The area had gold, but it also had caimans, piranhas, killer snakes, big cats, poisonous bugs and everything else you could think of.

"It took many years, but eventually, the Chibchas migrated to that area and became lost in the dense jungles, never to be heard from again. One reason they became isolated is that they bred the piranhas with larger fish to create giant killer fish, to protect their gold and tribe. The warriors became more fierce and aggressive, eventually preying on smaller, surrounding tribes, until they themselves became masters of the jungle."

John sat back in his chair. There wasn't a sound from his audience.

Jack was the first to speak. "And you say these devils are still around," he asked incredulously.

"So I've been told and, with all due respect to my friend Bill," he nodded his head toward Bill, "I believe it to be true.

"Charming. What about the Indians?" Jack asked.

Bill answered for him. "The Chibcha Indians are still real, but I only know of the good ones. Supposedly there are still bad ones where we are going, but still, no one knows about the Lost City of the El Dorado. At least, if they do, they are not talking about it."

"What about the *Conquistadors,*" Robin asked. "I thought they tore this area up and took out all the gold.

"That's the beauty of all this," said John. They did come here in the name of Cortés, plus the others and got the crap kicked out of them. They went back to the Aztecs for easier pickings."

"So now we have a new version of Jaws. Christ!" said Jack miserably. This really wasn't turning out to be Disneyland at all.

It was Bill's turn to laugh, "Listen to y'all," he said smilingly. "Get a little wine into you and a little old fairy-tail, and you are ready to run for the hills. Ha, Ha Ha!"

They all smiled and looked around as he continued. "What

you have to fear are the real dangers – the ones you can see and the ones you can't. Come with me." They all went up on deck. It was pitch black, except for the moon and the navigation lights. "Look at the water," he said. They all did.

"What are those red glowing things?" Kimmi asked. The PT boat's bow light was shining down and illuminating the water ahead of them.

"Caiman's eyes," Manolo answered. Fall in and they will chew you to pieces in seconds."

"See," Bill continued, "there are things that will eat you, but to stay alive you need to do just one thing - stay out of the water!"

After everyone went to bed, Bill stayed at the helm. He was scheduled to be relieved by Manolo at about 0400 hours. Then he would sleep for about four and a half hours. This was his pattern on these trips. He never slept much. There would be time for sleep later. Now he needed to concentrate. The currents were diverging and creating a rip tide, which was continuing to throw the boat around. He wondered if everyone was still sleeping. He gunned the engines to move out of the way of a large log which had suddenly appeared. He never would have seen it, except that it was making an even larger splash than the tide around it. He was good at this river and everyone know it. There were those who wanted him to lose his boat to the loan shark so that he might be forced to captain for them, on one of the large luxury steamers which went up and down the Amazon with tourists. The thought made him shudder. He would never fit in a tuxedo and didn't feel captain's bars were appropriate for a river pirate like himself. He settled in for a long night.

****

It was still very dark out. The river kept up its unsuccessful and endless quest to run out of water while it moved towards the Atlantic Ocean. Bill, still at the helm, jumped suddenly as the hatch in front of him opened and Manolo came out on deck. "It's only 3:15 little *amigo*," Bill said cheerily. He always was happy to see Manolo. He guessed he loved him in a fatherly way.

"*Si, Capitán* Bill. I can't sleep."

Bill thought about this quietly for a minute. "Your mind is becoming bewitched, my friend."

"From the river?" Manolo asked confused.

"No, by my niece, Kimmiko."

"NO! No, *mi padrone'!*" he said. "I would never betray your trust!"

"Relax son," Bill said easily. "She is just a little confused. It's okay that you look at her. I see that you treat her with respect...," he paused, "unlike others."

Manolo was still upset. *"Muy Dios mio!"* he said miserably, My God, Help me!

Bill handed him over to the wheel. "Do me a favor Manolo. Just keep an eye on her. I really love her and I don't really mind if you get attached to her. But I have to baby-sit the Professor and the good doctor, so I might need a little help with Kimmi."

"*Si, padrone,*" Manolo sounded a little relieved. "I like the doctor and your friend John, but *Senior'* Robin...," his voice trailed off.

"Don't worry about him," Bill said. He picked up his

Winchester and checked the rounds and the lever action. A sharp click was audible as the hammer fell on the first chamber which he kept empty. "I know how to deal with enemies if they don't behave."

He turned and went below for some sleep as Manolo was left wondering how his thoughts could be so easily read.

******

Dawn came late to the river, but by 8:30 everyone had risen, including Bill and assembled on the main deck. Robin, as though to make up for his behavior of last night graciously poured coffee. Kimmiko smiled into his eyes as he poured her coffee, but he looked hastily away. Now that he had had her, he was afraid to betray his mission. He noticed the hurt look that formed in her eyes. Manolo, still steering without a break since Bill had gone to sleep five hours before, was feeling the achiness seep into his shoulders.

Bill was the first to speak. "We will be hitting the village before long. I think they will be friendly, but if something should happen to me, I want you all to get the hell away from here." He looked over at Manolo. "I know your tired, son, but you will need to keep at the helm for a while longer." Manolo shrugged and smiled. "Doc, can you man the machinegun like you did yesterday?"

"Sure, it would be a kick in the pants!"

Bill smiled, "Just don't shoot me in the pants fella. Don't worry, when the time comes, I will teach you about controlling the gun and accurately firing the ordinance."

He looked over a Kimmiko. "Kimmi, I want you to stay on the bow when we hit the shore. Stay close to the helm in case you have to run. Sometimes the sight of a young girl will keep them from doing something violent."

John looked at Bill. "Don't you think she should stay below out of danger?" he demanded.

"John, you know I will protect her and," he added, "so will Manolo."

Robin felt a twinge of jealously and wondered for the hundredth time if he was really on the right side. "What about me?" he asked with a trifle of irritation. "I know how to fire a gun."

"Bill smiled, "Good, because you will be going ashore with the Professor and me and you can watch my back." Robin looked away, anger giving way to confusion.

They rounded a bend in the river and there was the village suddenly to their right. Along the shores were over one hundred men, women and children. Bill relaxed visibly. He saw one of the emissaries, a man named Regan, he had sent upriver, smiling and waving to them as they approached.

"How did they know we were so close," asked Robin.

"Because they have been following our progress since we hit this river over eight hours ago," Bill said quietly. "Doc, I still want you in that gun turret," he motioned to the forward gun mount on the starboard side. "But don't put your hands on the weapon. Just stand in the turret, okay."

"Sure." Jack slid around the front of the cabin and hoisted himself into the gun turret.

"Kimmi," Bill said suddenly, "what are you wearing beneath that sweatshirt?" He hoped it would be something.

"Bathing suit top, why?"

"Okay, I know it's a little cold, but these natives are not used to seeing women wear clothes." She immediately pulled off her sweatshirt and, shivering slightly in the morning cold, went and sat down on the bow, her back against the windows of the charthouse.

Manolo had slowed the boat and was expertly maneuvering to a spot he knew where there was still deep enough water, that they wouldn't run aground. The PT boat only drew four feet of water. Bill, John and Robin stood on the right side of the boat just forward of the first set of torpedo tubes. The boat began to yaw over with their weight and Manolo adjusted the thrust of the right engine expertly to compensate. John also took a step backwards to offset his weight.

The Indians drew closer to the shore. They were smiling and waving openly. Jack could see that many of them had even, white teeth. They must have great genes or a great orthodontist, he thought. He stared at the young children and the teenagers. His hands hung at his side. He knew that whatever the provocation, he could never bring himself to shoot these beautiful people.

The PT boat moved into the shore and Manolo swung the stern around by gunning the motor twice. He idled down and looked towards Bill who had jumped off the ship into the shallow water up to his knees. He strode over towards a bulky man, wearing white pants, a white shirt and a wide white hat. They embraced and the man whispered something in Bill's ear. Bill looked over to Manolo and made a slashing motion across his throat. Manolo idled down and began preparations to cut the engines. After a few more moments, the world went quiet as the three mighty Packard engines became silent. Just then, the Indians cheered out loud and what sounded like a million birds started yelling and shrieking in the jungle.

Bill motioned for two of the Indians to tie up the boat, which caused Kimmiko to squeal suddenly as one of the Indians splashed up onto the bow and quickly took the coiled rope off the bow without even looking at her. Once the boat was tied fore and aft, Bill motioned for everyone to disembark. Only Manolo stayed on board. This had been prearranged by he and John. As the others jumped off the boat, being helped by the friendly, grinning natives, Manolo casually picked up the Winchester rifle and laid it across the control panel as he continued to shut down the engines. It was likely they would be here at least for the next several hours.

******

Bill and three of the Chief Indians sat in a small hut not too far from the edge of the river, but out of sight of the boat. John, Jack and two of the other head Indians stood behind them. Robin and Kimmiko were outside the hut talking quietly with the emissary, named Regan.

So, what is it you are after this time, *Capitán* Bill?" the Head Chief began pleasantly.

"My friends are on a pilgrimage, your Honor."

"I see. A holy pilgrimage, perhaps, *Capitán?*"

"Perhaps," Bill said a little evasively. John started to say something, but one look from Bill silenced him. This was not lost on the natives in the room.

The Chief made a small motion, and as if by magic a young native girl with very long, straight black hair appeared wearing a silk wrap around skirt, and served them succulent fruit on her knees. He smiled at her and with a small sound in his voice, dismissed her. She stood, turned suddenly and disappeared as quickly as she had appeared.

This quick exchange had the chief's desired effect on Jack and John, who followed the young girl's naked back out of the room, losing track of the negotiations.

Only Bill had kept a straight face and stared intently at the Chief. "Your daughter, I presume?"

"Yes, my friend, you remember her?"

"It's been some time, I'm afraid. If she is the same one I held on my knee, then the years are catching up to us."

The Chief paused and looked down. This man deserved respect. He remembered when the guerrilla soldiers came down from the North. Their village would have been wiped out, but *Capitán* Bill and his boat had sailed in with many bullets and explosives and had saved his village.

"We are old friends, you and I," the Chief said. He gestured to the other two Chiefs sitting next to him. "My sons and I do not forget our debt to you."

At this, Bill made a dismissive waive of his hand. "I did nothing unusual, my friend."

The Chief would not be put off. "Let us speak plainly. The river speaks in whispers of your intent. The El Dorado may at last yield it's fortune to you, or else it's curse. You must always beware and be on guard. Because of your friendship to us, many of the guerrillas, soldiers and cocaine dealers leave us alone." He paused. "You see, it is not entirely out of love that we offer our protection. Our safety is ensured by your safety. I believe the Americans have a phrase from a movie. You are our Godfather, and we will help to protect you and those you love."

Bill stood up and bowed respectfully. "It is not just the gold of the El Dorado we seek." John looked at him sharply. The others listened intently. "This area could be an important source of information for my archeological friend. There are many mysteries to be uncovered and this area must be secure for our party and future exploration parties."

The Chief bowed his head. "It is good that we speak this way. The road ahead may lead to bloodshed and death and this could leave us with grieving mothers, wives and children. They must know their sacrifices are for the good of all and not a waste of life. Many are too young to know the life you have given them, as it was a long time ago.

"You must understand the area you will travel to is full of coca, gold and other valuable things. The Indians there are not of our own. They are the Chibchas, fierce warriors of another time. They are of two peoples. There are the good and the bad. The good will not hurt you, but they will not help you. The bad ones will hurt you and will feed you to the fish."

They were silent as they thought about his words. Jack was the first to speak. "The fish?" he said as he felt the hairs on the back of his neck rise up.

The Chief looked at them. There was no longer any joy in his eyes. "How much we help you may bring death to my people," he said sadly. "How much you know may help you help yourself."

Bill spoke up, "Your Honor, we do not require much. We will sail immediately and will travel," he paused, "to the left river when we hit the fork. I have seen the photos, but the fork is hidden under the mists."

The Chief smiled again. "Then you would have a pleasant trip, until you discovered the whispering falls, so named because men whisper their last breath as the falls draw them in and then smash their boats in a matter of moments. The river to the right is much more pleasant and may take you to waters you might find more to your liking." His eyes darkened again. "But I must warn you again. The fish of the right branch are much larger and not as cordial as you might find in these waters." He shrugged. It was a dismissal.

The others rose to go. Bill had remained standing. They all bowed low to the Chief. "Before you go," the Chief began, "I would like you all to join us for a feast this evening. It is not often we can show friendship and hospitality to those we care for. You will eat the freshest fruit, fish, manioc and we will drink *masato*."

"What's *masato*?" John asked.

Bill answered, "Fermented manioc plant mixed with spit," Jack grimaced and turned green. The natives laughed.

"You know, Your Honor," Bill began, I brought along several extra cases of beer. The ones you like and probably enough for the whole tribe."

The Chief smiled. "All would surely be grateful."

****

After they had left the hut, the Chief's sons turned to their father. The eldest, built large like his father asked, "My father, how much can we help them. The evil ones of the Chibcha's will hear it from the whisperings of the jungle and they will curse us and become our enemies."

His younger brother spoke up, also big and strong, he was more sympathetic. "My brother speaks the truth father. But that man was our savior once and we could help him again, perhaps so that those of the jungle or the river will not know."

The Chief looked at his two young sons, who had grown up so strong, but much too fast. He saw his own days were becoming shorter. "He reached out to his two sons and held their hands. He smiled to think of their hands, now larger than his own, were once so tiny that they could only hold onto one of his fingers. "My sons, your loyalty to our friend touches me. If we are to help at all, our help must be silent. If these men are able to even find the gold and get past the evil ones, they will still have to overcome the giant piranhas. No white man has ever come back from this area of the river. We will wait and watch. We may still help our friends, but we will not start a war."

The eldest spoke, "That is good. I too wish to help, but our debt should not bring death to our people."

"Agreed," said the Chief, "There are those I remember from many years ago, when the two of you were very young. Good Chibchas who live separated from the bad ones by the high rivers. It has been many years, but if they are still alive, then they might be of help to us. Perhaps we can get word to them to make contact with our friends here. We will assure them of their honesty. I will ponder this, my sons."

The feast was everything they had promised. Food was taken out to Manolo, who had stayed at his post all day and into the evening. The dancing by the natives was heady and sensual. Energetic dances, almost overwhelmed by the frantic drumming, gave way to slow rhythmic dances which stirred the emotions of the men. Even Kimmi, carried away by the pure ancient alchemy of the Indian rituals, reached under the low tables and found Robin's willing hand. They soon disappeared and became shadows in the darkened jungle.

******

Dawn came early and wet. The storm clouds had been moving in more and more and looked as though they would break soon. All had slept on the boat. Fortunately for Kimmiko and Robin, they had been the first ones back to the boat, even after making love three times in the jungle. Returning, they found a silent Manolo standing at the helm, looking out over the water, holding the Winchester. He acknowledged them only with a slight nod and wave of the rifle. The others showed up a few minutes later and all went to bed immediately. Only Bill stayed up. He had slept during the day and now relieved Manolo at watch for the night. He needn't have bothered. The Chief had sent ten of his best men to stand watch directly around the boat and another two dozen in the trees and bushes around her. He also had twenty more out in the river in open boats watching their flank.

Bill heard noise below and, thinking it was Manolo, bent low to tell him to go back to bed, because he was still not ready move ahead yet. He was surprised to see Robin Quigley round the ladder and make his way up. He stifled a grin and made it into a polite smile.

"Ahoy young man! What gets you up before the sun?"

"Bad headache, Captain Treese," came the reply. I don't know what was in that stuff the natives were brewing, but it was sweet and I have an awful hangover."

Bill smiled, a genuine smile this time. He decided not to tell him the whole truth yet. "Just a powerful elixir they brew up. It's a little strong the first time, until you get used to it. Want some aspirin?"

"Sure, what the hell."

Bill pulled the bottle out from a space below the helm. "Two's enough. Local stuff. Stronger than what's available back home."

"Thanks." He started back below, but turned around. "You don't like me very much, do you?"

The question, took Bill by surprise. "I like the fact that your direct and you don't pussyfoot around." He shrugged. "John likes you, and I guess that's good enough for me. But," he went on, "Kimmi sometimes gets a little confused and since she lost her mom, I've sort of played the long lost uncle, you know," he smiled a crooked smile and cocked his eyebrow and tilted his head to one side. "So if I come off as a jerk sometimes, it's just because I care about the girl and I want to protect her."

Robin smiled back at him. "Yeah I understand that. I like her too and I will do my best to protect her."

Bill's face straightened out. He stared into Robin's left eye.

"That's good. You should be glad that I will watch over her too." He paused, "To the end," he said quietly.

Robin stared back. It was a challenge. "To the end," he said. Then he disappeared through the hatch, leaving Bill to look out at the clouds which seemed to meet the water just up the river.

******

CHAPTER IV

THE FALLS AND
THE FORK IN THE RIVER

BY MIDDAY, THE RAIN HAD STILL NOT FALLEN. The boat moved up the river steadily, if not silently. The engines gave a mighty roar, whenever Bill goosed them around another floating log, animal or other interference. Breakfast and lunch had come and gone without incident. Jack, Kimmiko and Robin were surprised at the monotony of the trip. No one expected this to be dull, but it was. Little did they know the situation would soon be changing for them.

Bill had pulled up to one other stop since leaving the Indians. A small port town of natives, Colombian soldiers, mercenaries and obviously drug runners lived together in some type of unholy harmony. It was here that he got fuel and some supplies. His emissary, Regan had apparently made it here ahead of them and made arrangements - for large sums of money, of course. Bill had not seen Regan, but hoped he was okay. He had gone ashore alone and secured the necessary provisions, plus extra fuel for his thirsty engines.

Bill noticed he was being followed soon after they had left the port. He squinted back into the late afternoon glare. The sun fought the clouds, which, in return, filtered through dense jungle forest. Everything was getting too dark too fast. Suddenly he saw the boat break quickly around the corner. He grabbed his binoculars, while trying to steer and look backwards at the same time. It looked like one of the riverine boats from Vietnam he used to command. He could see twin gun mounts and what looked like someone holding a bazooka or rocket launcher. He pushed forward on the throttle. The river was heavy with flood waters and he was having more and more trouble seeing the floating logs. He pressed the siren to call for general quarters, which resulted in the loud "whoop, whoop", familiar to anyone with combat experience or has seen a W.W. II movie. Below, the others were napping, except for Manolo, who was preparing their dinner.

A small band of mercenary soldiers, once Colombian police who had changed sides, had earlier left the dock in their own armed river boat. This one was also outfitted with machine guns, and, while they did not have a 20 MM cannon aboard, they did have a surface-to-surface rocket launcher. Soviet made, this could blow Bill's PT boat out of the water. The catch was, that the Colombians wanted Bill's boat. They were smuggling large amounts of cocaine out of the country on fishing boats, with thousands of fish gutted and filled with the powder. The PT boat had infinite places to hide vast quantities of coke. It's size, speed and firepower would make and excellent addition to their fleet.

At the sound of the siren, everyone scrambled and piled on top of each other getting up the ladder, onto the deck.

"What the hell is happening?" John yelled above the roar of the engines. Bill swerved suddenly to avoid a large log, causing them all to fall over on the deck. Kimmi screamed as she was nearly flung over the side, but fortunately she fell against Jack who grabbed her before it was too late!

"We're being attacked!" Bill yelled back. He had clung to the wheel and had not fallen. He righted the boat. "Everybody grab a life vest. Now!" he screamed. "Kimmi, go below into the galley and get behind the reefer. Robin, go below and stay with her. There's metal there which will protect you against bullets," but not a rocket shell he didn't add. He was now in full command. Vietnam ended for him over thirty years ago, but his battle instincts were still intact.

"John, get on the starboard gun."

"The what?"

"The front machine gun on the right side! Jack, go aft and get on the port gun. Manolo, you get on the cannon. Jack and John, watch your fire. Don't hose Manolo down. Those safety rails should protect us against any wild firing." The safety stop metal tubing rails on every PT boat were installed so that the machinegun would only allow fire towards the enemy planes and at the sides of the boat. "I'm going to outrun these bastards. Now move!"

Everyone scrambled to their positions. Suddenly, the air was alive with bullets. The riverine boat, smaller and more maneuverable was gaining on them. Both enemy machine guns were firing simultaneously. The river had narrowed and darkened. Tracer bullets lit up the river and caused Jack and John to sink down lower in their gun turrets, one of the few places there was protective metal, which had been added by Bill. In addition to the life jackets they wore, there had been Navy surplus helmets which they put on. As Bill maneuvered the boat back and forth, partly to avoid logs and partly to avoid enemy fire, they found it almost impossible to fire on their targets. Jack, saying a quick prayer, was thinking, what the hell was he doing here. This situation had made his life a little too lively.

Manolo was also having his troubles. The cannon would not unlock and was too heavy to move manually. He finally got the cannon wheel unstuck and, quickly loading the 20mm rounds, began firing at the pursuing boat.

The shells, missing their target as the enemy maneuvered expertly, were exploding all around them. Bill had juiced his engines up and was trying to figure a way out of this. The pursuing boat was still gaining on them, when suddenly, their bullets found their mark and hit Bill's left engine. A fire-light went on as smoke began billowing out of the port side of his stern. "Damn it!" he screamed. He yelled at John who was next to him in the starboard turret, "John, go below and get Robin. You have to get the fire out or we'll explode!"

John had gone pale beneath his helmet. "Okay, okay!" He moved below to try to find Robin. He was now regretting ever getting into archeology.

Jack was still firing away, but his view was being blocked by the thick smoke still billowing out of the stern. He saw his tracer bullets hit the deck of the enemy, cutting a matching gash in their hull. Unfortunately, there was nothing vital in the bow, except small sleeping quarters. Manolo was also firing away. He got lucky as a round he'd aimed at the hull of the boat hit the man holding the rocket launcher. Seeing that the PT boat was not going to slow down or stop, he had been trying to take out the bridge, while sparing the rest of the boat. A tricky shot, but entirely possible, given the accuracy of these Soviet missiles. He never knew what hit him as he flew off the boat, his body instantly obliterated.

The PT boat was slowing and Bill had to cut the left engine, lest they become fireworks rivaling the Fourth of July. He saw that they had passed the fork in the river and, because of the enemy fire, had taken the left branch, which the Chief had told him not to take. He knew there was a deadly waterfall up ahead which, at this speed would draw the boat in under the falls and smash them to smithereens, even if the enemy wasn't successful. He noticed that the current had changed suddenly, pulling them forward, instead of pushing against them. There had to be some kind of undertow or freak of nature. The boat, in spite of losing an engine was moving forward faster. He looked back, but the Colombians had not reached the rip current yet.

He then made a decision which would either save them or get them killed. Either way, it would be over soon enough. "Hang on!" he yelled back. The gesture was useless as nobody could hear him. He maneuvered to his left and, gaining a few precious yards, and then spun the wheel madly to the right, at the same time reversing the starboard engine. The move caused the boat to heel over suddenly to the right, the starboard deck submerging briefly as the boat spun 180 degrees in the opposite direction.

Jack was thrown over into the gun turret railing, cutting a deep gash in his shoulder. Bill had braced himself and, using a special rope, had chained himself to the helm. Manolo had a similar chain which would connect him to the cannon, but because of the suddenness of the situation and all the confusion, he had neglected to secure himself properly. As a result, when Bill spun the wheel, Manolo lost his grip and went flying off into the water, narrowly missing the two active propellers, which were spinning at several thousand RPMs!

Below Robin and John, trying to put out the small fire in the tight engine compartment, were hurled against the bulkhead, but were kept from being burned by a firewall. Kimmi flew across the galley and was knocked unconscious as her head struck the wall. Fortunately, due to Manolo's instincts, and reacting to the "General Quarters" call, as he exited the galley, he had hit a gas shut off button, similar to those at all service stations, which shut down the propane delivery system. Had he not done this, the boat might have exploded or caught fire, due to the excessive yaw caused by Bill's maneuver.

Now Bill was heading directly for the enemy. Battle instincts had taken over. He was now in tactical command of the situation and he was moving forward on instinct. "What are you doing?!" screamed Jack, who had righted himself. He was too stunned and overwhelmed by what was happening to even fire his machine gun.

Bill didn't answer. He was focused now on his target. He was approaching his enemy from the right side of their bow.

They were approximately at his one o'clock position, and approximately two thousand yards away, both closing in at over 80 knots. His eyes narrowed as he reached down for the button which would launch his forward, right side torpedo.

The enemy boat viewed the sudden maneuver with some alarm. The captain, a 45 year-old Colombian mercenary thought he had seen everything on this river for the past 30 years. He thought the PT boat was going to try to pass him and go back down the river. He too knew about the deadly falls ahead, and, while this move didn't entirely surprise him, he had to figure out his own evasive tactics. It was much easier pursuing your target he thought grimly, but he always enjoyed a good game of *pollo* with a *gringo*.

Bill knew he had to fire quickly. If they were too far away, he might miss and not get a second shot. If they were too close, the explosion could out his own boat. He noticed another man had taken the bow on the enemy boat and was preparing to fire a rocket at them.

Instinctively he juked the throttle and wheel, taking them momentarily off course, but his action saved them. The stinger, launched with a small puff of smoke, streaked through the air and just missed their bow. Bill pulled his boat back on course and, suddenly, heard an explosion behind them. The missile had likely hit a tree or a rock wall from the sound. He sighted the boat now only eight hundred yards away and pressed the torpedo launcher. "Fire one!" he yelled excitedly, the adrenaline rush overwhelmed him. The forward starboard torpedo shot off the boat in an explosion of steam from the CO2 launcher. He rolled the wheel to the right causing the boat to go off at a forty-five degree angle to the approaching enemy. This brought Jack, in the port gun turret, around full in the face of the enemy's guns, but also brought them into his firing zone. He immediately ducked down, and regaining his senses, began firing again.

The captain of the enemy boat had seen the torpedo hit the water and, for a moment, was too stunned to react. He had forgotten that he was facing a fully dressed W.W.II combat boat. He tried to turn his boat, but his instincts failed him as the maneuver brought his starboard hull directly into the path of the torpedo, which had closed the distance in less than five seconds. There was a tremendous explosion as the torpedo ripped the boat in half and then the secondary explosions ignited! The smaller boat's ordinance then blew these halves into a million pieces. There was nothing left of the enemy, except falling parts and a burning, sinking hull.

Both Bill and Jack, the only ones left on deck, cheered as their enemy disappeared before their eyes. Bill immediately throttled down and scanned the sky for large wreckage falling down. The boat was hit by a few pieces, but nothing large enough to cause serious damage. Jack jumped out of the turret and ran forward to hug Bill. "Way to go, Skipper!" he shouted happily.

Bill started to turn the boat back to the left, to head back down the river and away from the killer current. He had missed the correct branch of the river that the Chief had quietly recommended to him. He also knew he needed to get past the destroyed hull of the enemy boat which was burning crisply on the surface. He started to make maneuvers around the boat when he suddenly realized someone was missing.

"Hey," Jack realized at the same instant, "where's Manolo?"

Bill spun the wheel around. "He must have fallen off. I've got to find him!" he said with urgency in his voice. He began moving back up the tributary slowly, looking for him.

Suddenly they heard John below, "Jack! Jack! Get down here! Kimmi's hurt! Jack and Bill looked at each other for a second. Bill nodded. "I'll find him," he said grimly as Jack hurried down the ladder.

Jack hit the galley in less than four seconds. He saw Kimmi lying on the floor, her hair matted with blood. She was unconscious. John was over her, crying and Robin was sitting on the floor, holding his own head and looking like he was about to pass out. Jack went over to her and took her carotid pulse. It was steady. He pushed back her eyelid, causing the pupil to contract visibly, even in the dim light of the galley. He checked her head and found only a small cut, but it had bled allot, as head wounds often do. She began to moan and her eyelids started fluttering. Jack reached over to John. "She'll be okay partner."

John looked visibly relieved. "Thanks Jack," he said gratefully.

Kimmiko began to whimper, "Daaaddieeee," she cried softly, her hands moving to her head.

"Just a second, John," Jack said. He made a quick assessment of her neck, back and ribs. He checked her arms, pelvis, abdomen and legs. "I think she's okay. Nothing broken. We'll know how she is when she fully regains consciousness. She probably has a concussion and will probably be dizzy and sick to her stomach." He touched John's arm, "Stay with her. We've lost Manolo and I have to help Bill look for him." John looked up in surprise and nodded. He moved over, wrapped his arms around his daughter and held her tightly.

Jack looked over at Robin, "You okay?" Robin nodded without looking up. Jack turned and sprinted up the ladder. "Keep her warm," he yelled back.

He made it to the deck in time to see Bill frantically looking left and right, in and out of the water. "Gotta find him, gotta find him," Bill kept saying softly over and over. "My fault, my fault." Jack put his hand on Bill's shoulder, but it was shoved rudely away. "Go up on the point of the bow and look for him," was Bill's rough reply. Jack obeyed at once. He suddenly saw the shape of a young boy floating in the water about 100 yards off the port bow. "Bill!" he yelled and pointed. Bill immediately revved up and covered the distance. "Jack, take the helm." He reversed the engines and went dead stop in the water. Jack scrambled back to the bridge as Bill dove immediately over the side.

Fortunately, Manolo was floating face up in the water, and came to immediately as Bill reached out for him. His life jacked had saved him. He and Bill looked at each other. The water here was cold. "You okay, son?" Bill asked with obvious concern in his voice.

"*Si, amigo. Muy Dios mio*, I'm sorry I fell out. *Por favor*, forgive me, *Capitán* Bill." They hugged each other, as Jack slowly and carefully brought the boat about to pick them up.

He idled the boat down and put it in neutral. He reached over the side of the boat and helped pull the two men aboard.

Jack noticed that Manolo had a small trickle of blood flowing off his temple. Manolo sat down in the bridge as Bill took over the helm. Jack reached over and began to clean out Manolo's wounds with a clean cloth.

"Hey, hey, Doc," Bill said happily, glad that his crew and boat had made it out alive, "I thought you were just a bone cracker."

Jack didn't even look up as he worked, "I'm a doctor, pal, same as any other physician. I just don't use drugs and knives to help people get well."

"Sorry, sorry," Bill grinned as he began to maneuver the boat back down the river, "didn't know you were so sensitive!" he laughed, obviously relieved at the turn of events.

Jack smiled. "*No problemo.* I don't usually do this medic stuff on daily basis. But I do know how to keep people alive and well, obviously, even on the battlefield." He looked behind Bill, "Hey what the heck is that?" he said pointing back up the river at a thick cloud of black smoke coming up over the jungle behind a bend in the river.

Bill turned around and looked back. It didn't look like a jungle fire. "Hey, that's oil burning!" he exclaimed. He wheeled the boat around, again heading back up the river toward the smoke. John stuck his head up through the small hatch in the bridge, "Why do we keep turning around?" he said with obvious alarm.

Bill motioned with his chin, "There's something wrong up ahead. That guy back there got off a stinger missile and I think he hit something up river." Just then, the boat began to pick up speed as it again hit the rip current caused by the falls up ahead.

The men looked at each other and hung on as they picked up speed. Bill throttled back and was ready to put it into reverse or spin the boat and try to make a run for it. As they started to turn around a wide bend, they could hear the roar of the falls. After a minute, the noise of the plummeting water got louder and louder. How's Kimmi?" Bill yelled to John.

She's okay. She's crying and that's a good sign. Robin is with her." He paused, thinking. "You know, Bill, I think that's the first time I've seen her cry since her mom's funeral. She's always been so damn tough." Bill nodded, but his response was drowned out as they came within in sight of the falls.

The sight was staggering. Four separate falls, the waters sometimes together and sometimes apart, fell from over a thousand feet straight down, creating what looked like a wall of pulsating water. All around the base, the water churned madly, frothing like some wild beast. Nobody said anything.

Suddenly, Manolo sat up on the deck, pointed ahead and shouted, "Look!" They then saw what was causing the thick smoke. A passenger steamboat, approximately 100 feet long was burning out of control, and at the same time was sinking. It was also moving toward the falls. They weren't sure which of the elements would get her first, the fire, the falls, or the depths of the river. On top of that, they could see huge caimans on the shore, and there were probably more in the water.

Bill began making evasive turns and began gunning the two remaining engines. With the port engine shut down it was like running on a broken leg. He had to get his boat closer to see if there might be survivors. The Law of the Sea said he had to investigate and save anyone aboard.

John yelled out, "Look! On the deck!" They could see what looked like two women and a young girl clinging to the stern deck railing. The stern was sinking and the bow was up. The boat was burning and they were drifting closer and closer to the roaring falls. Now they could see the caimans in the water circling for an opportunity to attack.

Bill began barking orders. They had less than a minute to save them. "Manolo get on the bow and get ready with a line. Lash yourself down or you'll be swimming again! Doc, get back on the machine gun. Don't fire unless I tell you to, and make damn sure you aim low. The caimans are the green ones in the water. John, get over here by the helm, I may need to go swimming myself!" He began to show John how to run the boat.

The situation was desperate. The flames were now over the superstructure and falling next to the women. They were screaming. Some of the spray from the falls began to hit the boat. A little of the fire went out as a result, but then suddenly the burning oil, floating on the water and saturating the deck, began spreading the flames faster and faster toward the stern. Gravity helped it, as the boat began sinking faster. Now one of the women began to slip, causing her legs to sink in the water.

"Jack, Jack!" screamed Bill as they saw a huge caiman start over toward her. Jack took aim at the reptile and with a single burst, hit it just before it closed its jaws on the frightened woman. "Great shot!" yelled Bill.

My lucky ass, thought Jack grimly. He couldn't have done that again in a million years, but he aimed again as more caiman started toward her. Fortunately, she had been pulled back up onto the deck by the other woman.

John was trying to bring the boat about next to the burning vessel. "Not too close, damnit!" yelled Bill. "Reverse, reverse!" John gunned the engines, throwing them into reverse. The current suddenly pulled them ahead, overpowering the engines. John had not compensated for his dead port engine and the boat began to spin around. Bill, who was now on the bow with Manolo, preparing to throw a line to the women, had to scramble back quickly into the cockpit. There was no time for niceties. He shoved John out of the way and grabbed the wheel. He gunned the engine and juked the motor back and forth. The boat responded to his touch. He knew this boat and how to maneuver her in the worst of conditions. His instincts as a skipper took over. "John, get on the bow. You have to help Manolo. Lash yourself to the boat and the secondary line to him. Tell him to release his harness. Move now!"

John scrambled onto the bow. He yelled instructions to Manolo, who knew what John wanted him to do.

Jack was holding the gun, frozen in place. "Doc!" Bill yelled, "Please get your thumb out of your ass and go up on the bow and help them!" Jack scrambled up and out of the gun turret and landed on the bow. Manolo looked back at Bill, who nodded to him. He suddenly dove in the water. John, looking stunned, tried to hold onto the rope, which was burning his hands as it played out quickly. They were now only ten feet away from the burning vessel. If Bill maneuvered the boat too far away, John and Jack both would end up in the water and would either drown or get eaten. If he got too close, then Manolo would be crushed and they would all join the sinking boat, which was now almost fully on fire.

Suddenly, Manolo jumped up on the stern deck of the burning boat next to the screaming women as if by magic. His sudden appearance next to them made them scream even louder. He never hesitated or looked back. He grabbed the young girl, who was about twelve, and flung her over the water onto the bow of the PT boat. Jack instinctively grabbed her, while Bill expertly maneuvered the boat closer. John took the line which was connected to Manolo and loosely wrapped a safety knot around one of the deck mounts.

One of the women, probably the child's mother, began hitting Manolo furiously. He bent under her wildly swinging arms and picked her up around the waist. By then, Bill had juiced the bow almost up onto the stern of the other boat. Manolo flung the fighting woman off him onto the bow of the PT boat and into the arms of Jack and John. The young girl was now safely in the cockpit with Bill. The last woman didn't wait for Manolo, but jumped onto the bow of the PT boat just ahead of the flames and just ahead of Manolo.

"Out, out out!" Jack screamed as they all pulled back off the bow and back to the outside of the cockpit.

Suddenly the flames of the boat intensified. They could feel the heat coming off of it in waves. All around them, the surface of the water was now aflame with burning oil.

"She's going to blow!" John shouted. Bill tried to pull the PT boat backwards, but the suction created by the sinking, burning vessel was pulling it down and forward.

Suddenly, as if by some miracle, the falls caused the burning boat to suddenly spin around and strike the bow of the PT boat, pushing it free. They were shoved forward with a mighty whoosh! The turning screws of the heavy PT boat suddenly grabbed and pushed it up and out of the water causing it to become momentarily airborne - the propellers biting madly at the air! The boat hit the churning water and the resulting wave bounced back against the PT boat, almost sending the two women, Jack, John and Manolo into the water.

The boat heeled over and spun around, as if controlled by some giant puppeteer. For an instant, it was facing away from the deadly falls and in that split-second of time, Bill rammed the throttle all the way forward. The engines screamed and the boat leaped forward as though shot from a cannon! It moved so fast, that Bill almost hit the opposite shore, but backed off with a quick turn of the wheel. Suddenly, a mighty explosion ripped through the passenger boat, shredding the old wooden vessel. For the second time, burning wreckage rained down around them. Bill raced down the river, never letting up on the throttle until they were past the rip current and almost all the way to the fork in the river. It was then that they all went below to recover.

****

The two women and the young girl shivered together in the small galley. Manolo had served the women hot coffee and the girl hot cocoa. Bill had fletched blankets for them. They were wet from their ordeal, and were now shivering. Robin and Kimmiko were also sitting at the table. Bill, John and Jack were standing, also drinking coffee.

They all looked at the new arrivals with curiosity and

sympathy. They looked to both be in their early thirties and the girl was no more than twelve or thirteen. Bill, as the commander of the vessel, spoke first. "So, who are you girls?" he said.

The three looked at one another. The one who had hit Manolo spoke first. "Hi," she put out her hand to Bill, "my name's Gwyndolyn Jones, but you can call me Gwen." They shook hands. "And this is my daughter Aleta." The young girl smiled shyly and took another sip of her hot cocoa.

Gwen looked over at the other woman, who, scowling fiercely, spoke up, "My name is Marianna Andolino. I demand to know who the hell are you and what the hell you were doing firing on our boat!"

"Whoa, cool your jets sister," Bill fired back. "We came to rescue you, not destroy you!"

"Sure, you just conveniently happened to be in the area when we were hit by a missile and then came to pick us up. What are you slave traders?"

"Ma'am," John spoke up, "my name is Dr. John Treese. I'm a research scientist from U.C. Berkeley on an archaeological mission up the Amazon. We were attacked just before we found you by an enemy boat full of mercenary gunmen. We too were lucky to survive. During the battle, they launched a missile that just barely missed our boat, but obviously hit yours. We saw the smoke and came to help."

This silenced the women. The young girl bent her head and began to weep softly. Kimmiko got up from her chair and went to put her arms around her. The girl, Aleta, put her head on Kimmi's chest and began to sob more. "What's wrong?" Kimmiko asked.

Gwen answered, "We had to leave our home and find a new life up the river. Not only have we lost everything we owned in the world, she lost her collie dog over the side of the boat during the fire." Aleta began to cry more now, as Kimmiko hugged her tighter.

"Where are you from?" Bill asked. They didn't look like natives of the area, more like dark skinned Asians. And the one named Marianna was obviously Italian, but mixed with something else. They were all pretty, Bill had to acknowledge.

"We're Americans," said Gwen, "but we have been living in Brazil for many years. Her dad," she gestured over towards Aleta with her chin, "left us last year and we haven't seen him since."

"What about you?" Bill asked Marianna, who was still obviously suspicious and very angry. "I'm an American," she began, but hesitated, not wanting to tell them too much, "I'm on business here. I was supposed to be exploring river sites in Colombia and Peru for...," she hesitated again, "my company."

"What kind of sites?" Bill wanted to know.

"You first," she said looking him in the eye. "This is obviously some kind of a combat boat, and ya'll don't exactly look like the 'Gilligan's Island' crew."

John and Bill laughed. John spoke up. "Like I said, I'm a professor of archaeology at Berkeley. We're exploring for ancient archeology sites, but at this time I can't say anymore." He looked at Bill, can we drop them off at that last village we got supplies at?"

"You mean the one the attack boat came from? What do you think would happen to them there? Or to us? They missed their target and they will probably come back." Bill paused reflectively. "You know, I did everything exactly like we talked about and planned, and they attacked us anyway." He shook his head sadly. "You just can't trust the river pirates anymore!"

They all laughed and the tension in the room eased.

"So now what will you do with us?" Gwen asked. She was still frightened, thinking about their ordeal. No one said anything, simply because this was a situation no one had planned for.

"Who else was on your boat," asked Jack.

Gwen continued. "Just the captain and mate. We had just dropped people off down the river at that last port and we were supposed to pick up more passengers further up river. Unfortunately, the captain had a side job to go up and take photos and videos of the falls and we started getting pulled by the current towards them. We had just started pulling away, when we were hit by that missile." Supposedly fired by the other boat, she thought suspiciously. The captain and the mate were both in the wheel house which was hit directly by the missile. It blew up and the fire spread quickly. I'm sure they both died instantly. So what are you going to do with us?" she demanded again.

Bill shrugged, "I guess we could take you back to the last port. But I can't say what will happen to you. I obviously don't have any more good contacts there and it's a rough town, especially for women."

"What's up the river?" Marianna asked, joining the conversation. Her anger was somewhat mollified. "Are there any ports of call that we can get safe passage to either Bogotá or back down the Amazon?"

"No," said Bill. "We're kind of trapped. We need to proceed up the river, but on the other branch. We will have to travel about two or three days more. There is a site up there that we need to explore. After that, there may be a loop we can come back down on, depending on the flood conditions. This would keep us out of harm's way from the port we just left. If not, we will have to come back down this tributary until we get to a friendly port. This means you will be with us for about a week."

The women looked at each other. "No way, *José!*" Marianna began. "You need to take us back, now!"

Bill smiled easily, "My name is Bill ma'am, not *José.* I don't work for you, I work for him," he motioned with his chin towards John, "and I work for myself. I don't take orders from anyone. I'm the captain of this 'war ship', and you are free to leave anytime. I will be happy to drop you off onshore whenever you like, but I warn you the natives around here are even less friendly than the bad guys who shot up your boat." He paused, "Or you can swim!" he added merrily, noting her rising anger.

When she did not reply, John said, "You know, you said earlier that you too were looking for 'sites' along the river for your company. Why not use this as an opportunity for you to continue your work? By the way, could you tell us a little about what you are looking for? I mean, if you work for Stanford University and are an archeologist, this could get a little uncomfortable!" he laughed.

Marianna thought about this. He was right - maybe she should be a little more cooperative. They didn't look or act like river pirates anyway. She looked down and smiled, "Okay, sorry, I'm just a little freaked out. I should tell you that I work for a communications company in New York. We want to establish a satellite link down here. It will help us to improve our speed and clarity immensely over our competition. If I can pull this off, it will put us ahead by years."

"That's fair," said John. He looked over at Gwen and Aleta, who was no longer crying. "Don't worry, we'll get you back safely. Unfortunately, we may have to encounter a little more uncertainty, before we get you back. We can't go all the way back and we can't drop you off at our last stop. That would be sure death."

"Or they might just try to sell you into slavery," Bill added. "Those mercenaries are ruthless and have no morals. They like children and attractive women. I can't totally guarantee your safety with us, but I can guarantee you will not be safe with them." At this, Robin glanced up and narrowed his eyes slightly.

Bill looked at his watch. It was almost nineteen hundred hours and it was fully dark on the river, due to the clouds and the dense jungle. The boat was moving forward at fifteen knots. He knew they would be at the fork of the river soon and he needed to pilot the boat himself around the turn. It was going to be a little complicated. Manolo could do it himself in the daylight, but not at night. "I'm going to send Manolo down to make supper and get you settled in for the night. We still have a long way to go and we have to make plans and get a little better aquatinted." They all relaxed now. The thought of food was a welcome one. As Bill ascended the ladder to the bridge, he shook his head at this complicated turn of events.

✳✳✳✳✳✳

Dinner was excellent and was welcomed by all. It was simple by design, South American style spiced chicken, rice and beans, but, because of their ordeal, they were all hungry and ate very quickly with little conversation. Oddly, no one smoked, but Bill did pull out his stock of special Puerto Rican rum and it was shared by everyone, except Aleta, who was content with a very excellent warm, sweet hot chocolate, made with thick cream by Manolo as a treat.

After dinner, they all relaxed and drank deeply. The alcohol had the desired effects. Only Manolo had excused himself to take the helm and was running the boat in a light current. Bill had been driving the PT boat and had executed the turn in the river bend two hours before. She was now merrily steaming up the new tributary.

"So, are you going to tell us what your quest is?" Marianna asked John.

John looked at Robin, who shook his head silently. John thought better of it. "Okay, you ever heard of the famous El Dorado?"

"Of course! Lost city made of gold! The chief, uh, uh...," she stammered, her lips a little thick with the rum, "they used to anoint him with gold dust and push him to the middle of that lake up in the mountains by Bogotá. Then the thousands of pounds of gold they used to throw into the lake every day for worship. I've read about it all. Is that what you're going after?" She began to laugh.

"What's so funny?" Robin demanded.

"Just that you are about a thousand miles from that famous lake, whatever they call it, and supposed city made of gold. I read they even drained the lake and only found a few trinkets."

John and Robin exchanged glances again. John spoke up. "The lake is in the mountains of Colombia near Bogotá." The lake is known as Lake Guatavita. They did try to drain it a few times and found some gold, but nothing substantial. That's all in the books, of course. What's not well known is that most of the gold was taken down river and transferred to a very secret, sacred location - a location that was guarded by great warriors and fierce denizens of the river. But that's all I can say for now," his eyes twinkled.

Marianna rolled her eyes, "I think we've stumbled across the 'fools on the hill', or the fools on the river. There must be a song about that!' She giggled. The alcohol was definitely taking effect.

"What do you mean by the 'denizens of the river'?" Gwendolyn asked.

John spoke again. "There are critters that are supposed to protect the gold and also the entire archeological site. Giant piranhas. But it's just a myth," he added.

Marianna spoke up again. She was getting very drunk now. I'm sure ya'll can protect little ol' us with those big ol' manly guns up there," she motioned up towards the deck. She giggled.

The men looked at each other. "Hopefully we will find the site, pull out enough gold to make the trip worthwhile, and then get back safely," said John. The others nodded. It didn't matter. Marianna had passed out suddenly and Aleta had also laid her head down on the table and was fast asleep. Only Gwendolyn was still awake. "All I want to know is, will we be safe?"

"Hopefully," said John. "But any way that we play it, you are safer with us than anywhere else on the river. Besides, I'm also a single parent and I want my girl to make it out of here alive, along with the rest of us." He shrugged.

Gwen yawned. "Let's get some sleep. I really hope things will look more promising in the morning." With that, they all said good night and turned out the lights.

****

The United 747 aircraft moved quickly through the bumpy skies over the Brazilian jungle at exactly 0235 that same morning. Leon Scarborough pulled his seatbelt a little tighter and at the same time looked out the window at the darkness. He could see a few smatterings of lights down below, indicating small towns or cities, mostly broken up by the thick rain clouds rolling by and of course. the thick jungle canopy. A cold moon which seemed to care less, illuminated all.

He sat back in his seat and sighed. He had been awake since just after midnight and, try as he might, couldn't get back to sleep. There was no food or beverage service on this transport either. He'd eaten only once since leaving New York, and that was a standup box lunch, eaten with the crew and twenty or so other military passengers. There had been no conversation. Leon just wanted to get the plane on the ground and meet up with his contact, Thomas Reichen, who would be on the ground waiting for him at the airport.

The airplane gave a sudden jump and then shuddered.

Suddenly, the pilot banked sharply to the left and, executing a slip maneuver, that is, where he punched his right rudder while at the same time rolling the ailerons to the left. This had the effect of causing the aircraft to lose altitude quickly as it slid or "slipped" down to the left. The pilot brought the aircraft down and leveled it out. Suddenly, Leon heard the whine of the flaps dropping and the immediate reduction of airspeed. In a matter of seconds, they had dropped beneath the cloud cover and had the "numbers" as the pilot landed safely on the controlled field.

Leon stood and was the first at the door. He didn't feel like screwing around and wanted off this aircraft. Even though he thought this was a better cover for the operation, the flight had been less than pleasant. He made another mental note to task his father for one of the shared corporate jets they had leased at his disposal.

The door opened with a slight scream of metal-on-metal. The new paint did not help the stiffness of it, but it was now half past three in the morning and, by the look of the outside, it had been raining. He walked down the ramp, while covering up against the sudden gust of wind and rain. He was surprised it was so hot. A wet, smothering heat, that clung to his clothes and made him wish that he was about 40 pounds lighter. Immediately, he began to perspire.

When he neared the ground, a man came up to him and, beneath the black hooded cape, looked down to greet him. Leon looked into the dark shape, which seemed to change with the rain and the darkness. "It" stuck out its hand.

"Leon! Nice to see you again!" Thomas Reichen, said.

Leon looked up at the big man. For some reason foreign

to him, now that he was on his hired killer's home territory, a chill shot up his spine and wrapped around his brain. This man was indeed dangerous. Leon didn't doubt that for one second. He had been around Middle Eastern assassins long enough to smell the presence of death. But this man, in spite of his overt friendliness, had all the kindness of a scorpion about him. The man smiled at Leon, but it never touched his eyes. Leon shivered unconsciously, "Good to see you again, Mr. Reichen."

"Thomas, if you please," was the easy reply. "I try not to stand too heavily on formalities." This young puke was already trembling in his presence, thought Reichen. This kid was a real momma's boy - a lamb sent to do a man's job, he thought. If it weren't for his father's money, this fat popinjay would already be dead. He smiled. Never let it be said that Thomas Reichen would turn down a buck just on principle. In this case, two million bucks, just for starters. He would take him to where he wanted to go and then the real mission started. He wasn't about to let this boy get in his way, even if he had to tie him up and leave him behind. The boy's father was practical and wanted this laser site and possibly the gold, but he also did not want his only son killed. So now Thomas was in a bit of a predicament.

"Thomas," the boy said amicably. "Can we sleep before we travel, or do we have to leave right away?"

"The helicopter is spinning up even as we speak," Thomas smiled. "But you can sleep on the aircraft as we make out way into the jungle. Our prey is steaming their way up the deep back waters, even as we speak. We will have a twelve hour stop-over tonight, then will proceed by porter and meet up with our contacts near the treasure."

"You have secured our position with the local natives, right?" asked Leon.

"Of course, my friend." He said it without emotion, as though he were playing an elaborate game, with Leon as the guest king about to be hit with a checkmate.

Leon looked tiredly toward him. "Lead the way, my friend." They walked off toward an old military UH-1 Huey with its rotors spinning and ready to take off.

****

The clouds had still not given up their mighty tonnage of water. Bill, at the helm, looked up toward the sky. It was 0700 and he had been on the bridge since 0400 hours. There would be hell to pay when the clouds finally broke – and he figured they were due to let loose pretty soon. The river was amazingly calm now considering that there was a storm about to break. They were doing about twenty knots and there was no floating debris in sight. In fact, there was really nothing in the water they had to dodge. It was, however, hot and steamy.

Jack hit the deck first, wearing only shorts, a tee shirt with "The Olympic Club of San Francisco" displayed proudly across his chest, and deck shoes. He had had to surrender his forward bunk to the girls and had slept in the main cabin with the men. He smiled at Bill, "'Mornin' Capn'!" he saluted smartly.

Bill grinned, "You're pretty damn chipper this morning sailor!" as he returned the salute. "But you're a little underdressed for an officer."

"My rank has been changed from the Commanding

Medical Officer aboard to Gunner's Mate First Class, sir!"

"Naw, Bill replied with some amusement, "You can still be the doc. Your better at fixing necks than blowing away bad guys. You're the guy they should have called 'Bones' in Star Trek. Isn't that what you chiropractors do?"

Jack smiled. "Sort of. Plus, my insiders at Universal Studios told me that DeForest Kelley was really playing a twenty-second century chiropractor. You notice he never used medicine or cut into his patients, right?"

Bill shook his head. "You're nuts, but nice work yesterday,"

"Thanks, but I'm supposed to be a healer, not a fighter. You think we might have more trouble ahead?"

"*Quien sabe?*" Who knows. "We might see more action from the river pirates or the native Indians, depending on if my sources and funds arrived intact."

Jack nodded. "What do you think happened back there?"

"I don't know. The only thing I can think of is they either got really greedy, or else the buyoff never happened. They were out to get us, though."

Jack pondered this. "Do you think we will run into any mean ol' creatures in the water?" he asked, trying to stay calm.

"Naw!" Bill laughed heartily. He wasn't faking it. He really was laughing. "You mean like the giant piranhas?" He slapped his thighs in amusement. "John's nuts! There's no such thing. It's all a myth! Haw, haw! There are a few caimans and snakes, but they won't bother us!" He wiped away a tear from one of his eyes and continued to chuckle.

"Those ones back at the falls, didn't look too intimidated," Jack added.

Bill smiled. He liked Jack. "Jack, do you know how to water-ski?" he asked suddenly.

"Yeah, I like to ski." He looked around. "The water is pretty flat, but I still remember that scene in the old movie *The Sea Wolf*, where they threw the cook in the water and a shark chomped down on his leg."

"They're no sharks around here and you might have some fun. Tell me later, if your game."

"More like bait," Jack muttered, but he thought a quick dip might be fun. It really was hot out here.

John and Robin came out on deck, both wearing shorts and tee shirts. The morning was getting a little brighter, as the river widened and the jungle backed up some.

"Good morning, guys," John said. He rubbed his head. "Still hurts where I hit that bulkhead. Are we going to stop to repair that engine?"

Bill thought a moment, "Possibly. I can still make good speed on two engines, but I have to compensate for a slight yaw when I navigate. The further we get up river, the less likely I can find parts, if we even need any. I really haven't had the time to check it out, but I probably should." He looked at John. "Take the helm, for a minute, I'll be right back."

In less than five minutes he was back again. "Looks great!" he beamed. "You guys did a good job yesterday. The fire came off and some spilled oil on the deck. A bullet probably ricocheted off it and caused it to ignite. There are a few holes in the transom, but I nailed up a plank over them and we are again water tight. No apparent damage to the engines, but we'll check them out." He made preparations to fire up the port engine.

"How are we set for gas?" asked Robin casually. He was still calculating out what his mission would entail up ahead and he needed to know as much as possible.

Bill regarded him silently. "Plenty," came the reply. He started the third engine. The boat, which had been moving forward at a slight angle against the current, known as "crabbing", straightened itself out and moved ahead perfectly. "Excellent!" said Bill.

There was suddenly commotion below, as the women had obviously woken up and were making their way to the deck. They emerged sweating already in the morning heat. Marianna came first wearing a halter and short shorts. "Damn, it's hot." She wiped a sweaty forehead.

Behind her was Gwen and Aleta, both dressed similarly. They both smiled at the men, who had moved forward to make room for them in the cramped bridge. Kimmiko came up last wearing her usual bikini top and cut off blue jeans. The men eyed the girls appreciatively.

"It seems the landscape has changed," John observed dryly. He didn't mind the presence of attractive women, but their arrival may have endangered the mission. Oh well, he shrugged.

"Any coffee?" Marianna asked hopefully. She was a little hung over.

"Manolo," Bill yelled out, "any chance of coffee, *amigo?*"

"*Si!* I'm coming up," came the reply. He appeared with a large tray with several hot cups of coffee. "Sorry, there's no ice at the moment, or this could be ice coffee."

"*No problemo*, Manolo," Bill said cheerfully reaching for a cup. He was surprised he was so happy. The addition of the women complicated everything, but he was enjoying himself immensely. "What do you think doc? Want a little tow before breakfast? This is the safest part of the river that I know of. No logs, caiman, snakes or scorpions here. No monster piranhas, either!" he added with a grin.

Jack paused reflectively. He thought if he was looking for adventure and bragging rights to his family and friends, then here it was. Water-skiing up the Amazon River behind a W.W.II PT boat. it didn't get any wilder than that. "Sure, what the hell! I need to cool off anyway." He looked at the water, which seemed innocent enough. He had been skiing in lakes dirtier than this one. "Just a short one, though, right?"

Bill laughed. "Sure, sure."

John looked at them. "What are you two meat heads up to?"

"Doc's gonna' take a little dip," Bill said merrily, "While I test out the engines."

"Cool!" said Kimmiko.

"You guys are crazy," said Marianna. "What if there's piranhas out there?"

"Don't worry, my boat will outrun 'em. Besides, after you guys see the doc havin' fun, you'll all beg me to be next!"

Manolo took over the wheel as Bill headed to the stern with Jack in tow. Bill had slowed the boat to almost a full stop. He reached into a long storage chest anchored to the deck and pulled out two Maharaja skis. "Think you can handle this doc?" his eyes twinkled.

"Yeah, but let's get it over with. I'm starting to chicken

out." A sudden gust of hot air revived his interest in getting into the water. He pulled off his shirt. By then, the girls had joined them on the stern.

"Nice bod!" Marianna said enthusiastically. It was true. In spite of being in his early forties, Jack was in excellent shape. He worked out five days a week, played a lot of sports and was a serious martial artist, specializing in the Bruce Lee inspired art of Kung Fu known as Jeet Kune Do.

Even Kimmiko was checking out her dad's best friend. "Hey Uncle Jack, when did you get all those muscles?"

Jack smiled and looked away shyly. Bill had taken out a tow rope line and tossed it in the water. The boat was idling slowly, but was moving fast enough against the current in the water to stay almost still. The current pulled the rope out to the end and held it taunt. Bill turned and looked at Jack, who was looking around. "No critters around here, right?" Bill nodded.

Jack put on the skis and a safety flotation belt, grabbed the line and jumped in over the stern. He had not expected the current to be so strong, since the river looked so still. He was glad he was holding onto the rope. He moved quickly to the end and grabbed the ski handle. He wanted to get moving. He would feel safer when he was on top of the water. He couldn't escape the feeling that there were large things swimming beneath him. He held a thumbs up signal to the boat as he positioned the tow rope between the tips of his skis and held his arms out straight as he maintained a tight sitting position in the water.

Suddenly the boats engines growled as Bill thrust the three

throttles forward and Jack was pulled up onto the skis. He made it up the first time. It was a little difficult at first. PT boats as a rule didn't exactly jump up and move out like jet ski boats do. But Jack had never felt anything so powerful pulling him on the water. Over the roar of the engines, he could faintly hear the sounds of music coming back from the speakers on the boat. He recognized the Rolling Stones song, "Start Me Up". He grinned. The feel of the boat, the cooling sensation of the water and the song got his blood pumping and he began laughing at the absurdity of what he was doing – skiing up the Amazon River behind a vintage W.W. II PT boat! What a kick! He began cutting across the wake of the boat – he was having a really great time!

So intent was he that he didn't notice the women pointing back at him and yelling to the skipper.

What they saw, that Jack couldn't see, was a large frothing boiling mass of water several yards behind him. They didn't know what it was, but it was heading straight for Jack and was gaining on him. Bill saw it too and his blood went cold.

"John, John!" he yelled. John had started below to get his camera. "Look back there. What the hell is it?"

John's mouth froze. He tried to speak, but he couldn't say anything. He finally croaked out a hoarse whisper, "Speed up, for God's sake. He suddenly cried out, "SPEED UP FOR GOD'S SAKE!!"

Something large and sliver jumped up in the frothing mass of water. Something larger jumped again. It looked like some sort of giant fish, but they both knew that only piranhas swam in a mass like that.

Manolo jumped up from the bridge and ran back to the stern. He tried to grab the line to pull Jack in, but it was too taunt. The speeding boat hit a wave and he almost went over the side, but miraculously hung onto the stern cleat, *"Mi Dios Mio!"* he cried.

The women had run towards the front and were yelling for Bill to do something. "Manolo," he yelled, "get back up here!" Manolo came running back up to the helm. "Take over! Do exactly as I tell you to." Manolo nodded. Bill reached under the console and grabbed his Winchester rifle. He headed back to the stern and laid down on his stomach.

Jack finally noticed the commotion on deck and looked back. What he saw made his heart leap into his throat. The giant frothing mass of fish towered above and was almost on top of him. He didn't know how big or how many, but he knew his life was in danger. He bent his knees and pulled hard on the rope. Although the boat was moving fast, his move brought him up even faster along the left side of the boat. This pulled him away from the mass of fish behind him.

As Jack moved to the side and forward, Bill got up on one knee and, holding the rifle under his arm like a shotgun, fired off a rapid assault of bullets. Since the trigger was tied back, he simply cocked and squeezed the handle back and forth, over and over like "The Rifleman". Bullets flew out rapidly. His aim was true and he hit the center of the mass of water. He emptied his chamber and looked back. Even after the shooting, there was no change. In fact, the mass of water seemed to move even faster, and began to close in again on Jack.

Manolo saw this and sped up the boat. He also steered it

a few points to the right, allowing Jack's rope to move back to the stern position. His speed had compensated for the approaching piranhas and they were again behind him. Suddenly, Manolo had an idea. *"Capitán* Bill," he shouted above the roar of the engines, "hold on!" He took the boat in an even wider arc to the right. He slowed the engines, then suddenly began turning the boat to the left again.

Jack felt more than saw the approaching fish, moving even faster. He knew they were almost on top of him. He saw Manolo's maneuver and knew what he had to do. Once again, he bent his knees and began speeding off to the left side of the boat. He was almost even with the bow as Manolo suddenly turned the boat in a 180 degree arc, and cut the forward motion of the engines, but he didn't shut off the motor. His bow was now facing back into the approaching fish. Jack's momentum carried him completely around the bow, almost doing a 360 degree turn around the boat.

The current, plus the forward motion of the fish caused them to crash into the bow of the PT boat, which shuddered with a mighty crash. The mass of the fish pushed the boat backwards and caused everyone to fall down on the deck. Only Bill, maintaining his sense of command, had held on. He started running forward to the bow and again emptied his magazine into the mass of fish which was still boiling in the water, but was not nearly as violent. Some of them must be stunned or dead, he thought.

Since Jack's momentum had carried him completely around the boat, because of the distance covered, the tow rope, instead of going over the deck in a 360 degree circle, it ran along the hull of the boat and shortened considerably. This brought him back alongside the stern. He kicked off his skis and started up the ladder.

Kimmiko had run back to the stern to help him. She suddenly screamed, "Look out!" as something hideous head and a huge mouth and long sharp teeth reached up and tried to grab Jack's leg. Its head was over two feet wide and, after it missed, suddenly regrouped and launched itself out of the water. It struck the transom with a shudder and almost knocked Jack off his feet, who had gained the deck with Kimmi's help. It fell back into the water. It then resurfaced and seemed to grin at them. Kimmiko screamed and then moaned as she started to faint into Jack's arms.

Jack, still loaded with adrenaline, shook her, "We have to get up to the front." She nodded as he started to half pull and half carry her to the bridge where she would be safe.

Bill was still on the bow, emptying his magazine into the now circling fish and then reloading. There looked to be about twenty of them.

John came up to Bill. "They look like they're about fifteen feet long," he said.

Bill had stopped shooting. It didn't seem to do any good, anyway. "Damn! Giant piranhas! Guess you were right. Jack are you okay?"

"Yeah, "said John, "but I hate being right all the time." The fish were still circling the boat, but no longer frothing at the surface. They seemed to be leering at them.

By then, everyone was looking over the side. Fortunately, the boat was high enough out of the water that the fish couldn't reach the deck without some difficulty.

Suddenly the fish began gaining speed as they circled the deck. John knew what was going to happen. "They're going to charge the boat and try to get up on deck!" he shouted.

"There's no way they can get up here," Bill yelled back.

"Do you want to find out?" John said plaintively. Just then one of the piranhas jumped out of the water and landed on the bow. Marianna and Gwen, who were standing close to the bow screamed and moved quickly back to the safety of the bridge. The fish was almost fifteen feet long and stretched completely across the bow. It was huge and had the mouth and head of a piranha, but the body of a very fat and large pirarucu fish, coupled with the much longer pirarucu fish. It moved its mouth rapidly, looking for something to eat.

Bill jumped back and took over the controls from Manolo, who looked at the fish with a shocked expression. He gunned the boat backwards, causing the fish to roll harmlessly back into the water.

He continued backing up for a few hundred yards and then spun the boat around sharply. The piranhas were keeping up. As his boat turned so that it was facing back up the river, he juiced the engines and stared racing back up to full speed. He didn't know how fast these things traveled, but he wanted to put some distance between him and them. "Get the women down below and get them squared away," he yelled at Manolo. Robin didn't need any encouragement, and was the first to run down below. Bill shook his head.

Jack, now shivering, more from his ordeal than from the wind-chill factor, jumped into one of the gun turrets and was preparing to fire behind them. "Save your bullets," Bill ordered. "I can outrun these bastards."

Jack, his adrenaline still running high, nodded and joined Bill and John at the bridge. He looked at Bill. "Nice day for a swim, eh? He mimicked Bill's voice, "You mean like the giant piranhas? John's nuts! There's no such thing! It's all a myth! Haw, haw!"

"Okay, okay, so I was wrong." Bill looked Jack over. He smiled, "You don't look too badly hurt," he said smugly.

Jack replied, "It's like they say, 'first you say it, then you do it.' Excuse me while I go check my pants!" Bill and John laughed as Jack went below.

Bill looked back. He didn't see anything except the river. "I guess we lost them," he said to John.

"You know there's no losing them. They will not only be back later, but as we get closer to the El Dorado, they will increase in number. And probably in size and aggressiveness too," he added.

Bill didn't say anything for a minute. "Manolo," he yelled down the hatch.

Manolo appeared immediately. "*Si, Capitán* Bill?"

"I need you to make breakfast and then relieve me at the wheel. I need to discuss our course with Professor Waales, here." Manolo nodded and went below to make breakfast and continue to calm down the girls.

Bill continued. "I think we are entering the area hidden by the clouds on the photos. It's hard to tell, but I think we will be at the next tributary in a few hours."

John nodded. "After breakfast, we'll chart our position

using the GPS, if it's still working." The Global Position Satellite, was being used by mariners, the military and now anyone who owned a newer model Lexus, BMW, or other high priced car. It had proved to be invaluable and John intended to make good use of it on this voyage. Unfortunately, it had sustained some damage during the attacks and the rough travel conditions.

****

They all relaxed around the cramped galley table. Breakfast was excellent - coffee, bacon, fish and rice. There was even some sourdough toast with butter and, for Aleta and Kimmi, grape jelly. Jack had calmed down, but became a little nauseated when he found out he was eating pacu fish, a close relative of the piranha. "Better them in your tummy, than the other way around," joked Bill.

John spoke up chuckling, "Well, what do you think about that old legend about them giant piranhas now?" he asked Bill. He would have gloated except that his life and the lives of his daughter and friends was suddenly tied up in this turn of events.

"Are you trying to say, 'I told you so?'" asked Bill without humor.

"No, actually I'm adding this to our situation and I am considering strategy."

Gwendolyn looked up. "What do you mean? We just outran them and if we don't see anymore, then that will be the last of them. Right?"

John looked at her with some sympathy. "Unfortunately, that may not be the last of them. You see, one of the legends of the El Dorado, at least the new ones we have discovered at the University, involve the treasure being protected by large killer piranhas. So, there may be more as we approach the uncharted waters that we are heading into."

Marianna joined in, "So why don't we turn around and get the hell out of here? I need to scout locations for my firm, but there are a lot less dangerous places we can find, you know?"

Bill spoke up, more for John's sake than his own. "As I have said before, our path lies up the river. We're on a mission that will not be diverted. Besides," he added a little more gently, "there seems at this moment to be more danger behind us than ahead of us."

"Do we know exactly where we are going?" Jack asked. He had dried off with a towel. The food and an out-of-character morning drink of "torpedo juice," a mixture of grapefruit juice and vodka, with salt, popular with W.W.II PT boat crews - had steadied his nerves somewhat.

John looked sadly at his friend. "I guess I can speak plainly, since none of you are terrorists." This caused Robin to flinch momentarily. "You see," John continued, "we have a map of the Amazon, which includes this tributary. We also have satellite photos, which are a little blurry and not completely clear. Finally, we have local maps, some modern and some from antiquity. The crowning jewel is that we have acquired recently taken aerial photos. All these things are good things. The bad news is that there are conflicting stories, even among the Indians who are supposed to still be guarding the treasure. Throw in the complicating weather patterns, low clouds and dense foliage and you can imagine the difficulties."

"So how will we find it," asked Gwen, "and still get out of here alive?"

John smiled, "Luck, a great crew and a great boat."

"And what about the piranhas?" she continued.

Bill took this one, "I've got a lot of ammunition, and, besides, I'm really more worried about the natives who are supposed to be guarding the gold and the ancient city of gold. We have to be very careful. They are supposed to be killers who prey on the innocent local tribes for barbaric ancient rituals involving sacrifices and slavery, even in these modern times."

"Right," spoke up Marianna, "If you just plundered the gold for yourselves, it would then be okay, right? But, then, wouldn't you just be doing the same thing the Conquistadors did in the past?

The room was silent for a minute. John spoke up, "You are right Marianna. If we were here to plunder, then we would be as guilty as those in the past. But our mission is supposed to be a relatively peaceful one. We are looking for a stake in the gold, but also, and more importantly, the priceless archeological finds which surround it. Any gold we take out will be used to finance this expedition and help the University finance more expeditions. According to legend, there are several thousands of tons of gold up there, which is more than enough for everyone. More gold taken out would help the local people with food and needed medicine. If the Indians are agreeable to what we want, then actually most of the gold would be left in their hands to sell or keep as they see fit. But if they are engaging in some sort of human genocide, even on a small scale, then we would report it to the local authorities and they would, hopefully, take action. People like that need to be put out of business."

"Not exactly a mission of mercy, but also not exactly a mercenary takeover for profit, then." said Marianna.

"Right," said Bill. "But we all do have a certain amount of gold fever, which is unavoidable," he admitted. "My boat is at stake. I'm up to my neck in debt and a successful outcome would help me out a lot." He paused, "I'm no saint, but I'm not a river pirate either."

Gwen nodded, "Sure, everyone should be paid for their services. From what I've heard down the river, there's trouble in these waters. Many avoid these tributaries and speak of dangers both in and out of the water. I guess we've seen the trouble in the water..." she let her voice trail off.

John and Bill looked at each other. "We are being followed, even as we speak," Bill said mysteriously. "Manolo was the first to warn me. He said that the jungle has eyes now, and that we are entering very dangerous territory. We will be living by our wits and our means. Right now, we have to make plans." And, so, he began laying out strategies for their success.

Suddenly Bill looked up. "Damn," he snapped his fingers. "I need Manolo down here for a minute." He looked casually around the room. "Robin," he asked innocently, "do you think you can take over at the helm for a spell. Just have Manolo show you how to keep her steady as she goes."

Robin looked suddenly angry, but he forced the look on his face to go away. He smiled at Bill, who noticed the smile was false and never reached his eyes. "I'd love to," he said, and turned quickly to head out of the room and up the ladder to the bridge.

A few seconds later, Manolo appeared in the room, "Yes *Capitán* Bill," he said.

"I want you to listen in on our plans because you will be needed." Bill continued, "I cannot stress how dangerous this mission could become. We will try to be friendly, but the locals here may object to our presence. Even if we can overcome the natives, we still only have less than a ..." he looked over at John, "ten percent chance of recovering any gold or treasure."

John continued, "On the other hand, we have been near here before, but our entry was up a different route and a different tributary. Unfortunately," and he looked over at Bill, "our intelligence at the time took us into a blind canyon where the walls rose over two thousand feet and ended at a giant waterfall. We figured that the city and treasure were beyond the mountain, but there was no way we could get over to them That was three years ago and it's taken us this long to get the finances together for this trip. The difference then was we had no aerial pictures and what we thought was a reliable course, turned out to be a dead end."

"The other difference," continued Bill, "was that it was just John, myself and a couple of locals. We didn't have all this..." he paused.

"Baggage." finished Marianna.

"Something like that," said Bill. He sighed. "Anyway, our first priority is to protect everyone and get us all out safely. But you must know the enormous stakes we are playing for here."

"Yes, like our lives," Gwen said. She continued, "If it was just me, I wouldn't worry, but I do worry about the safety of my daughter. Obviously, she's already been through enough," she said firmly.

"Agreed," said Bill, "but that's why we are going over this right now. I'm a very cautious man. I don't like surprises. I always like to think of the worst-case scenario. And this is it." He looked around. "We could come under fire from the land or the river. We may be forced to repel boarders if we can't make a run for it."

Marianna spoke up, "This is going from bad to worse. I demand that we..."

Jack surprised everyone by standing up and interrupting, "You're in a position to demand nothing. If it wasn't for us risking our lives, you three would be working your way through some reptile's digestive system!" He hated the way he sounded right now, but the shock of the morning was wearing off and he was suddenly getting really mad. "If you want to, you can just stay down here below decks for the next three or four days, and wait to see if someone overcomes us and finds you here for the taking, or you can come up on deck, pick up a rifle or a hand grenade and help us all get through this!"

Bill leaned over and whispered, "Jack, we don't have any hand grenades." This broke the tension and caused the others to giggle.

"Okay, okay, but, dammit, we've got to pull together on this! If it wasn't for Bill and Manolo, and the rest of you, I wouldn't be here right now. We are not in a safe place and it will probably get worse before it gets better." He sat back down. "Sorry, I guess I'm just a little rattled."

John reached out and touched his friend's shoulder, "Your allowed." He looked around. "I'm really sorry ladies, but this is our only chance. If we can get to where I think the lost city and the gold is, there is a way out, possibly on the other side, on a parallel river to the one we were at three years ago, but behind the high canyon. We couldn't find it then because it is well hidden by the jungle and," he added, "probably more piranhas."

Bill asked, "How many of you ladies know how to shoot a gun or a rifle?"

Marainna, Gwen and Kimmiko all raised their hands. Gwen spoke up, 'But it's been awhile, so I would like a little review first. Also, I want to know how to operate the machine guns and that big gun on deck - just in case," she added.

"Okay," said Bill. He looked over at the young girl. "Aleta, are you afraid of guns?" he asked easily.

She shook her head. "Good," he added. If we do need you, then it will be something you can handle, okay?" She nodded without speaking. Gwen reached over and held her daughter's hand.

"One last thing," Bill said quietly and very seriously. There could be other players around here other than the local Indians, who are sworn to protect the El Dorado. Our progress and probably our mission may be known to others. We wouldn't be the first to be set on by claim jumpers after we find the gold." They all nodded in agreement.

Afterward, Bill and John were standing on the bridge. It was evening and everyone else was below enjoying another excellent dinner of chicken and rice, complete with local spices, corn and hard biscuits, all prepared by Manolo. They were all teasing Jack in a good-natured way about his skiing abilities.

"John," Bill spoke up quietly, "I have to talk to you about Robin." John felt the hairs on the back of his neck start to stand up.

"Okay, we've been over this before. What's the problem with Robin?" He noticed he was getting defensive, but he didn't know why.

Bill smiled. "I want to start by saying that I'm probably wrong." He paused and held out his hands, "I'm probably wrong, but I have a very bad feeling about him. Please don't ask me to explain it. I just get the feeling that, somehow, he may be planning to compromise our mission."

John shook his head slowly. "You are dead wrong, buddy. I've been his mentor for years and I think he has feelings for Kimmi. Even if he was going to wreck the mission and kill us, what would he do with her?"

Bill shrugged. "I don't know. All I'm asking you to do is keep an eye on him. Like you said, what would he do with her? That means, you and I can afford to gamble somewhat, but we can't jeopardize her life or the lives of the other women. Right?"

John was clearly upset. He didn't like this turn of events and he cursed the day that he decided to bring Kimmi along. "So, what should we do, confront him? Or should we just shoot him? Hell, no one would know. We could just say that he fell in the water and was eaten by large, mythical piranha fish, ha, ha, ha!" his voice was rising.

Bill stepped forward and gently took John by the front of

his shirt with both hands. He leaned in very close, causing John to flinch backwards involuntarily. "Listen, John. I'm first of all your friend. I'm hired to watch your back and, as Captain, protect our passengers and crew. If I screw up, then we will all probably die, so cut me a little slack, okay?"

John nodded. He pushed away, causing Bill's hands to drop away. "Unfortunately, I've been getting bad vibes too, and not just because I think he's been screwing my daughter." The reality of what he had just said was sinking in. "Oh God," he moaned, placing his head in his hands.

Bill continued, "I just want us to keep an eye on him. I have total faith in Jack and Kimmi, you and Manolo. I even think the girls are square. But I want us to watch Robin. Anybody," he paused, "anybody who screws with your daughter, us or this mission, will get this," he held up a big fist and shook it. The shadows on the river became longer as the night fell and the clouds still held their mighty tonnage of water like an enormous sack poised over them.

******

The incessant *WOP! WOP! WOP!* of the Huey's rotors made it impossible for Leon to sleep, in spite of the converted jump seat which had been modified to tilt back into a reclining position. He looked over at Thomas, a large and imposing sight even in the tight confines of the chopper. At the moment, he was looking out the side window at his reflection in the window. The dawn had not yet broke and it was still dark in the jungle below.

Leon yawned loudly. "So, why do we have to deal with these tourists when we know where the gold is and the location where we will build the laser site?"

Thomas waited a full twenty seconds before answering him and when he did, he did not turn around. "We don't know exactly where the gold is and I have never been to the site," he said while continuing to gaze into the window.

"What? I thought you had it all sewn up? I thought we were going into the valley after the professor had stripped the gold out and we could then off him and collect?" he asked boldly.

Thomas turned and looked him fully in the face. "You ever 'off' anybody in your life, kid?" he asked plaintively.

Leon swallowed hard. This wasn't how it was supposed to be. This guy was supposed to work for him and his father. "Well, no...., not exactly. But I know something about fighting. And shooting a gun too," he added.

Thomas smiled and turned back to the window. "Kid, you may be rich and you may think you're in charge, but if you want to survive this little excursion, you need to grab onto the back of my coat and hide your silly face." All the affability was gone from his voice. It was cold and flat like the outside hull of this chopper.

Leon turned beet red. He felt the fear and embarrassment rising up in his throat. He wasn't used to having people talk like this to him. "You're supposed to be working for me," he said hoarsely.

Thomas turned around. "Sure kid, you're the admiral on this little *tête-à-tête* - owner, boy scout and boss." He moved his face within an inch of Leon's. "But I'm the captain. If you don't do what I say, you'll probably die. Simple as that. Do we understand each other?"

Leon nodded sullenly. "So why don't we know anything. I, we," he corrected, "thought you had everything ready to take over."

"Nothing is as easy as it sounds, especially in the jungle. We have to find a way in to get near the site."

"We have the helicopter. Why don't we just fly there and land? You have your contacts with the natives and they are supposed to help us, right?"

"It's the mist and the valley is thick with the jungle. The only probable approach has a waterfall, which blocks our entrance. Plus, they may or may not help us. It depends on their mood," he added.

"So, fly over the falls and enter that way. Do the trees and vines grow over the river which leads to the falls?"

"No," repeated Thomas, "It's the mists. 365 days per year, the mist hangs over the river and the jungle like some huge blanket. You can't get any sort of aircraft in there. Penetration is impossible."

"Can't your pilot fly in IHR, or something like that?"

This boy was getting on his nerves, Thomas thought. "It's IFR, sonny. Instrument Flying Rules, and no, we can't get in there, even with GPS, that's Global Positioning Satellite to you. There are no controlled airfields in the area and we can't fly over those falls into a blind forest through that mist. Can't be done."

"So how do we get in and are the natives really going to help us?"

There is a way. Through the jungle, up the river and to a

landing spot I know. There, the natives will meet us and take us in. I have arranged for large sums of money to be placed into their hands. I hope you brought it," he said seriously.

Leon licked his fat lips slowly. Now he was on solid ground. They may not need him, but they needed the money he'd brought. "I have the funds you requested. But it seems to me the price is a bit high for just promises....," his words trailed off as he saw the look in Thomas Reichen's eyes. The man's smile was one of evil and showed no emotion. His smile was like a shark - teeth and black eyes only - which showed only the promise of dangers to come. Perhaps he had better warn his father he thought quickly.

"Promises, boy. Promises? You and your father could never get this close without me and you know it. I don't demand much, but I do demand respect. Do you understand?"

Leon nodded weakly. What had happened to him being in command? His father always said he would someday lead the company and its business adventures. So why was he agreeing to everything this man was saying? Prudently, he decided to let it pass. But he promised himself he would think more about this later. "Can we trust these Indians? We didn't bring any blankets, beads or firewater." he chuckled.

"Boy, remarks like that will get us both killed. Just follow my lead and try not to screw up. I haven't dealt directly with these people before and I don't want to get killed, okay?"

"So, we'll touch down and then they will meet us?" he asked, but Thomas had already turned back to the window and, in a matter of five seconds, was already asleep. Leon looked at him for a minute and then decided to roll over and sleep as well. His last thought was that this may be his last real sleep for a few days. Then his mind went blank.

******

CHAPTER V

THE LOST EL DORADO

BILL WAS ROUGHLY SHAKEN AWAKE WITH A START. It was Manolo, but it couldn't be because he was supposed to be at the helm, running the river. Bill could still hear the motor purring and felt the forward motion of the boat.

"Capitán Bill! *Capitán* Bill! You must wake up now!" Manolo said earnestly.

"What? What? What time is it?" Bill asked.

"0600, sir!" Manolo saluted more out of reflex and posture, than out of respect.

"So what's the problem?"

"You must come up on deck, sir. There are river people in the water ahead of us." He added earnestly, "We cannot pass, sir!"

Bill leaped out of his bunk. The others were still sleeping and he thought he would check out the situation before waking them. "Let's get up to the bridge. Who's running this tub, anyway?" he chided Manolo, just to let him know he did the right thing by waking him.

When he got up on deck it was still dark on the river, but his eyes were still used to the darkness of the cabin and he could immediately see there were about twenty open boats in the water, each filled with approximately ten natives. Simple math, he thought, outnumbered two hundred to eight, including the kids sleeping below.

They weren't blocking his vessel, but running alongside and in front of it. Manolo had idled down and the PT boat was moving ahead at only six knots. Bill noticed Manolo had lashed down the wheel to keep a straight course while he went below to fetch him.

Manolo started to turn on the powerful search light, but Bill reached up to stop him. He wanted to see what they would do if he just kept on course. They were not necessarily friendly natives, but they didn't seem to be hostile either. If they were, they would have attacked without warning and killed them all as they slept.

He took over the helm. He started to increase his speed and the natives picked up their pace also, rowing with fury. They also began to close their forward boats in front of him. He slowed down and they also slowed down. It was an interesting situation. He could make a run for it, or he could get the men on deck and start slaughtering them with machinegun fire. For some reason, however, he felt he should just keep going straight ahead and wait and see what they were going to do. He could always enact Plan B.

They kept up their quiet game of cat and mouse. "Manolo, go below and wake up John and the Doc."

"What about Senior Robin?"

"Just wake up John and the Doc!" he snapped.

"*Si, señor!*

Bill began quietly checking the ammo in his Winchester. A visual check confirmed that the two machine guns were fully loaded. He could not see the Oerlikon cannon, but knew that Manolo would have secured it ready for action in a moment's notice.

John and Jack appeared on the bridge within seconds, their eyes instantly alert. "Battle stations," Bill whispered quietly.

Jack jumped in the starboard machine gun, while John scrambled back into the port gun. Manolo, ran backwards to the cannon. All immediately took offensive action, including putting on their battle helmets and life jackets. Within seconds they were armed and dangerous. And waiting.

Now it was Bill's turn. The dawn's light was coming up over the river. It didn't appear the natives had guns, but you never knew. He was not going to blow them out of the water without provocation. He really wanted to see what they were up to. He yelled back at John, "Who do you think they are?"

A voice next to him on his left said quietly, "We are the Chibchas."

Bill spun quickly to his left, the shock and surprise plainly on his face. He turned. The Indian had somehow gotten on the boat and was standing on the bridge to his left. "You are a ghost," he said quietly. He was surprised, but not defeated. Not yet.

"It is quite lucky for you," the Indian replied in perfect English, "that I am Casper the *friendly* ghost!" he smiled.

Bill started to back up and began to reach for the Winchester. He was inches away from the stock when the

Indian smiled and quietly raised a long, thick knife. With one quick move he had the blade at Bill's chest. Bill froze.

"*Amigo*," said the Indian, "if I wanted you dead, you would now be laying on your deck. My people do not wish to face your guns of destruction, but we must speak with you now and in peace, *por favor*."

Bill let his hands drop silently. "Okay *amigo*, who are you and what is it that you want?"

"As I said, we are the Chibcha's. We are the true descendants of the original Indians. They were the guardians of the El Dorado."

"The El Dorado, what's that?" asked Bill innocently.

"Don't insult us, my friend," he said, in a slightly mocking voice. "There are few who dare to journey up the river this far and this direction. You are obviously treasure hunters, but ones who do travel bravely with protection. Your women down below owe their lives to you, but have also put you in danger."

Jack, who was on one of the machine guns, made an audible noise and started to turn his gun on the Indian. It was a useless gesture, however, as the metal tubular limit stop around the gun turret, called a tubular limit stop, prevented the .50 twin caliber machine gun from moving into a position where it could shoot up the boat or anyone on it. It would shoot down to the water on the sides, but would only shoot upwards if it were aimed amidships, forward or to the stern.

"Jack!" said Bill sharply, "Belay that! Jack obeyed immediately.

The Indian had not moved a muscle. "My life is expendable, *señor*. I do not fear your guns. But I know all about you and your crew." He gestured out toward the others in the boats, now becoming more visible as the day became lighter. They know about you also, but do not fear you. We do not wish to die, but we will board you and kill all of you if that is what you wish us to do."

Bill stood resigned to whatever fate had in mind. "Okay, who are you exactly and what do you want?"

The Indian smiled. He was handsome and had even, white teeth. He was well over six feet tall and very muscular. I am Mondo Salvaci'on. My father, who was good, helped rule all of the river around the Lost City. I am now the ruler here as we have no further contact with our tribe and the others."

"Why have you separated from the others?" asked John who had actually taken his hands off the machine gun's trigger.

Mondo smiled. "They are the evil ones. They control the evil fish and make sacrifices as the ancients used to do."

Jack and Bill both felt their skin crawl. Only John was perfectly calm. "Mondo, where are the others?" John asked.

Mondo looked him over. "You are the professor from America."

They could see that this startled John, who was not accustomed to being recognized, let alone deep in the Amazon jungle by a native. "How did you...?"

"Years ago, you tried to come here through the backside. We all had a great laugh as you were turned back by the mountains. You are the only white ones who ever make it this close to the treasure, but you are still not there yet."

John looked a little piqued, "Yeah, funny like a crutch!" he said.

Mondo, looked confused, "What's a crutch?"

John rolled his eyes, "Never mind!"

"We know about you from your travels and your books." He gestured toward Jack. "That one over there, he is the *'curar de la mano'*."

John translated, "What do you mean the hand healer?"

Jack spoke up, "He means a chiropractor. 'Chiro means hand', or one who heals with his or her hands. How did you...?" he started to say to the Indian.

"I read a great deal, *señor.* I have read your books also." Jack too looked surprised. His books on chiropractic and natural healing had been sold around the world, but were hardly on the NY Times Best Sellers List, especially along the Amazon Basin.

Mondo continued, "Unfortunately, we do not control the gold and we do not live in the city of gold. We came here to this jungle over four hundred years ago. After awhile, some of our people revolted against the sacrifices and the violence the others did. We were not favored by our brothers and after a time, we split up. My wife's father and brother live in the city of gold. They sacrifice to their gods and the bastard evil fish. They are vile in our presence and they would kill you all and us too if they could."

Bill spoke up, "So where are they and this Lost City of Gold?"

Mondo looked down. "Up the river. But we cannot take you there. Our laws forbid outsiders to look on the city. It is said that if one takes an outsider there, he will die a horrible death in the jaws of the giant piranhas. Our sect has been outcast for over twenty years, but we still fear and respect many of the old laws.

"Why have you split with your tribe?" asked John.

"Many years ago, my wife, the child of Chief Sanek Omagua, and I fell in love. He did not approve and neither did his son, my wife's brother Prince Sajava Omagua. I was the leader of my group of warriors, and my father was a leader also. There was no reason for them to deny us, but they hated me. They knew we did not believe in the sacrifices," he shuddered.

"So why do you reveal yourselves to us now?" asked Bill.

"We see in you a chance to regain our rightful place. We are the ones who should guard the El Dorado. Those ones have sinned before God. Yes, we believe in the one God, not the gods of the river who the other's make evil sacrifice to."

John spoke up, "How can we help you and how can we find our quest? The treasure has been lost for over six hundred years."

Mondo smiled. "*Si amigo*. The others have been looking in the wrong place!" He began to laugh. The other Indians in the canoes surrounding the PT boat began to laugh also. "You will keep going up the river. It will become more dangerous for you. We will try to help you, but we will not protect you. The other tribesmen are much stronger than us and are in greater numbers. Beware the fish!" He said as he jumped over the side into a waiting boat. Within seconds, they had disappeared, rowing into the mists. Then the river became flat as though they had never been there at all.

Bill, John and Jack just looked at each other.

Jack jumped out of his gun turret. He went over to John, who was now standing beside Bill on the bridge, "Sure enjoyed that, buddy!" he said, slapping him on the shoulder. "You could have invited me to Tahiti or Maui or even Mexico, but noooo…, we had to go to the Amazon on a treasure hunt. You never said there were people down here who wouldn't like us!"

John looked at his friend and smiled sheepishly. He didn't know what to say. "At least you can quit complaining that no one ever reads your books," he smiled, shrugging his shoulders.

Bill spoke up. "The crew will be awake soon. We need to plan for the day and the next two days."

"What about the others they spoke of?" asked John.

"That I do believe. It makes sense. We know there are those who protect the treasure and will kill anyone who gets close. Those natives seem to be okay, but I don't believe they will help us. I do believe they will try to take over if we do their dirty work for them and get rid of their evil cousins." He shrugged. "Oh well, always on the outside!" He reached around and clapped them both on their shoulders. "Better to not get in the middle of family squabbles." He smiled.

******

The rest of the morning was spent traveling uneventfully up the river. All three engines were firing now and Bill wasn't lying when he told Robin they had plenty of fuel. He'd installed extra tanks which would keep them out on the river for a long time. He also had his secret supply people that he could pinch in an emergency.

However, they didn't know that Mondo's prediction

would come true so quickly. They were getting very close to the unfriendly Chibchas and at that moment, they were being watched by many eyes from the shore. The evil sect of the ancient tribe could become ghosts in the jungle and protected their gold and territory with a deadly vengeance.

In truth, other than their outcast cousins, they were really the only ones who knew the location of the new El Dorado, which was not really a city at all, but rather a series of small to large sized temples and houses built of gold bricks. The largest and most ornate temple was near the river, up a small hidden tributary. The water appeared to be seldom more than a trickle when it hit the river the PT boat was steaming up, but as you moved inwards, the thick jungle foliage parted to reveal a much wider, true river. This was a freak of nature, which was the result of a combination of deep, underwater drainage, level land and a contributing spring. The jungle itself also housed quicksand, deadly reptiles, insects and, of course, the giant piranhas, who slept around the giant hanging ferns and foliage.

The fish were fearsome. They were tended to by only the bravest of the Chibchas. The last temple was so large, it actually straddled one branch of the maze of streams which made up the river. There was a breakaway, elevated platform there, used for the past 500 years as one of their sacrificial altars. There were probably 50 or more giant piranhas circling the area and slipping back into the main river and also back upstream looking for food. They were always ravenously hungry and would turn to cannibalism, eating the smaller and weaker ones, or those fish which became old or sick. They would eat any animal which had the unfortunate luck to drink or bathe in this part of the river. They could leap out of the water through the air and attack prey, even ten feet away from the water's edge.

****

It was late afternoon before the rain began to fall. At first, it was a light drizzle, then it poured until the water rolled off the deck of the PT boat in sheets. Bill had put up a canvas cover over the bridge, but it only protected him slightly from the rain starting to blow in as he crouched behind the small windshield. He put on his foul weather gear that he had stowed below deck. Here, the river narrowed until it was only about 75 yards across with thick jungle foliage on both sides. John and Jack joined him at the helm also wearing their rain gear.

"Can you see forward?" asked Jack.

"Enough," replied Bill, "but if you want to man that forward turret and work the search light, you might spot something I could miss."

Jack nodded and jumped in the starboard gun turret. John looked at Bill. "You know," he said quietly, "we are in the region of the river where there is supposed to be another tributary leading up to a maze of rivers. Somewhere around there is the Lost City."

Bill nodded and smiled, "Don't worry, we'll get her this time. The only thing which can interfere with us are the bad guys and the weather."

"And the piranhas," added John.

"Right, how could I forget. You know, John, it's entirely possible that those fish we saw are the only ones."

"Want to bet your life on it, pal?"

"No, I wouldn't," said Bill.

Jack called over to Bill, "How far do we have to travel before we get to the area we are looking for?"

Bill looked at John. "What do you think buddy?" asked Bill.

John swallowed hard. "I don't know, people. The maps, the photos and the intuitions all stop here. The only thing I have left is luck."

"Hey, what about changes in the river?" asked Bill suddenly.

"What do you mean?" asked John.

"We can put the boat in slow forward motion and there may be a sudden surge as the tributary takes over and pushes us out into the river." said Bill.

"Even in this head current?" asked John.

"Yeah! Where's Manolo," asked Bill.

"Down below making dinner," said Jack. "Do you want me to get him?"

"No leave him there. We need a good dinner. It may be our last chance to eat well before we truly get busy."

The rain continued to pour down as they moved forward slowly, each intently feeling for any change in the current.

******

The Huey rolled and banked to the right, descending in a sharp angle to get through the trees and avoid the mists and the clouds. The last thirty minutes had been bumpy and Leon had slept badly. Thomas, on the other hand, had slept deeply until it was time to rise. In an instant, he was fully awake, ready and looking for the landing area.

"Over there!" he called over the intercom to the pilot. Dawn was breaking and he could see the clearing, hacked out of the foliage, shaped into a large X with a full circle inside. It was approximately one mile from the river and approximately five miles from where the Lost City was reported to be. The pilot swung the Huey down and flared it out expertly until it touched the ground.

The bump as it touched down startled Leon awake with a "Huh?!"

Thomas looked over. "We're here sonny."

Leon blinked rapidly as he looked around. The indirect light from the sun was barely lighting the jungle. The clouds had almost fully closed in now and the mist coming off the ground mingled with the steam from the jungle, always moving upward, touching the clouds as they descended slowly toward the earth.

Thomas, along with two native porters, jumped out and quickly removed their gear. He had supplies for several days, including food, water, guns and ordinance. They had a small burro onboard for the heavy items. Thomas lifted it off the aircraft and set it onto the jungle floor.

"Hurry up!" shouted the pilot. "I have to get out before the visibility drops anymore!"

Leon jumped up and helped grab the last of the bags. As soon as everything had been dropped, the pilot quickly spun up the aircraft and was up and away almost instantly. Leon gazed up at disappearing bird, which was quickly enveloped by the mists. He turned to Reichen. "What now?" he asked.

"Grab your gear and let's move out!" he commanded.

"On foot?" was the surprised reply.

"Of course! If the Indians find us worthy, they will find us."

"Which way do we go?"

"You sound like a cartoon character! Which way did they go? Which way did they go?" Thomas chuckled. "This way son. Toward the river. We may have a bit of a walk, but don't worry, I know you can handle it."

Leon shouldered the equipment. In spite of the bulkiness, it wasn't overly heavy. Together they struck off into the jungle and were quickly surrounded by the steamy mists.

******

The current was changing in the river. It's urgent surging against the PT boat was now more from the side and not as much straight onto the bow. Bill was at the helm, Jack was on the forward gun turret on the starboard side and Manolo was on the port side gun, aft of the main cabin. They were at full alert now - continuously at general quarters. John and Robin were below decks trying to figure out where the tributary was exactly. The women were trying to make something decent to eat in the galley. Although they appreciated and enjoyed Manolo's cooking, they all agreed they could do better. They also, in somewhat whispered tones, felt they could probably out fight the men and would likely be better leaders as well, but this they didn't dare voice. The male ego was a delicate thing and, besides, it was their boat and their war. They had no interest in fighting. They just wanted to go home. Even Kimmi, had had enough of the jungle and longed to be back in Berkeley, where she could eat pizza at Blondie's on Telegraph Avenue with her friends, followed by a smoky bratwurst at Top Dog on the South Side and then go to a Cal football game on a Saturday afternoon.

Bill slowed the boat. He had to feel the current. The changes were subtle. You would think you could see the tributaries, but because of the heavy jungle growth, this was not always possible. It was especially hard when the natives didn't want you to see it. It seemed the more he slowed the boat, the more the bow pushed out to the right, away from the center of the river. "Hey John," he called down the open hatch, "you got any idea how close we are?"

After a moment, John stuck his head out of the hatch. "According to the GPS and our maps and pictures, we should be less than a mile from the mouth of the main tributary."

"How will we know when we are there? The entrance is reported to be hidden by the jungle and we could be stuck driving up and down this damn river for days."

"Give me about twenty minutes. I've almost got the coordinates down. How's the river?"

"Changing. But it's so subtle, that I can't tell if it's a new feeder stream, or just a rip current. We need something to float behind the boat to see the direction it's taking. He looked over at Jack. "Hey doc! Want to take another ski run?" he chuckled. Jack just smiled and looked away. "Guess not, huh?"

The boat continued to crab slightly into the changing current as the day gave way to the evening and the evening gave way to the night. The endless river seemed to move even slower as the men continued their vigil.

******

Thomas Reichen had no intention of staying in this hot, steamy jungle more than two days without contact with the natives. He'd been told that the tribe would be there at the river to meet him and take him to the golden city. There had been no assurances made that he would receive any gold, but only that he would be allowed to set up his satellite position and that there would be Indians to help him. He knew and understood the local customs and had procured extra money from Leon's father to ensure the complete cooperation from the natives. Everything had been arranged according to his plan. There was the additional lure of the cocoa production and the distribution of cocaine. This, he thought with relish, could net him over five million dollars alone, plus the supply network it would generate. This could last years and produce billions of dollars for him and his associates. Even he had partners who needed to be satisfied.

The two native porters who had flown in with them aboard the Huey, carried the bulk of the equipment and also the weapons. Thomas was convinced he would have to do this alone - this fat popinjay of a boy would wilt at the first sign of a fight. He did, however, have a mole aboard the attack boat. He had promised the young assistant professor a goodly sum of money and a chance to run his new research and satellite project if he would help him overthrow the crew of the boat.

He smiled. It was never certain how the mole would react. The inherent dangers of combat made predictions impossible. The only thing which was inimitable was man's unquenchable greed. He knew that the enticements would be too much for this assistant professor. He was young and handsome, but was also impatient. He couldn't wait for full tenure. He could make a name for himself immediately and also earn a bloody fortune if he just played along. He was certain he'd make contact with the young assistant within the next two days. He would then be on the outside with a man on the inside. He chuckled.

****

On shore, Prince Sajava Omagua and two of his native tribesmen looked out silently at the PT boat. Even in the darkening light of late evening, they could make out the captain at the helm and the two gunners on either side of the boat. There was also someone at the stern cannon. Although the natives had never seen a World War II PT boat, they knew it was a heavily armed gun ship. It was longer by over 30 feet, than a similar boat they had hidden away. Their sources down river told them that these men would be looking for their City of Guatavita. That was the name for the golden lake their ancestors left behind hundreds of years ago when a tribal feud had split them apart. They were sworn to protect the gold and their way of life. There were still Chibcha Indians left at Lake Guatavita; distant cousins, perhaps. They were a kind, friendly people. But the new warriors here in the lower reaches of the Amazon Valley, were fierce fighters. Prince Sajava was proud of this. His father, Chief Sanek

Omagua had taught him the old ways, even the sacrifices which were necessary from time to time.

The prince had a way with the fish. He fed them and they respected him. He thought of his sister, Cornelia - the woman of that peasant Mondo, gone now these many years. He shook with silent rage. His younger brother, Prince Damien was weak and didn't know the ways of the fish. He was still too young to know the power of his tribe. Damien was not yet twenty, almost fifteen years Sajava's junior. He still yearned to be with his sister, whose name had been stricken by the tribal council since she left. There was a bounty on her and her husband. He could be killed on site, but she must be brought back alive to pay for her sins.

These people would also pay if they dared step ashore. The fish were always hungry. For now, though, it seemed the boat would keep going away from the mouth of the tributary. Nature had hidden it well and they had done the rest. Only the fish glided in and out at will. For now, the natives would watch and wait. Prince Sajava turned and whispered something to one of the natives, who turned swiftly and ran back into the thick jungle. The city was well hidden and he had to travel the two miles by foot quickly to deliver his message to the chief. The two left behind to observe were silent shadows in the dark.

******

It was midnight. There were no stars and no moonlight. An eerie mist mingled with the clouds. It was somehow evil and, along with the dark jungle which seemed to lean in on the boat, it was not a good place to be. The PT boat was idling in neutral. Bill had found a spot in the river where the boat would hold its position, not moving forward, backwards or to the side. It was a complete freak of nature. The usual sounds of a busy jungle at night still accompanied them. Monkeys and other animals screeched, roared or yelled their indifference at the people and their mission. They had their own path to follow and it was according to nature's own recipe.

No one could sleep. It was hot and even the air was oppressive. Bill was at the helm, Jack was on the starboard machine gun and John manned the port gun. Manolo was at the stern on the cannon. Robin was on the tip of the bow looking forward, his eyes straining in the darkness. Although Bill had sent him forward to look for the tributary river, he was really looking for a different signal.

Gwendolyn and Marianna were next to Bill, whispering in the dark. It wasn't as though they needed to be quiet, but the very nature of the place forced you to whisper and made you want to keep silent. Only Kimmiko and Aleta were below, in their bunks and excitedly talking about boys, their favorite pop groups, (*NSYNC and the Back Street Boys were their favorites) and how old was old enough before you could "do it." They had formed a fast and close friendship. And, in the romantic ways of youth, they even giggled their opinion about Kimmi's father and Gwendolyn's mother falling in love and then they could be sisters, although this thought caused Kimmiko a little more pain at the thought of her mother than she would have thought possible. It had been years since her mother had passed, but the pain was always near the surface, ready to rear its ugly head. They couldn't sleep either, but for different reasons. This was fun and they felt the adults would protect them. To them it was one big adventure. Even the piranhas were a distant memory.

Gwendolyn whispered in the dark to Bill, "How long will we stay here and what, exactly are we looking for?"

Marianna spoke up, "Why don't you just put the boat ashore and in the morning, we can just go exploring for the mystery river?"

"Sure, we could find it easily on foot," continued Gwendolyn, "if it really exists!" Both girls giggled.

Bill looked at them. He really hoped they would all live through this. These women had no idea how much danger they were really in. He decided to let them in on a little of what was going on. "You know, it probably would be a good idea to land. Maybe we will do it right now. Of course, you know the natives know this jungle really well. And they probably wouldn't even need to use their blow guns to hit us if they came out of the dark. Hell, they could probably just climb aboard and use their knives, or guns," he added hastily. "This is the new Millennium after all! No sense in staying out here in the water out of reach until we know its light, right? Say, you girls know how to fire a machine gun?" By the look in their faces, he knew he had gone too far. They were both silent. "We'll go ashore at first light," he continued, "unless we can't find the tributary. Then it will have to wait. I don't fancy traveling in these jungles, unless I know we are close to our quest." Both of the women nodded, and by unspoken consent, headed down the hatch to the decks below.

Jack looked over at Bill, "Subtle, very subtle buddy. Nice to have them on deck, but I guess they are safer down below."

Bill nodded. He didn't say anything, but continued to concentrate on the movement of the boat and the possibility they might really find the Lost City. The sudden movement in the water, made him hiss sharply, "Check your mounts!"

Instinctively, the men on the guns snapped the slides on their magazines up and took aim, although no one knew what they were aiming at. Robin scrambled back up from the point position on the bow back to the helm. He leaned across the windows of the chart room towards Bill and whispered, "I saw a flash , then a splash. I couldn't tell what it was."

"Piranha," came Bill's nonchalant reply. Then the answer came to him. "We'll follow the fish. They must know the opening, because, according to John, the legend says, that's where they're bred. Look alive!" he called sharply to his gunners. He throttled down the boat and, against all caution, hit the search light. The ten-million candle power beam reflected off the water. He could just make out the tip of a slivery dorsal fin slice through the water and, impossibly seemed to disappear beneath an intact shore. He thought it could have turned around and dove under the water. He shined his light on that exact spot. Over a minute passed. He was just about to give up when he spotted another fin, this time emerging from under the shore. Impossible, he thought. But then as he raised the light towards the thick jungle shore, he realized his light was shining through the thick growth, rather than bouncing off it. In fact, he thought it was possible that he was seeing water on the other side of the thicket, but then it could simply be a trick of the light. He turned the boat around towards the shore and powered up quickly.

Everyone fell back towards the stern, as the big boat moved instantly towards the mysterious shore as though slung from a giant slingshot. Bill increased his speed. He was determined to find out what was behind that thicket of jungle, or die in the process.

Jack and John, both alarmed at Bill's temporary loss of sanity, screamed their protests over the roar of the engines. Only Manolo, knowing Bill's capabilities as the captain of this craft, wisely hung onto the cannon's cleats, figuring it would be the safest place if he crashed into the shore. Bill, keeping his spotlight trained on one area, chose to hit the shore at the spot that seemed to be the thinnest. "Hang on!" he called out to no one in particular.

The heavy PT boat hit the wall of jungle doing over thirty knots. It burst through the jungle thicket like a giant swatting away some tiny flies. Instantly, Bill cut the engines so the three turning props would not get tangled in the heavy vines, nor would they be damaged if he was wrong and they crashed embarrassingly into the shore.

As they hit the jungle shore, Bill, Jack, John and Manolo ducked down instinctively. Robin, with a scream, scrambled over the bridge and dropped down into the cockpit beside Bill.

For an instant, as they crashed through the jungle foliage, they found themselves slightly airborne, then they then splashed heavily into the river beyond the thicket and into a different world. Here, the water was calmer. Since Bill had cut the engines, there was only the forward movement of the heavy boat's momentum, which stopped quickly due to the jungle vines. They had made it through, but now the boat had come to a full stop. Oddly, it didn't move back towards the river they were just in, but rather stood still where it had landed. Slowly, the men stood up and looked around. It was dark. The jungle seemed to lean in on them. Much of the jungle chatter had stopped. At first, they thought it was because of the crash of the boat. After a few minutes of silence, they realized that it stayed quiet. It was as though there was no life on this tributary.

Bill waited and looked around. By mutual consent, no one spoke to each other. Bill whispered down the hatch, "Are you girls okay?"

"Yes," came a frightened reply, "are you okay?"

"Yeah, but be silent for a few minutes, please."

John, Jack and Manolo, resumed their positions at the guns and Robin went back to lie prone on the foredeck. It was now so dark, that he used his own flashlight in addition to the bow light. Bill also scanned the area with the big search light, which had, remarkably, survived the crash intact, in spite of the thick foliage. They all felt as though they had entered a different world, and it was not a friendly world at all.

"Jack," Bill whispered, "look alive now. They are probably watching us, even as we speak. He looked back at John and Manolo. He could just barely make them out in the darkness. "Look alive, boys!" he hissed. We're going to keep moving for about a mile or two and then shut 'er down. We'll have to keep watch all night from now on, though. We'll be taking shifts - mine starts now. Jack and I will stand watch for the next three hours.

Then John and Robin will come back up on deck and then Jack will get some sleep. Manolo, I want you to sleep for the next five hours and then relieve me an hour before dawn. Tell the girls to get some sleep. I'll knock off between five and seven. Then we'll land and do some exploring and hopefully no more fighting."

"Why do we have to leave the boat?" Jack asked, pain and fear plainly showing on his face.

"Well, doc," Bill chuckled, "if you have a way to make the gold march itself onto the deck, then I'm all for it. But I think we have a little more work to do before we call it a trip, don't you?"

Jack nodded silently and looked down, thinking about his family. You never knew how good you had it until the time came when you could lose it all he thought.

"Okay," said Bill, "everybody please move out. It'll be dawn in a few hours and," he looked up into the darkness, "hopefully the rain will hold back."

The rest of the night was uneventful. At various times, those on the deck heard a faint swishing through the water and occasionally felt a jolt as though something large carelessly bumped the boat. Other than that, there was nothing but darkness and silence. There wasn't even the screeching of the monkeys in the trees which had followed them since they had left their home port. It was as though nothing lived here in this silent tributary except something unseen - and dangerous.

Below decks, the women were asleep and even Bill was sacked out. John and Robin were on deck as lookouts. Jack lay in his bunk but couldn't sleep. His mind moved in a million different directions. As a chiropractor, he worked with the natural flow of energy on a daily basis. Asian cultures called this Chi, others called it God or Nature and believed it lives inside all of us. Chiropractors call it the innate and believe it helps them direct the course of their care for each patient. As much science that existed supporting the validity and the effectiveness of chiropractic care, it always came down to the art of the doctor's sense as to what was the perfect adjustment this one patient needed at this moment. It was that feeling of what was to become which robbed him of his sleep.

He knew this place was fraught with danger. He did not expect this to be a Caribbean cruise, but he didn't think he would have to shoot at and possibly even kill people. He was a healer, not a soldier. But now he knew to his very core that they would all have to fight - and fight to win.

He silently slipped out of his bunk and, after retrieving an object from his grip, he walked silently into the small galley. There, in front of a mirror, he started running his nunchakus. The Chinese weapon was fearsome - two metal, telescoping round poles, extended to about one foot on length each, and held together by a small chain, the "chaku sticks" could generate up to 25,000 pounds of force. He started slowly and then worked his way up to high-speed revolutions, moving the sticks from one hand to the other. He was a very good martial artist. Not an expert, but the nice thing about *Jeet Kune Do*, the type of kung fu made famous by Bruce Lee, was that it blended well with American fighting arts. Jack's mind was clearing. He did some fighting stances and silent punches along with the chaku sticks' movements. He stopped, sweating in the hot galley. Wiping his forehead, he looked in a mirror and pondered for a moment what he was doing here. The thought passed and his mind began to steel against whatever was out there. They had guns, of course. But he had been trained as a martial artist and he would use whatever he had at his disposal to protect himself and his shipmates. With that thought, he compressed the nunchakus to their 3 inch size, turned out the lights and went back to his bunk, where he fell immediately asleep.

******

Leon Scarborough sat down on a large rock. He swiped at his sweaty brow with a fat forearm, unconsciously knocking back the wide brimmed hat he wore to protect himself from the sun. But here in the deep jungle, it wasn't really the sun. It was overcast and the thick canopy of the forest covered him as he walked. It was the sweltering, oppressive steaminess of the jungle. It was hot and wet. He could not shake the humidity. It was wearing him out.

Thomas Reichen and the two native porters were handling it better. They had been in the jungle a long time and had fought many battles here. They were standing by the river, waiting for their contact. Actually, they were just inside the foliage, so that they couldn't be seen by anyone on the river. They were hidden, but knew that they would be found by their "friends" if this was going to work.

Leon looked up in pain. "How much longer do we have to wait?" he asked plaintively.

"Hard to say." Thomas said, without looking up. "Our friends should meet us soon enough. If not, we'll be hitchhiking home." He smiled.

"That's comfor-," he began. The words froze in his throat as the bushes behind Reichen, seemingly fixed began to move up and towards them as the hidden natives stood up.

Thomas, startled, but determined not to show it, turned around slowly. He smiled, knowing that it was better to smile than to show any type of aggression. With his fighting skills and the fact that he was armed, he could probably handle at least a dozen natives on his own. But the problem was there were always a whole lot more natives watching and waiting. This meeting had been prearranged and, to a certain degree, prepaid. But in the jungle, nothing was guaranteed. He always had to be careful. "So," he said to the largest native who was in front and seemed to be in the lead, "you have found us. Skillfully, as we had been told."

The native moved forward and slowly separated himself from the rest of the natives, who were still rising slowly up from the underbrush. He did not smile. "You have brought the money, yes?"

Thomas nodded and motioned towards one of the native porters. He brought out a leather grip and handed it to Thomas, who unfastened the buckles and unzipped the zipper. He held out the contents for the native's inspection. "One hundred thousand U.S. dollars cash," he said.

The native leaned forward and looked over the money carefully. He did not touch it. "The medicines?" he asked.

Thomas looked over at the other porter, this one, tall and overweight, with a surly look on his face. He obediently stepped forward and placed two very large suitcases on the ground at the native's feet. Thomas reached down and unsnapped the catches.

He opened both suitcases and stepped back.

The native peered down. He was looking into a large array of vials, syringes, needles, I.V. bags, sutures, bandages and other medical supplies. He looked up at Thomas. "The rest?" he asked.

Again, Thomas looked over at the first porter, who had been leading the small burro through the jungle. He pulled several large packs off the animal's back and sat them down immediately. They were heavy and he was not that large.

Thomas and the native walked over to the packs. Thomas opened them and several small handguns, rifles and shotguns in one bag. The other bag contained boxes of bullets and shells. "Good." the native replied.

"We have also brought special foods and liquor as extra offerings for your chief," Leon said.

Thomas looked at him silently. He was unhappy at this breech of protocol, but was not surprised.

The native smiled. He motioned toward the jungle and about two dozen other natives appeared and picked up the provisions. "This way," he motioned. The party moved out through and hidden path in the jungle. Thomas and Leon were separated from their porters and did not see them again.

******

Chief Omagua ruled this nation completely. He was a man with a large belly and had a great force about him - not unlike the Mafia chiefs of the 20th Century. He was a dictator who ruled with an iron fist encased inside an iron glove. Punishment was carried out against those who opposed him with a lightening quickness. He was judge, jury and executioner. Many were crucified. They were tied spread-eagle on trees and vines in the jungle. They were left to the mercy of the wild animals, who seldom showed any mercy. Others were more fortunate. They were simply fed to the fish, and consumed in a matter of seconds. The villagers were forced to watch these executions, which were an effective deterrent to misbehavior.

The chief was surrounded by men and women, who had sworn to die to protect him. He had noticed lately, though, as the food and medicine began to run out, that some of his people had become restless. Others, the younger ones of the newest generation looked away during the sacrifices and the punishments. He sighed. The old days were better, he thought. It had begun to get bad after his daughter had left with that *pendejho.* She was a *putah,* and had brought shame on him and his tribe. He vowed the day would come when he would have his revenge. His evil heart had no love or pity for her or anyone else for that matter. He had been born and raised by evil parents. His religion was the fish and the gold.

At one time, he could sell the gold and get provisions for his people. That had stopped in recent years as the traders had given him less and less for the gold. Eventually, he had become angry with them and, in a moment of rage, had fed several of them to the fish. He smiled now, at the thought of their cries for mercy, even moments after they had contemptuously offered him a bag of beans and rice for a man's weight in gold. Unfortunately, with their demise, no others could be found to trade with his people, and so he had to make other arrangements.

Many whites and some native Colombians desired the white powders they made from the region's coca plants. These plants were also sacred to the natives in their rituals and in their celebrations. Coca also helped men get through their daily work and then to relax at night. These natives chewed their plants, mixed with limes acquired from crushing seashells from the Caribbean. The limes activated the chemicals in the coca leaves to produce the effect sought the world over. Cocaine in any form was a drug which stimulated men to a higher level of desire.

This man, Thomas was reputed to be a man of great influence. He was also said to be of great personal strength and also one who could bring much needed supplies and restart the trade they had enjoyed in years past. One other thing appealed to the chief -Reichen was rumored to be a very bad man. A man equal in deeds to the Chief himself. He should meet such a man, thought Omagua. He looked over at his son, Prince Sajava. He was like his father. Ruthless and cunning. He would help him judge this man, Thomas. He was as proud of this son as he was disappointed in his other son Prince Damien. True, Damien was of a gentle spirit, but he was still young and could still be turned. Too much like his sister and their mother. Still, like any father, the Chief had hope that Damien would eventually see the light. While he thought nothing of sacrificing his daughter for bringing shame onto the tribe, he did not want to lose a son, as he placed more value on his son's life. Males were much more highly prized here, as in many countries of the world.

The familiar approach of footsteps in the jungle alerted him. Most could hear only two sets of feet. The natives who accompanied them walked silently, and could not be heard.

The thick jungle brush parted and the party stepped into the bright clearing, blinking in the sudden light. The sun, unable to break the cloud' s thick barrier, none the less still lighted this area much more than through the forest canopy.

The Chief looked at the two men. Instinctively he knew that the taller and bigger of the two had to be the man, Reichen. The other looked soft and fat. A momma's boy who did not work, but lived off the sweat of others. He had heard through Thomas Reichen's emissaries, however, that this boy held the purse strings of his father's wealth. And for that, his life would be spared - for now. He motioned for them to move forward.

Thomas looked straight into the face of the chief. He had no illusions that this man would have him killed if he failed to keep his promises. He did not look around, but kept his gaze open and friendly. He did not, however, smile. He simply waited until the Chief made the first move.

Leon, on the other hand, could not stop looking around at the native women, who wore only small, wrap around skirts. He blinked rapidly, as his eyes began to water from the heat and humidity, as well as the stimulation.

The chief noticed this with some amusement. He placed out his hand. Thomas immediately leaned forward, and, as was custom, kissed the large, ornate ring on the chief's hand. He stepped back and now he smiled.

"I have been told you are a great chief and a great warrior. I hope we can do business together which will be profitable to both of us."

The chief nodded. "My messengers tell me you have brought us the agreed supplies and," he stopped, wondering how benevolent he should be, "a few additional offerings."

Thomas nodded. "It is my custom to give more than the agreed amount. I reward friendship with kindness. This has kept me alive for a long time in a dangerous business."

The chief nodded. "I agree, this business is dangerous, but," he looked around him, "danger too has its rewards."

"Yes," he said, also looking around, "you are blessed with strength and beauty surrounding you and also inside you."

The chief smiled, "The stories about you I hear are true, Mr. Reichen. My only question is, once our trade has started, will your friendship and fairness run away like the water over our sacred falls? Other relationships we have enjoyed in the past have similarly been profitable at first, only to vanish as the whites become greedy and think of us as fools."

"I do not think of you as fools. As I have said, I have lived long and prospered because I am careful and I do not become greedy. I offer a business which will profit us both. This may last us many years. I have learned that time will bring riches slowly and steadily to the man who is wise and does not seek instant fortune."

Chief Omagua nodded. This man was, as they said, wise enough to stay alive and connected enough to be of service to them. "What of your friend there," he nodded toward Leon, who could not seem to take his eyes off the breasts of one of the prettiest girls. She smiled at him. "Leon!" hissed Thomas.

Leon snapped his head around, his eyes wide. He did not observe protocol and did not smile or kiss the Chief's ring. He looked up at the big native, who looked scary to him. "What?"

No one spoke. Leon looked around nervously and said, "How do we know we can trust these guys?"

Thomas stepped back, leaving Leon alone directly in front of the chief. He did not want to be in the way in case the chief decided to swing his large sword, which hung menacingly at his side.

Leon, not knowing what else to say, continued down the path he had already started, "I mean," he blurted out, "Why do they need money and guns when they live in a city of gold? And where is it anyway? All I see here is more of this lousy jungle."

Thomas looked up at the chief. He was trying to read his reaction, and, more importantly, what he would do with this fool. The chief, thinking this young rich boy would make an excellent meal for his fish, decided to humor him. "The trinkets you bring us, my boy, are the initial offerings we need. Your father wants to use our land to set up a powerful weapon, no? You also want our cocoa and some of our gold. Since you cannot just take these things without a fight, then you must trade. We cannot get some of the medicines you bring us, as they come from your country. Gold, that we have plenty of, will not buy us other needed things as readily as your American dollars will. Perhaps, we will both profit, and live," he added, "if we follow the lead of your Mr. Reichen here."

Leon wanted to be in charge of this operation, but he was unsure of how to lead. If only his father was here, he thought. "I think we can do business," he said plaintively, the nervousness creeping into his voice. "But now I am hot and tired. I want to see this legendary city of gold, then we will do business."

It was all Thomas could do to keep from grabbing him around the throat and strangling him.

The chief, older, wiser and more tolerant, at least at the moment, toyed with him like a cat does with a small mouse before pouncing. He smiled, "We will show you our city now, my boy. Melina will show you personally, then you may visit with her and some of her friends. They will take care of you." He added, "And so will I." He snapped his fingers and the girl Leon had been staring at came over to him. She was followed by four other beautiful native girls. To Leon's surprise they took his hands and led him out of the clearing and through the thick jungle toward the Lost City.

The chief looked at Thomas. "Now we do business," he stated bluntly.

******

Bill woke up suddenly and snapped his head up. It felt as though he had just laid his head down, but the early light had moved through the small port hole and, along with pure instinct, told him that it was time to move out. His eyes burned. He'd been asleep for only about two hours and his body screamed for rest.

He moved toward the small galley by feel, as his eyes were still tightly shut. He could not shake the graininess inside them. He felt the heat of the large coffee pot as he stepped over the bulkhead, beyond the water tight doors into the galley. The coffee was hot and fresh, thanks, probably thanks to Manolo, who was well trained and looked after his boss and his charters with care. Bill was used to Navy coffee and drained his cup quickly, in spite of its heat. He poured himself another cup, this time with his eyes partially open. The caffeine was already taking effect. He started towards the foredeck, but decided to go aft and go up onto the stern deck, instead of moving back forward towards the bunk area and then up through the chart house.

He exited the stern hatch next to the 20mm Oerlikon cannon. He looked around and decided he had not slept too long. The jungle was still mostly bathed in darkness and the sun would not likely burn through the thick clouds and mist on this day. He shrugged silently. As long as he had some light and a compass, he could find anything. He chucked the last of the coffee down his throat and set his cup down on the ammo box, next to the cannon. He was surprised no one was stationed at the cannon. He moved forward on his boat towards the bridge.

John and Robin were in the gun turrets. Bill noticed with a mixture of amusement and alarm that both of them were dozing. He noticed Manolo was at the helm looking around. Bill thought he could sneak up on the boy but, just as he made it up to the cabin roof behind him, Manolo spun around with Bill's Winchester held under his arms as though it were a shotgun. He smiled. "*Olla, Padrone!*"

I'm no *padrone, amigo*," smiled Bill. He nodded toward the two sleeping men. You let your guards sleep at their posts, eh?"

"These are your *amigos, Capitán*. They rank above me and it is my job to protect you first and the others after, *si!*"

Bill nodded silently,

"Besides, *Capitán*, they will need their rest. The jungle was restless all night. We may not return alive," he added quietly.

Bill looked around. "You will, my little *amigo*. You will stay at the boat and wait for us today."

"I think I would rather stay beside you, *Capitán*. That seems to be the safest place, even on these evil shores."

Suddenly a loud scream, not quite human and not quite animal erupted from the shore. High pitched, like a woman's desperate scream, it was impossible to tell where it came from. It stopped almost immediately and was followed by a long sinister growl, which then also abruptly stopped.

Both of them felt the hairs on the back of their necks stand up straight. Manolo, his eyes wide said, *"Muy Dios Mio!* It's okay, *Capitán*. I will stay on the boat and protect you from the river!"* He had lived on the Amazon, next to the jungle his entire life and he had never heard sounds like these, or, even more important, felt anything like this in the air. This is why the old ones back at home forbade them to travel up these dark rivers, he thought.

Bill smiled. The sound had alerted both John and Robin. Each of them jumped up and looked around suddenly. Fortunately, neither one of them had fired their weapons. Bill was steadfast about keeping the safeties in the "off" position at all times.

From the sounds emanating below, the scream had woken up everyone else as well. The early morning darkness was giving way to the dawn, dampened as usual by the promise of more rain, possibly heavy today. The hatch in the console opened suddenly and Jack, followed closely by the girls came up on deck, bumping into each other and trying to rub the sleep out of their eyes. Bill noticed with amusement that no one had bothered to dress completely in the darkness and confusion. Jack only had his briefs on and the girls were only attired with tank tops and underpants. John looked away out of respect, but Robin gawked lewdly, especially at Kimmi.

"What the hell was that!?" asked Gwendolyn, clutching her daughter Aleta tightly to her side and looking around at the dark jungle.

Marianna also moved closer and put her arm around Kimmi. "I don't like this place," she whimpered.

Bill noticed with some satisfaction that her characteristic toughness had suddenly disappeared. Then he felt a little ashamed of himself. She had a right to be tough and, in fact, he needed her to be tough. "Just some friendly night sounds," said offhandedly. "We need to plan out the day, and we should probably get you folks into some clothes and have some coffee. It may be the last you have for a day or too," he added ominously.

The girls looked at each other. Jack was the first to head below, as he suddenly realized his nakedness. The girls all followed, embarrassed, but still laughing and smiling, racing each other down the ladder to get their clothes.

"Manolo," Bill turned to see him looking a little green at the prospect of being here on the ship alone, "would you please run below and whip together a quick breakfast - oatmeal would be fastest. I wish I could give 'em a proper meal, but we have to get off this boat and into the jungle within the next hour. I don't like what I feel here."

Manolo nodded. "*Si Capitán* Bill. The jungle has eyes." He turned quickly and left the bridge.

Bill turned to John and Robin. "You two can go below and get ready. The jungle will be hot, but it may rain and it will get cold around nightfall." They both nodded and got out of the gun turrets.

"Hey John," said Bill, "wait a minute, will ya?"

Robin continued down the ladder and pretended to go around the corner below, but he stayed within hearing distance. He thought no one could see him in the darkness.

John had a funny look in his eye as he turned to his friend. It looked to Bill like a mixture of fear and gold fever. "What's up?"

Bill looked around as if there might be someone else on deck listening. "John, no matter what happens, we gotta get back on this boat safely - all of us. You and I both know we're close - closer than we have ever been and we want this treasure. But," he added seriously, "we can't lose out heads, or our lives. I want the girls to go ashore, except for Kimmi and Aleta. They can stay with Manolo. He'll wait for my signal and if it doesn't come, he knows how to get them out of here and down river to some friends of mine. If that happens, then the *Federales* and my friends will come back and find us, or what's left of us."

John nodded. he saw the sense of his plan. "What about Gwendolyn? Won't she want to stay with her daughter on the boat?"

"Maybe, but we need her with us. Between you and me, Jack Robin and the girls, we have six guns." He hesitated, "Well, actually five. I don't know if I can trust your assistant." In the darkness below, Robin's hands tightened instinctively around the ladder rail.

John nodded, "He's probably okay, but I know that this is now life and death. I feel the danger all around us. Now that we know that the legend of the giant piranha is true, will we discover temples of torture, cities and walls of gold, sacred altars for sacrifice? It blows my mind that this world down here can exist in the new Millennium."

Bill nodded. "I thought the same thing on the Mekong Delta in Country, John. The horrors! My God, what men can devise to do to each other. I still have nightmares!" John nodded silently and started below.

Robin quickly turned to drop down the ladder and was suddenly grabbed in the darkness and pulled into the forward compartment, through the bulkhead. He started to strike out and then realized it was Kimmiko. She closed the hatch and turned on the light. He blinked rapidly in the light. Her eyes blazed up at him. "What the hell were you listening to?" she demanded. "I want to know what you are up to. I thought you were on our side!"

"What, what have I done wrong?" he stammered.

"I've been watching you. You are acting like you are going to try something funny."

His blinking eyes caught the sight of her still wearing only the thin tank top and panties. He reached out suddenly and grabbed her breast. "You mean, funny like this?" he grinned lewdly.

Kimmiko took a quick step backwards and slapped him as hard as she could across the cheek. "You bastard!" she hissed, not wanting to alert the others.

Robin, who was not that large or tough staggered

backwards, hitting his head on the top bunk. "You bitch," he snarled back at her. "Go play your games with the Indian boy and leave me to my business." He put his hand to his face and pulled open the hatch. He was gone in an instant and Kimmiko sank to the floor and began to cry. She hung her head and sobbed quietly, wishing her mother was here, to be back home in Berkeley - eating Blondie's Pizza. She wanted to be anywhere but here in this dark, dangerous jungle. Suddenly she felt strong arms around her, pulling her close. Manolo had been outside the fo'c'sle long enough to hear what had been said. Fortunately, Robin, in his rage and fear of discovery, had sailed past him toward the galley. He gently held her until her sobbing stopped and she regained the toughness she was known for. She clung tightly to Manolo, "Be careful of him, Manolo. He is going to do something. I just know it!"

Fifteen minutes later they were all assembled in the galley. If anyone other than Manolo had heard the fight between Kimmiko and Robin, they didn't let on. For their part, the two combatants stayed as far away from each other as possibly, a difficult thing in the tight quarters of the tiny galley. Manolo, emboldened by his increasingly strong feelings toward Kimmiko, sat next to her and looked menacingly toward Robin, who did not return his stare.

John spoke first, "I don't want to mince words with you. We've entered a dark and dangerous area of the Amazon. All of you all have a sense of what's out there, both in front and behind us. There are dangers ashore and in the water."

Gwendolyn sat, holding her daughter tightly on her lap. She spoke as though she feared the worst. "So why the hell don't we just leave this place?" she demanded. "We could just turn around and sail back to one of the ports behind us."

Bill spoke up, "That would be our plan, except that there are some bad guys waiting for us down river. Remember the ones who tried to shoot us out of the water and sank your boat. There is a way for us to go up stream and to navigate around them. Ahead of us is a point on the river which will bring us to another tributary which will ultimately dump us back downstream further below the bad guys. The only problem is, we don't know exactly where this second river is. Where we are now is very close to the Lost City of the El Dorado. Legend has it that the small tributary we need is behind and adjacent to the city." He paused looking around.

John continued, "This area is also our quest. We have good reason to believe that we can find the city and the gold and also fulfill our mission. We know there are dangers, but we are being as careful and proceeding as prudently as we can."

Marianna spoke up, "So what exactly is the plan and what, or who are we going to encounter when we go ashore?"

Bill smiled, "So does that mean you're volunteering to lead the mission?" he asked happily. They all laughed.

She smiled back and shook her head, "Not hardly, but," she added, "I was planning to go ashore and help you hunt for the city, and a way out of here. Don't forget, I have my own mission. My company will be most happy with me if I find a suitable site for their interests, even if it is a little out of the way."

Bill looked up at John, who nodded back silently at him. Without a word, they had decided to tell them all the plan, even with Robin in the room. "John, Jack, Robin, Marianna and myself will be going ashore in a few minutes. Manolo, Kimmi and Aleta will stay behind on the boat." He looked at Gwendolyn. "That leaves you. I would prefer it if you went ashore with us. I know you would rather stay here with your daughter, but I can guarantee you that Manolo will protect her, and will get her back to safety if anything happens to the rest of us."

Gwendolyn shook her head, "So why do you want me to go ashore then?"

John spoke up, "Because you've lived here and you know the native people. We may or may not encounter some of the Indians around here. The ones back there," he gestured with his thumb behind him, "seemed friendly, but having one more person with us carrying a rifle, especially a local, could help us out tremendously. It's up to you, but your presence with us could be the difference between success and failure."

"Or life and death is what you really mean," Gwendolyn added sadly. She hugged her daughter tightly and whispered something in her ear. Aleta listened intently, nodded, squeezed her eyes shut tightly and turned to hug her mother. She began sobbing quietly. Everyone looked away.

Jack spoke up, "So, the plan is that we will go ashore armed, follow the maps and photographs you have to where we think the Lost City is located. Then, if we can find the right tributary and mark our location, we can leave, right?"

"Yes, but first, we'll do some preliminary archeological prep work," answered John. "Best case scenario is that we go in unopposed and unmolested. We can then take photos and set up some excavations. We'll try to take out a little gold and, if all goes well, find Marianna's site. If we encounter any natives and they're friendly, then we'll try to strike a deal with them to return on a larger scale. We'll then make sure we're in full compliance with the government and then start a full-scale archeological project. This involves treaties, contracts, exchanges, etc. The government will either pay us up front for the finds, or, as happens more often, they'll take a smaller percentage and let us do all the work. This method is less of a risk for them and probably more profitable in the long run."

Marianna spoke up again, "And so what's the worst-case scenario?" she asked.

Bill handled that one. "The absolute worst case is that we won't make it back onto the boat and Manolo and the girls will take off back down the river and take their chances going past the unfriendly towns. We have some back up plans available, but this is our best chance."

Robin spoke up for the first time, "So what exactly are our chances?"

Bill looked directly into Robin's eyes, "I give us better than a 50% chance of success, even if we encounter a hostile enemy and have to shoot our way out." He smiled evenly at Robin, but his smile was cold and was meant as a warning.

Robin nodded and looked away. He was getting the message that they had figured out he wasn't a part of the team. He was beginning to have doubts about whether he was a part of either team. His actions toward Kimmiko had confused him and made him wonder why he was doing any of this. He had family back in the States who were proud of him. Growing up, he had never thought of himself as the bad guy. Actually, he never thought of himself as "Robin," but pretended he was really "Batman," the hero who vanquished the villain and got the girl in the end.

Bill continued, "It will be light in less than an hour. When we go up on deck, I'll issue everyone a weapon." He held up an Uzi submachine gun. "This isn't a game. If you feel threatened, you have to shoot first, but please make sure you shoot the enemy and not a friend. I will be giving each of you an Uzi. They have a setting for single fire and automatic fire. They will be set on single fire. Marianna and Gwendolyn, have you ever fired an Uzi?" They both shook their heads. "Then I will have to give you dry fire lessons." He looked at Gwendolyn, "Are you coming with us?"

She let go of Aleta who turned around and looked at her mother. They gazed at each other for a long time. Aleta nodded and Gwendolyn hugged her tightly. She was crying as she looked up at Bill and nodded.

"That's good," said Bill, "You just increased our chance of survival by 20%." He looked around the room. Everyone get a canteen of water. Manolo will bring you a backpack of dry rations. Get clothes for the heat and coverings for the cold if we have to spend the night ashore, which we probably will. Your pack will contain a small sleeping bag, which is not very heavy. Now assemble on the deck in 10 minutes."

******

Thomas and the Chief had made their plans carefully. They agreed that Leon would have to be kept alive at all costs. The Chief informed Thomas that his spotters had seen the boat carrying the professor just offshore, less than three miles from their position. In fact, if those onboard the boat knew their exact position, they would have sailed up river another 2.5 miles, turned left up another vine-obstructed river and they would have been right next to the Lost City. Fortunately for Thomas and the Chief, they didn't know these details and would be moving through the jungle right into a trap. Then they would get the information they sought from their captives, seize the boat and sacrifice them all when they were no longer of service. They had gathered the natives around them and made their plans.

Leon was lying on his back, naked. He looked at the ceiling of the grass hut as two of the girls worked their magic on him. The other two native girls held his arms out to his sides and rubbed his stomach and chest. The first two were using their hands and mouths on his body in ways he could never imagine. He suddenly felt waves of pressure as he convulsed into another orgasm, his third, actually, in less than an hour.

The girls, naked as well, washed and massaged him after each session. They kept him drinking a strange, warm flavorful liquid which made him sleepy and at the same time aroused him again and again. The pretty one, named Melina, who had serviced him a moment ago, looked up with a smile on her lips. Slowly she moved up until her dark brown breasts were near Leon's mouth. He took her hungrily into his mouth, and, like a greedy infant, began sucking her intensely. This time he didn't even lose his erection, as one of the other girls, kept him hard. He felt her small body climb on top of him and, as he entered her, he let out a gasp.

Two of the Chief's guards watched them through the slats in the hut. One nodded to the other one, who took off through the jungle to tell the Chief that Leon would be asleep for at least the next 12-24 hours. The concoction he had been drinking was called caldo, a soup made from water, salt and the boiled head of the pacu fish. The head was loaded with fat, and the soup it produced, was popular up and down the Amazon, as it caused heavy sleep to anyone who consumed it before bedtime. The natives here had mixed it with one of their locally grown herbs which was a very powerful aphrodisiac. The combination would ultimately wear Leon out and cause him to sleep for the entire day and through the night. The plan was to get him out of action, but keep him alive and happy until they secured the full cooperation of his father. After that, it didn't matter what happened to him. Once business had been established and the money was flowing to everyone's satisfaction, poor Leon would probably have some kind of unfortunate accident. His father would be sad, but the jungle was full of danger, as everyone knew.

******

Bill was up on deck in full battle gear. Despite the early morning heat of the place and the increasing humidity which would become almost unbearable in the afternoon, he was wearing fatigues, boots and a jungle vest. He had his Colt .45 automatic pistol at his side, a Bowie knife and, of course, his Winchester. John and Jack were both wearing long pants and similar vests, but without shirts underneath. They both held

Uzi's and had knives, but no pistols. Gwendolyn and Marianna were wearing shorts and tank tops. They had refused long pants, preferring comfort to whatever the jungle might do to their bare skin. Gwen was succinct when she said she was really a native and knew how to get around the jungle, thank you. They both held their Uzi's tightly in their hands, but away from their bodies, as though to touch the thing was in and of itself a bad omen. As taught by Bill, their fingers were off the trigger.

Last was Robin, who, like Bill, wore fatigues. He had brought them aboard in anticipation of his secret mission. He had also brought his Smith and Wesson 586, a stainless steel .357 magnum revolver, which hung at his side. He noted that when Bill had handed him his Uzi, he had a strange look on his face, as though he shouldn't be doing it. It didn't matter, the scream and growl they had all heard earlier was the signal to him that everything was in place and that he would be met shortly. He had no way of knowing what the trap was to be, but that he should be ready. He was a little disappointed that Manolo and Kimmiko were staying on the boat. He wished he could take out Manolo and keep Kimmi as his prize. She could stay alive as long as she cooperated and made him happy. He smiled inwardly at the thought.

Bill maneuvered the boat gently toward the shore, scanning constantly for traps. Manolo went forward to the bow to give hand signals back to Bill where to land. Jack stood at the starboard gun mount, ready in case there was an attack. John was at the 20mm and Robin was at the stern ready to toss a line onto the shore if needed. The rest were in the bridge, huddled together tightly and ready to duck down in case fire erupted from the jungle behind the small beach they were moving toward.

Manolo suddenly waved his right arm frantically as he lay on his stomach behind the running light on the bow. "Starboard 20 degrees, Captain!" he yelled back. Bill turned over the wheel sharply, but the PT boat was moving slowly and its 45 tons of plywood and armaments took a several seconds to respond. They all heard a loud thud as the port bow hit something heavy and bounced off. It proceeded forward, as though there was no damage. "Sorry, Captain that was a big log- I think."

Bill looked over to his left as they passed the spot the log should have been. He didn't see anything, but the small wake that the slow-moving boat was making, was broken up here, as circles of water moved against it. He also noted large bubbles coming up through the concentric rings. He shuddered to think of what down there was large enough to make those bubbles and move his boat off its course. His mind went back to the giant piranhas, as he put his engine into neutral and set up his approach into the seemingly soft sandy shore. There was always the possibility of hitting roots and logs which could tear a hole in his bow and sink his boat. This time, however, he felt the comforting mild crunch as the boat's bow hit the sand, about three feet below the surface. The angle of the boat as it touched the shore, would enable them to all drop onto the sand without getting their feet wet.

Manolo scrambled over the bow and tied up to a thick rubber tree. He cinched a quick release knot and jumped back onto the boat. He replaced Bill at the helm and Kimmiko replaced Jack in the forward gun mount. Both Bill and Manolo had shown her how to fire the .50 caliber machine gun just in case. Aleta, after hugging and kissing her mother went over and stood by Manolo at the helm. He put his arm around her small shoulders and gave Gwendolyn a thumbs up. She smiled and followed Bill, Robin and Jack over the bow onto the beach. Marianna blew a kiss to Kimmiko and jumped onto the soft sand. John was about to go over, but walked back to Kimmiko in the gun turret. He gazed into his daughter's brown eyes and said, "Kimmi, I love you. I don't think I've said that enough to you, but I do and I am very proud of you. If anything happens to me, get back to Berkeley safely and call Professor Meyer at Boalt Hall, the Law School at the top of the campus. He's my attorney and will handle everything.

Kimmiko blinked rapidly, suddenly overcome with emotion and love for her dad, who, like her, she realized, had never gotten over her mother's death. "Oh Daddy," she threw her arms around her father's shoulders as she leaned under the gun turret railing which partial obstructed her dad's reach, "I know you do and I love you - more than anything." she added.

She started to cry and her dad held her head in his hands. Her head used to be so tiny, he thought, with little braids and a pony tail. Now she was turning into a woman and somehow, he had lost the last several years with his daughter - time that would never come back. He sighed. "I'll be back sweetheart, and then you and I need some time together, just the two of us. Somehow, I lost the last ten years with my baby and I want to try to make that up to you, okay honey?" She nodded and wiped away her tears. "Now make sure you don't shoot the old man as I make a break for the jungle, okay?

Kimmiko nodded again, still blinking away her tears, and took up her post behind the gun, scanning the jungle fiercely. Suddenly she felt a lioness' strength and courage, ready to shoot anything that dared tried to take her father or his friends away from her. She had lost one person she loved with all her heart and she would be damned if anyone would take anyone else away from her. Ever.

****

The natives under Mondo, had not been up this stretch of the river in many years. They knew approximately where the Lost City was, but many of them had been only infants and young children when their parents left. Now they were treading in unfamiliar waters, both geographically and philosophically. The older ones in the group knew the area fairly well and relished the chance to see their ancestral home. Many had a strong desire to return there and spend their last days in the place of their childhood. Unfortunately, they knew, however desirable this might be, it could never happen under Chief Omagua or his evil son. They were outcasts and there was a price on their heads. They were guilty of high treason. They had left their home and had left their religion. They were outcasts, even as they pinned away for their homes and culture. They had grown and prospered down river and raised their children to be good. They wanted nothing to do with the evil sacrifices or the evil fish. Once, one of the giant piranhas had wandered too far downstream. After a fierce battle with the natives, it had wound up as an unhappy guest at a giant barbecue in its honor. One thing about the giant piranhas, pacu and the pirarucu, they all tasted great.

Mondo held up his hand to stop the ten boats, each carrying around ten natives. In the last boat was Corneila, Mondo's wife and their infant son. Although Corneila was the exiled daughter of Chief Omagua, he had not seen her since she had run off with Mondo. He had no idea that he even had grandchildren by her, not that it would have affected his evil heart. The boats stopped before they reached the next bend in the river. They were less than 200 yards from the PT boat. They would hide their boats in the jungle and try to get around the landing Americans, passing them inland on their flank. They knew their old Chief would be waiting for the Professor and his party. This was not only their chance to help them, but also to possibly vanquish the evil ones and regain their rightful lands. Silently, they cruised in and hid their boats. They then set off for the Lost City, careful to give a wide berth to the enemy.

****

The PT boat landing party had been moving through the jungle for only about an hour, but the heat and the oppressiveness of the place was wearing them down. Only Bill, ever on the alert, was still fresh. He felt a constant supply of adrenaline kept kicking in. Now, as exhaustion began to set in, everyone sat down heavily on whatever they could find. They were all dripping with sweat. Marianna wiped the back of her neck with a handkerchief. "I can't believe how hot it is," she moaned. "There are clouds, but not even a hint of a breeze. How much farther is it, anyway?"

John held the map next to the aerial photos. "We need to look for a small stream, winding like a snake," he said. "We'll follow it to a small pond and from there, the city is less than a thousand yards away."

"A thousand yards which way?" asked Jack.

"I'm not quite sure. The map is inconclusive and the photos are obscured. There are other signs, however, we may see once we get close."

A sudden snap of a branch in the jungle behind them, brought Jack, John and Bill to their feet. Robin, also alert, moved closer to the two girls, as if they needed his protection. Both Gwendolyn and Marianna had their guns out, loaded and ready.

They listened intently for over a minute, but heard nothing except the usual jungle sounds which had started again at the first light.

Bill shrugged. "Let's move out," he said quietly.

******

Chief Omagua's natives were in position less than one mile up ahead of the path from Bill and John's search party. Mondo's good natives were behind them by about the same distance. One of the natives trailing the Americans had just inadvertently stepped on a fallen tree branch, which had snapped in half. Two other two natives had grabbed him and all had moved silently back into the dense undergrowth, so they would not be detected.

In the thick jungle, ahead of the Americans, Thomas was waiting with Prince Omagua. There were twenty other natives with them - some in the trees and some hiding in the jungle. They were heavily armed with guns, knives and bows and arrows. Some carried blow guns with darts dipped in a poison they derived from the local plants in the area. Certainly, there were enough of them to capture all of the landing party and carry them unharmed back to the City. There they would be stripped, searched, then interrogated. Thomas needed information from the Professor. If he couldn't get any, then they would just be eliminated. He'd take their boat, which had some value, and please the native's gods with a bounty of a sacrifice. He looked over at the Prince. "I've heard you have a brother and a sister. Where are they?"

He sniffed disdainfully, "The brother is Damien. He coward. He is afraid of the fishes. The sister - she dead. She run off with a traitor. She no more."

Thomas did not know if she was literally dead, of if she had just been disowned. He decided to leave it alone. He did not want to anger the Prince and small talk wasn't in his nature anyway. "Remember, we have a man inside the group who may be with them. He is younger than the rest, but that's all I know about him." The Prince nodded. Thomas turned back and looked into the jungle, and listened for footsteps.

****

Bill and John were on point as they made their way through the thick underbrush. John was looking at his maps and photo, as Bill moved carefully forward. Jack was out to one side, flanking the main party which, of course, was only the girls. Robin was covering the rear. The jungle was getting hotter and wetter, if that were possible.

John and Jack had unbuttoned their vests and the girls had both wrapped their shirts around their waists. They were wearing bathing suit tops, but were still dripping with sweat. Only Bill kept his clothes on and, more importantly still kept his cool. He felt like he was back in Viet Nam and that they were walking into danger, but was unable to stop. They had a mission. The orders were specific and could not be denied. No matter what happened to him, he wouldn't go down without a fight and he would get a few of the bastards.

"There has to be a stream around here," said John. "It shows here on the map. We are within yards of the formations."

"Formations?" asked Bill as he scanned the jungle thicket ahead.

"Deep foundations in the ground made of stone near the stream. The natives believed that they need to protect the City from those who walked above the ground in the light and from those who float through the dark. The idols which sit above the foundations are there to ward off the good and the evil alike."

Bill shivered. He could hear the wind moaning through the trees. It seemed they were in a very isolated part of the planet and he, like the others wished he were somewhere else. He was poking through the brush at a very thick part of the jungle, when he was stopped short. His Winchester had tapped against something hard, unlike a tree trunk. "I think we found one," he said dryly.

The others moved forward as he parted the thick foliage, to reveal a squat, ugly idol about four feet high. Behind it was a small stream approximately eight feet wide. From the flow of the water, it looked to be about three or four feet deep.

"Ugly, isn't it?" said Gwendolyn.

"Sure is," replied Marianna, "ugly and wicked looking.

They all tensed as the jungle suddenly became silent.

Jack looked around, "Hey, where's Robin?" he asked.

Suddenly the jungle parted all around them and natives came out of everywhere. They had guns, bows and arrows and blow guns. They completely surrounded the Americans and had advanced to within inches before anyone could more or react. A tall, white man wearing jungle fatigues similar to Bill's, although his were black instead of green, stepped out of the jungle holding an automatic pistol. He smiled. "I would advise you to drop your weapons. All of them please, or these natives will be forced to shoot you, starting with these lovely girls." He smiled easily.

Bill's eyes narrowed. He could see they were outnumbered and outgunned. "Drop you weapons," he said reluctantly. They placed their guns and knives on the ground. Unarmed, they felt naked.

The man looked around. "So, Professor Waales, we meet at last. Your capture went much smoother than I had anticipated."

John's eyes went wide at the use of his name. "Just who the hell are you and what right do you have to capture and detain us?" he demanded.

"My name, sir, is Thomas Reichen. I'm a big fan of your work and your theories. I have followed them right into the heart of the jungle and right to the Lost City. If it wasn't for you, I would never have known about the true location of the El Dorado. Happily, I've made friends with the local natives and have struck a deal with them. While you've wasted your time on photos, idols and streams, I have already seen the Lost City."

Bill spoke up, "So what do you want, you bastard?"

Thomas smiled and motioned to the natives. Swiftly they grabbed the men and women. After a brief struggle they had them bound with their hands behind their backs and all together in a chain to keep them from running away. Marianna screamed and struggled when one of the natives grinned as he dragged his hands across her chest while he wrapped a thick coil of rope around her. Jack reached out to help her and was knocked to his knees by two of the natives. He fell forward as they kicked him in the side.

"Stop it, stop it, you bastards!" hissed John. They grabbed Jack and pulled him to his feet. He looked up at the two who had abused him and smiled. He was tied up and without his gun, but he still felt the comforting weight of his telescoping nunchakus, hidden deep in his underpants, strapped to his groin. He would serve these two a lesson if it was the last thing he ever did.

"Move out," Thomas said quietly to the Prince, "your father awaits.

******

Manolo and Aleta stood at the helm of the PT boat as Kimmiko stayed at her post in the starboard gun turret. They were scanning the area in a 360 degree sweep, using binoculars and their eyes. In spite of the thickening clouds, the heat was getting more and more oppressive and the humidity was becoming almost unbearable.

"Do you think they'll come back alive?" asked Aleta fearfully.

"Yes, I do," said Manolo. "I have seen *Capitán* Bill in the worst fight you can imagine, *niña*. He has won every time. I would trust my life and the life of my children to *Capitán* Bill."

"This place gives me the creeps," Kimmi said looking back from her gun. "I kind of like this machine gun, though. It makes me feel like a super-chick!" They all laughed and the tension broke for a minute.

"Aleta," Manolo said, "I want you to look at the water a lot. The fish are *muy malo* and there could be *bandidos* in small boats, *comprende?*"

She nodded. "I can see a long way. Mom always said I had great eyes."

"Kimmi, keep an eye on that jungle. Anything can happen at any time."

"Way ahead of you. How long does it take to fire up this boat if we need to get out in a hurry?"

"Quickly, I can get away. *Capitán* Bill keeps the magnetos hot and the injectors primed. It is different from most engines. He thinks of everything," he said almost wistfully. In his heart, he was praying mightily for *Capitán* Bills return. Other than his immediate family, he loved Bill more than anyone, although, if the truth be known, he was falling hard for Kimmiko as well.

****

They were being led, tied and blindfolded, through the jungle single file. The Prince was in the lead and Thomas brought up the rear. Between each of them was two natives, ready at a moment's notice to knock them on the ground if they misbehaved, or to pick them up if they stumbled. The blindfolds were the idea of the Chief, who didn't want them to know the way to the Lost City. They all wondered what had happened to Robin. They hadn't seen him since before their capture. This confirmed John, Bill and Jack's suspicions of him, but the two girls just feared the worst.

They broke into the same clearing, where a few hours earlier, the Chief had welcomed Thomas and Leon. At this point, they were led to separate huts. John was taken by Thomas Reichen and two natives into one hut, Bill and Jack into another hut by the Prince and four of his main guards. The girls were led into a third hut by four of the natives and were joined there by the tribe's medicine man. He would look them over and see if they were suitable for the ceremonies later that day. All of them were searched thoroughly and tied down. The men were interrogated and the women were gagged.

Thomas and the Chief questioned John. They needed to know how many more knew about his plans. They also wanted to know the extent of the University's and, thus, the entire scientific community's dedication to the project. They knew it would be a little hard for them to pretend there would be no one else coming to search for the professor and his crew. But they thought they might be able to make them all disappear if there weren't too many who knew where they were.

They had sent a party of natives out to get the boat, the young boy and the two girls, then bring them back to the village. They knew from their lookouts and from Robin, who was resting comfortably with the same girls who had taken care of Leon before he passed out, that one of them was Kimmiko, Professor Waales' daughter. They knew that the thought of harm coming to her would force him to cooperate. Even now, he was tied to a chair, wearing only his pants as the natives cut very tiny slashes in his arms and back. They held handfuls of salt, but had not rubbed any into his cuts yet. He too was gagged, but not blindfolded.

Bill and Jack would be questioned, tortured and either killed or sacrificed to the fish. The only thing they had to contribute was to confirm whatever John Waales told them. The older one, Bill, might be useful to teach them how to operate the PT boat, but they had captured a smaller, similar boat many years ago. It was a Mark II Riverine Boat, otherwise known as a Mark II PBR, or a Patrol Boat River, used in the Viet Nam War. They kept it in running order. One of the last heroic things the smuggler who had owned it did, before his unfortunate dance with the fishes, was show them every detail of how to run and repair it. They had absolutely no use for Jack. They wondered what he was even here for, but it didn't matter. They thought an extra hostage wouldn't hurt anything. Both he and Bill had on their baggy swim shorts. Everything else had been removed and buried. They were both tied tightly down onto wooden boards, blindfolded and gagged.

Gwendolyn and Marianna had suffered the most so far. They had been stripped, bound and gagged. The Chief and the Medicine Man, had, after carefully examining them, spoke in excited whispers. As the girls both moaned and writhed on their boards, the Chief came over and whispered something into each of their ears, which caused them to struggle even more and they began to cry with fright.

****

Mondo and twelve of his most loyal warriors were moving as fast as they could back to their boats. They had stumbled on the area where John and the others had been captured just as they were being led away. They had crouched in the dense underbrush, watching their former cousins and, in Mondo's case, his estranged brother-in-law taking away the Americans. One thing they didn't understand was the way two of the natives were treating the one young American. They laughed and slapped him on the back as if he had done a good job over something. They then led him away a few steps behind and to the side of the others. Mondo sent three of his swiftest men to follow them and then to report back to him at the boat. He needed to know where the Americans were to be kept. He had no illusions about what was to happen. It was his wife's father's ultimate joy to torture, humiliate and ultimately to sacrifice his victims to the fish. The fact that they were Americans and two of them were attractive women whetted his infernal appetite even more.

They reached the boats and gathered the other tribesmen. They had to get first to the PT boat and warn the children there - why anyone would leave children alone on a ship of war baffled all of them - before the Chief's men captured it and sacrificed all aboard. The problem was the young ones probably had no experience in combat and would likely shoot them all first, thus bringing a swift conclusion to their rescue operation and an immediate conclusion to their lives. Fortunately, Mondo's wife, Cornelia, joined the conversation and it was she who came up with the best approach of all.

****

Twelve-year-old Aleta could not contain herself. She walked about the deck like an angry tiger confined to a cage. Balling and unballing her fists, she knew, she just *knew* that her mother was in trouble. They communicated that way all their lives. Each could talk to the other without words ever being spoken. Her mom was only half American. The other half was pure Colombian from the back countries. Even now she could hear her mother saying, *"...run, run, it's a trap, it's a trap, please get far, far away from here, sacrifice, sacrifice, sacrifice..."* The words kept eerily coming back again and again.

Kimmiko also knew there was something wrong. She had felt this same gut-wrenching, emotional plunge before when she finally realized that her mother was gone and there was nothing on Heaven or Earth that could change that. She squeezed the trigger mechanism on the .50 caliber machine gun over and over again. Had it not been for the safety mechanism, the gun would be out of bullets by now.

Even Manolo knew he had to do something, but he didn't know what. It was only 1500 hours and he was supposed to stay here until noon tomorrow and then leave if he did not hear anything.

Suddenly, out of the corner of his eye, he saw a native canoe coming toward him with a woman in her late thirties who held a small baby in her arms. A single, small native man rowed the boat. She was waving her free arm furiously as though she were desperate to talk to them. At the same instant, Kimmiko caught sight of the canoe and, without realizing what she was doing spun the machinegun around, until it was pointing directly at the canoe. In that one motion, she had expertly flipped off the safety and started to turn to let loose a volley of fire directly at the woman and baby. Manolo lunged at the machine gun and, with all of his weight, crashed into the twin barrels, elevating them enough so that the one second burst of bullets flew harmlessly over their heads. Instantly Kimmiko realized with horror at what she had almost done. She let go of the gun's handles, jumped out of the gun turret and dropped to the deck, flat on her stomach. She reached out for the canoe, which had gone dead stop in the water and said over and over again, "Oh, I'm sorry, I'm so sorry!"

She, Aleta and Manolo helped pull the woman and the child aboard. The man stayed in the canoe. Badly shaken from the fact that she and her son had almost been killed, the woman began to speak slowly, "I am Cornelia and this is my son, Damien, named after his uncle, who he has not met. We are part of the Chibcha Indian tribe. We are the good ones. The bad ones are ahead of us. They are our cousins, many of whom are, like us, still good but could not escape. We left the City of the El Dorado, over fifteen years ago. We have come to help you. I am the daughter of the bad Chief Omagua. My brother, Prince Sajava is helping him. We have come to help you."

Manolo knew he was supposed to be in charge, but he wasn't sure what to say. He looked at Kimmiko for help, but she was still in shock over the fact that she had almost killed this young mother and her infant son.

It was Aleta, the twelve-year-old who spoke up, "Do you know what has happened to our families?"

"Yes, they were captured earlier by the Prince and a tall White man. There was also a young one in your group who seemed to be friends with them and must have helped capture them."

"Son of a bitch!" cried Kimmiko angrily. It all became instantly clear to her. She turned to Manolo, her eyes blazing, "Robin is trying to kill my father and take credit for his work!" She slammed her fist into the wall of the bridge angrily.

"What of the others?" asked Aleta fearfully.

Cornelia placed her hand on the young girl's shoulder. She placed her son down on the deck and put her other arm around her. She was taller than Aleta, so she bent down and spoke quietly as she looked in her eyes. "One of them is your mother, yes?" Aleta nodded. "My child, first they will all be tortured and then, as midnight comes tonight, they will all be sacrificed to the gods of the river. The piranhas will consume them so that the Chief can show to all, his power is that of the gods."

"Nooooooo...!" sobbed Aleta, as Cornelia held her close. She became wracked with tears. Kimmiko reached over, and, as Corneila backed away, hugged her tightly. "Shh, shh," she soothed.

Manolo spoke up angrily, "How can you help us if there are only the two of you and the baby? And how do we know that you have not been sent here just to lure us back to the El Dorado and kill us as well?"

She smiled and picked up her baby, "My son, I knew you might have doubts about us, so I came ahead of the others."

"What others...?" he asked, his voice trailing off. He suddenly spun around to see at least twenty of the most fearsome looking natives, all wearing full war paint and holding a mixture of rifles, pistols, knives and bows and arrows standing not five feet behind them on the deck of the PT boat. Somehow, they had come onboard completely silently and undetected. He looked over the side and saw another fifty in the same canoes that had met them in the early morning hours of the previous day. Several held their weapons pointed at him, as though he might try to do something.

"You see, my son," Cornelia added gently, "if we wanted you dead, you would be so already!"

******

The burst of gunfire had, as Mondo feared, alerted the Chief's guards sent to seize the boat. He knew they had to work quickly. He and his men pulled and pushed the PT boat off the shore, no easy task in the soft sand and with the ever-alarming possibility of the presence of the giant piranhas. They tied ropes to the PT boat and with five boats and fifty men, began towing the boat upstream against the current. Manolo steered and the girls, now both of them at the machineguns, prepared for the worst. The boat had been covered with jungle vines and branches, and, although it would never pass for a native barge, the camouflage did help it some. A light rain had begun to fall and, as the shadows lengthened, they all knew they had very little time to spare.

****

Mondo had left twenty of his most experienced guards behind to deal with the Chief's assassins, who, as they suspected, had orders to kill the boy and bring the girls back.

The assassins had volunteered eagerly for this job because they were told they could take a few hours to enjoy the young girls before they brought them back. They were to arrive alive, but damaged was okay. These were bloodthirsty young men, being trained by the Prince himself to be handlers of the killer fish. They in turn, because of their savage instincts, enjoyed letting out their wild bloodlust on sometimes the most helpless of victims. In this case it was to be Kimmiko and Aleta. As they advanced through the jungle, they boasted foolishly, more like boys than men, about what sexual perversions they would soon enjoy.

Mondo had instructed his men to show mercy if they gave up without a fight, or, if they recognized a cousin or a nephew and did not want to harm him out of respect for a grieving aunt or uncle. This was not the case, however. The five Indians simply went to where the boat was supposed to be, they had heard Kimmiko's machinegun volley after all, and discovered nothing there, except the ripple of the waves against the small beach. Suddenly, the men of Mondo's army descended on them and attempted to capture them peacefully. The evil natives would have none of this, however, and foolishly tried to fight against the twenty warriors. Of course, they were cut down instantly and thus, Chief Omagua lost five of his best and most feared fighters. It would not be all he would lose, as he was soon to find out.

****

John had held back the screams as long as he could. The salt bit deep into the wounds inflicted by the Indian's cruel knife. The natives, obviously masters of torture, ground the salt into each cut, one at a time. John thought he might pass out, if it not for the new and agonizing pain each time they rubbed in more salt. He had not told them anything, even though he knew they would not stop. They had told him that they were preparing long shards of palm needles to place under his fingernails if he would not talk.

Thomas was weary of this game. He reached out and grasped John under his chin. "I want to know right now, who else is preparing to follow you to this place and who else has seen the map and the photos?" he demanded harshly.

John shook his head, "No one else is close. We couldn't risk it," he lied. In truth, over twenty other scientists were working with him on this project. There would be enough gold and fame to go around. Dr. John Waales would be the first and would get the headlines, but he knew that this project was too big for one or two men. Like a true scientist, he had shared it with others, even those at Stanford University. He smiled inward at the joke. Strangely, he had not told this to Robin and some of his other close colleagues at Berkeley, who he felt would not understand this. He didn't even know why he had held back from them, but he had. Now he was glad.

Thomas smiled as John gasped while one of the natives poured salt water into one of his wounds. "Gag him for a minute." He looked down benevolently. "Soon your lovely daughter Kimmiko will be here. Even now she is being escorted here by five young natives. Actually, they have been told to take their time and enjoy her first," he added cruelly. This had the desired effect on John Waales. As a father, his mind revolted against someone touching or hurting his daughter. He lunged for him and, struggled madly against the ropes, until Thomas stepped behind him. With a swift blow to the back of John's head, the lights went out.

****

Bill and Jack had fared no better. They had been whipped by the natives until their skin bled. They were both weak. One native took out a knife and was preparing to deliver a fatal blow to Jack's chest, when the Chief came in and spoke harshly to him. They would be sacrificed to the fish, he told them, not to the butcher.

The Prince stepped back to look at them. He turned to his father and, in their native tongue said, "Are we to sacrifice them all at midnight, tonight?"

"Yes, my son. I grow weary and the sacrifice will be a nice demonstration for our two new friends." He corrected himself, "I mean our new three friends. The one they call Robin, he is resting comfortably, yes?"

The Prince nodded. "He has found comfort in Melina's arms and that of her friends. Why do we allow these white devils to use our women so, Father?" He spat in the sand floor of the hut.

Chief Omagua smiled, "Never underestimate the power of the woman, my son. You yourself have tasted the pleasures of these girls and so have your elite guards. There are many forms of warfare, and the women are simply fighting our battles in the only way they know how. They will get information from Robin by using their tongues, rather than their fists, just like they have done with the fat *pendejo* Leon."

"Was the information useful, my father?"

"Indeed it was son. We must use this Reichen, *gringo*, for a while and also his two friends. But soon, each will lose his life in turn as we gather our outside contacts."

"Didn't you tell the man Reichen that we would all prosper together over the years."

The chief sighed, "My son, it is simply impossible to trust the white eyes. They will lie skillfully to your face and tell you what you want to hear. Then they will cut your throat and that of your wife and children when you are not looking!" He made a slashing, motion across his throat as he said this. Jack, looking up, thought this gesture was meant for them and he let out a moan. He was still gagged and could not say anything.

"Let us leave, my son and prepare for the feast and the

sacrifice. Are there girls picked out for our guests?"

Prince Sajava grimaced, "Yes, my father. Indeed, we have many beautiful girls who will dance for us and then, as if by accident, will pick out the *estupido* white ones as mates for tonight. Let's hope we get the others from the boat and that they too will be worthy of our fish."

After this, the Chief nodded to the guards. Jack and Bill thought their time had come and started struggling against the heavy ropes. Like John, they were both hit on the head and knocked unconscious.

****

Mondo and his group of natives had towed the PT boat up to a second hidden opening, leading to the next tributary. In this case, there was a complicated delta of several flowing streams, creeks and rivers, all cascading around the Lost City, which was still hidden by the thick forest canopy. Mondo had made his plans, but he was sure that things could still go wrong. He had approximately 100 soldiers - hopefully the twenty sent back to intercept the PT boat raiders were still okay - but they were outnumbered by at least ten to one. That didn't even count all of the women, who could also be loyal to the Chief. If their long-lost cousins recognized them and befriended them, then they might get through this and regain their rightful home. On the other hand, if all of their lost relatives were unfriendly, then they realized that they probably wouldn't survive.

In one of the canoes, Mondo looked lovingly at his wife Cornelia. Although the shadows had long since darkened and the rain still fell lightly, this wasn't enough to hide his wife's beauty. He loved her dearly and their several sons and daughters left behind in their own village left downstream knew of their parent's love. Cornelia smiled back at him. It was at her insistence that they brave this chance to regain their City of the El Dorado – their ancestral home. The young ones only knew of the city through their stories. She also felt pity for these young ones they were escorting. She had little feeling, however, for the adults of the party. To some extent, she and Mondo felt the white men were simply grave robbers, who would try to enrich themselves with the bounty of the El Dorado's treasures.

Mondo looked around at his warriors. They would soon be in position. The river, at this entrance, would lead them right next to the city and its sacrificial altars. He also knew they would be heading into the thickest of the guards and warriors. The worst of which were, of course, the giant piranhas. He remembered having to watch them eat the sacrifices. The victims of war with other villages, hostages, criminals of his own tribes and, when there were no people, the animals of the jungle. All died horrible deaths. In spite of the heat and humidity, Mondo shivered violently.

They would wait here until full darkness. Hopefully the clouds would obscure the moon and help hide them. Even now, fifteen warriors left various boats and made their way on shore to act as lookouts. Their orders were the same as the others. If the enemy would convert or come peacefully, they would not be harmed. But if they resisted, then they could not be taken prisoner. Mondo cocked a round into his old Savage .30-30 rifle and sat back in his boat.

CHAPTER VI

THE ATTACK

ON THE PT BOAT, below decks, Manolo and Kimmiko prepared themselves for war. They dressed in camouflage and blackened their faces against the night. Kimmiko pulled back her long dark hair and tucked it under the back of her shirt. She held up a Walther PPKS .380 automatic pistol and a W.W.II Luger .32 pistol. "Where shall I hide these?" she asked Manolo.

"*Senorita...*," he began.

Kimmi, said, "Manolo! We are too close to death and," she added somewhat shyly, even for her she thought, "too close to each other for formalities."

"Kimmi," he continued, "you must hide these on your lower body. If they capture you, they will strip you to the waist and include you in their sacrifice to the fish." He blushed, both at the revelation of what he had said and also at the candor he had displayed, although it was somewhat inadvertent.

She smiled at him. She unbuttoned her black pants and hid the two small weapons in her underpants.

Manolo, sensing he was now closer to her, but still afraid of her rejecting him, turned away as he strapped several weapons to different parts of his body. "We will soon move out and the young girl Aleta will stay here on the boat where she will be safe."

"I don't know about that," said Kimmiko. "She's manning the .50 caliber machine guns. I think she is enjoying herself. Of course," she added, "she's still worried about her mother and getting out of here alive, as we all are."

Manolo nodded. He hoped he was doing what his *padrone*, *Capitán* Bill, wanted him to do.

****

The guards were everywhere. John, Jack and Bill had been bathed by the Indian women and led, with their hands tied, still in their shorts, out to the center of the huts outside the city. The two women, also bathed by the girls, had been dressed in ceremonial skirts and heavy wooden beads laid over their chests. They were tied, brought out and were led to the same area as the men. It was eleven o'clock and the night was at its darkest. The clouds obscured the sky and rain continued to fall lightly.

Torches, mounted on the buildings, and outcroppings of rock, burned brightly and lit up the path. They were led single file with their hands shackled behind them through the thick jungle for over 500 yards. Their blindfolds and gags had been removed, as the Indians expected no interference or resistance. They could hear drums beating an evil, intoxicating sound just up ahead.

John, Bill and Jack were led, with Gwendolyn and Marianna at the rear, past the huts and shacks, through the dense jungle. As they walked into a clearing, they suddenly stopped short. They stared unbelieving at the sight ahead.

One and two story buildings, over twenty score of them, lined the river and flowed back into the jungle. They were lit by torch light and looked to be made of solid gold. The buildings sparkled brilliantly, looking all the more dramatic by the cleansing rain. The gold looked heavy and thick. There were hundreds of structures, each more ornate than the one before. Their tired and painful eyes could only grasp a small part of what they were seeing. Had they been able to calculate the enormity of the lost City of the El Dorado, they would have realized they were looking at over 100,000 tons of gold, literally two hundred million pounds of the stuff. Never mind the historical significance and the ornateness of the carvings, but the sheer melted down value was in the hundreds of billions of dollars.

John, the first in line, reacted with a small sigh then closed his eyes. His lifelong quest was being answered, but not the way he had imagined. Now, his body and mind strove not for gold, but for life, a commodity more precious than anything else in the world. He knew that his life and the lives of his friends and family were at stake.

Bill was holding up better than John. He was behind him and saw the city. "Your quest," he whispered, before the nearest guard clubbed him to his knees.

Jack and the girls saw the City of Gold, but didn't care. They knew they were being led like animals to the slaughter.

Their only concern now was for life. Silently, each of them resolved that they would fight to the bitter end. No matter what.

****

Mondo's twenty-man guard who had vanquished the Prince's five guards, made their way silently and undetected through the jungle. They were close to the chosen sacrificial site and had climbed up in the trees. They positioned themselves and covered the site with their weapons. Arms ready, they had nothing but contempt for their former evil tribesmen. They hoped they wouldn't have to fight their loving, lost relatives, but they were ready for the fight and, if need be, the end of the world.

****

John, Bill, Jack, Gwendolyn and Marianna had been led past the City of Gold, to the river's edge. Here, they saw the sacrificial altars - flat, squat, evil things which resembled large, wooden crosses laid horizontally, and elevated three to four feet above the ground. Guards pulled John away from the group and tied him with his hands over his head to a large palm tree. There he would watch the sacrifice of his friends. The natives began to chant, as the drums began beating in earnest.

The rest of the crew was laid out on separate crosses to be blessed and anointed before they were sacrificed. Their feet were strapped down to the base of the altar. The guards untied their hands in preparation of tying their hands at the far ends of the cross pieces. The river water near their feet began to boil with the presence of several large predatory fish. A loud clap of thunder broke across the rhythm of the chanting and the drums. Women in native dress writhed in front of the drummers in an unholy dance of sacrifice.

****

Mondo and his natives had moved the PT boat up to within five hundred feet of the sacrificial altars. It was very dark on the river now. They could hear the chanting of the ancient rituals. The drums were mesmerizing, and for a moment, Mondo and several of his older guards felt themselves moving to a beat well remembered from their childhood. Thick and evil, like excrement, the sounds oozed down the river. Cornelia, seeing her husband being drawn in, turned and slapped him sharply across the face. "Mondo!" she hissed. "We are here to free them, not sacrifice them!" Mondo rocked backwards, and shook his head. He whispered something sharply in his native tongue, and the other Indians reacted as though they too had been slapped.

The PT boat was tied to the shore by a long rope attached to the bow. The current here was strong and made all the worse by that which was unseen, buried deep in the current. The native boats emptied their men on the shore, where they fanned out as planned to surround and take out the enemy soldiers of the Chief's army. They would not attack until they received the signal from Mondo.

Kimmiko and Manolo jumped over the side of the PT boat quietly and took up their position beside Mondo. Several of Mondo's men jumped onto the PT boat to stand with Aleta. One of them got into the gun turret not occupied by Aleta and one went to the Oerlikon 20mm deck gun. Manolo had shown them how to operate the gun mechanisms, just in case. There was no time, however, to teach them how to drive the boat or fire the torpedoes.

Mondo knew he had a problem – he had no way to communicate with his warriors to coordinate the attack. He had men up in the trees, men in the jungle on the ground and men, including himself and the *niños*, advancing forward from the water. They had a standard set of animal calls to each other but this situation was far too complex for that. He could only rely on the fact that his men were trained warriors and would do their best to execute their duties without being carried away by the smell of blood. He only hoped that once the attack started, everyone would only do what was minimally necessary for success.

He looked over at the boy and the girl. They were too young and inexperienced to be here, he knew, but he could not do anything about that now. Their presence was necessary to pull off a needed distraction. He sighed. He really had no plan, if the truth be known, and he would just have to wait and see how everything would play out when the action started.

Kimmiko and Manolo scrambled up the rough river bank onto the dry land and dropped to the ground. They had a full view, only partially obstructed by the jungle foliage. They could see the dancers, altars and river that led around the bend to the PT boat's location. They could hear the music and its frantic beat coupled with its insane meaning. Even now, they saw the victims being led into the circle before the fire pit and illuminated by the thousand torches which lit up the clearing and beach area. Manolo tensed and swore silently. Kimmiko gasped and almost cried when she saw her dad, her Uncle Jack and Uncle Bill. The seriousness of the situation was now fully upon them. Unfortunately, even in their rage and anguish, they themselves did not know exactly what to do.

Monolo turned to Mondo, "When do we attack?" he asked with the reckless abandon of youth.

Mondo turned slowly back to whisper in his ear, "My young friend, we are outnumbered ten to one and your loved ones are being tied down even as we speak. We can surprise them, yes, but the chief can step on a lever next to his foot and drop them immediately into the river. Then they would be gone," he added needlessly. Silently, they all decided to wait for a few more minutes.

****

Jack was in a quandary. He had to get away. He'd be damned if he would die on this damned altar in this damn jungle, while his wife and kids thought he was on the equivalent of a Caribbean cruise! Today was NOT his day to meet God, he decided. He had, unknowing to the natives, purposely forced them to tie his ropes loosely. Twenty years before he had read a book by Stephen King, one of his favorite writers, who had described how a young boy outwitted a vampire's helper by keeping his fists bunched up in knots while the man tied him up. When the boy relaxed, there was some slack in the rope and he was able, with the help of sweat and patience, to further loosen the ropes enough to escape. Even now, as the natives tied him down to the cross on the altar of sacrifice, he held his hands taunt and elevated. When they were done, there was some slack in the ropes. Now, he worked his hands up and down, as well as his feet, pumping them gently like small pistons and ever careful that he was not being observed. The heat of the night produced enough sweat to make it easy to further loosen the ropes.

He looked at the others. The girls were both tied down securely and could not do anything at all. Bill was in the same predicament and John was tied to a tree - obviously being forced to watch his closest friends die in his own service. He continued to move his fists and feet in circular motions and could actually feel the ropes beginning to give. He shifted slightly and the comforting weight of the metal, telescoping nunchakus, moved against his groin. If he could get one more layer of rope off his hands and feet, there would be hell to pay, even if he could just get at the chief. He was no longer thinking like a doctor or a healer. Now his mind had reverted to that primitive place where he lusted for blood. He wanted to kill these savages. It was only after his third beating of the afternoon and also hearing Bill and the others scream throughout the day as they were tortured, that his mind began to implode and change. He was becoming an animal.

Bill was far colder and more calculating than Jack. He used

his military intelligence to do recon work of the enemy. He knew or more likely he felt, that his boat was near and he guessed that there were reinforcements just over the hill. The only problem was that he had no way to confirm it. He relied on his gut instinct and knew he would be fighting for his life in a few minutes. He didn't know how, but that was enough to keep him in the game, even with the deck stacked against them.

John Waales was crying softly. He couldn't get it out of his head that his lust for the gold and the conquest of the El Dorado had brought them to this. Now he, his daughter and his two closest friends would die because of him. Even these two young women, the little girl and probably the boy Manolo would all be dead because of HIM. It boggled his mind how yellow fever and also rock fever, the lust of archeology, had brought so many of them to their demise. After a few minutes, he stopped crying. The pain and fear he felt, instead of wrecking him, began to stoke away at a small fire in his belly. Somehow, he would get away, and then these bastards would pay dearly for their evil ways. Even as he looked out on the Chief in his royal robes, the Medicine Man sharpening his knives and the seemingly endless numbers of natives chanting and moving to the sounds of the drums, he knew they would live to fight even now.

Chief Omagua was in his moment. He would show these white eyes that he knew how to conduct a ritual. Thomas Reichen had been joined by Robin and a very sleepy Leon. They sat at the head ceremonial table. The Chief sat, of course in the middle. He raised his hands high. The rain which had been merely a light drizzle, now began to shower harder. The drums continued, but the women stopped dancing. They dropped to their knees and surrounded the entire scene in a crude circle with the victims of the sacrifice in the middle and with most of the warriors behind them. In the background, the river, churning madly with increased activity, was alive with the fish.

The Chief clapped his hands sharply twice. Nine warriors, dressed in ceremonial skirts and fearsome war masks - sporting spiked collars and matching bracelets - moved forward, each pair attending to one of the victims of the sacrifice. Even John, who was at this moment only a witness, was included as one native moved toward him, and held his chin up roughly, forcing him to watch.

Once again, the Chief clapped sharply. The Medicine Man selected a long, evil looking knife, over two feet in length, which was thin and straight. It had both a point and an edge, good for both stabbing and slicing. They had decided there would be bloodshed before the fish were fed. This was going to be a fit ceremony, remembered for a long time by their guests. This was crucial for their future cooperation. The medicine man advanced first toward Marianna.

Strapped down to the altar, she was totally helpless. The Medicine Man pressed his long knife gently onto the beads covering her chest. With a flick of his wrist, he cut the strand which held the beads. They fell harmlessly to the sand, leaving her exposed and vulnerable. He smiled as she screamed and squirmed on the altar. Turning efficiently to his right, he did the same thing to Gwendolyn, who made no noise, but squirmed for her life nonetheless. Again, the Medicine Man smiled. He turned back to Marianna. Chanting an ancient, evil intoxication, he raised the knife high in the air and took aim at the sweating, heaving sternum between her breasts.

Suddenly, a loud bark split the sound of the chanting and the drums! With a deep and menacing growl, a medium built collie dog, dashed into the clearing, causing a great commotion. He jumped at the surprised Medicine Man, biting him on the wrists with a vengeance!

At the sudden, unexpected intrusion, Jack, threw off his ropes and in a single motion, pulled the nunchakus out of his shorts. In less than a second he started spinning them and, with a single motion, cracked both of his surprised native attendants across their faces, felling them both. He turned around, with a deep growl he leaped toward the Medicine Man. The dog jumped clear as Jack swung the sticks, which could generate over 4400 pounds of force per square inch. The end of the metal sticks hit the Medicine Man across the temple, causing a cerebral hemorrhage. He dropped to the jungle floor with a scream and a thud, blood pouring from his nose.

******

Now all hell was breaking loose. The good natives swung out of the trees, attached to vines shooting arrows, darts and a few automatic weapons. Jack, pumped up with adrenaline, moved to his next target, the Chief, seated next to Robin, Leon and Thomas. Everybody started moving at once, and yet it all seemed to happen in slow motion. Jack swung the nunchaku sticks around rapidly from the right toward the Chief's head.

Prudently, the Chief, ducked, but Leon, still dazed from his deep sleep, sitting immediately next to the Chief, took a full hit to the side of his head. Screaming, he fell over. Jack, next swung the sticks down, trying to hit Thomas, who fell backwards while the metal nunchucks hit the ceremonial table, causing it to break in half.

The Chief, barked out a command and several warriors moved in with knives drawn to take out Jack. Suddenly a sound came out of the jungle like the screech of a monkey and several arrows flew into the cleared circle, instantly killing many of the Chief's elite guard. Everyone looked toward the jungle next to the river as Mondo's troops, with a yell reserved for only the most desperate of times, charged into the clearing.

The Chief screamed out orders in his native tongue as Thomas and Robin pulled back, looking behind them for their weapons. The clearing was suddenly full of natives fighting each other hand to hand. It was as though this scene had been written over a thousand years ago and nothing could change the mighty force of destiny.

Manolo and Kimmiko leaped into the clearing behind Mondo, who was fighting his own battle, and made their way to the girls and Bill. Manolo cut the ropes binding them, while Kimmiko ran to her dad and, using one of Bill's long, thin and extremely sharp fish filleting knives, cut him free. They hugged each other fiercely as John almost started crying again.

In an act of desperation, the Chief, lunged toward the lever and pulled it. This caused the altars to begin to slide into the river. The ropes securing Marianna had only been cut part of the way through, and, as she was dragged by one arm across the sand toward the river, she began screaming and pulling back frantically. Manolo desperately clung onto her as the 5,000 pound gold altar, slid down a metal track toward the boiling, angry river. At that instant, the head of one of the monster fish appeared above the water and, with its giant mouth agape, seemed to grin in anticipation. Suddenly, a huge native appeared and swung a long sword at Marianna. Her scream stopped in her throat. The sword cleanly cut the rope binding her wrists. Freed, she found herself being flung backwards in the sand, falling on top of Manolo. The altar, cartwheeled over by design, and would have dumped her right into the jaws of the giant piranha.

They looked up to see Mondo grinning in triumph. "Don't feed the fish!' he warned sarcastically. But there was no time to laugh as he turned and went after the nearest enemy warrior. Manolo jumped up, picking up the still shocked Marianna and fled toward their shipmates.

The fish needn't have worried. Several natives had been wounded or killed in the struggle. As a few rolled down the bank into the river, the fish began their infernal feast on the dead and the dying.

Jack, in his rage and his inability to keep track of what was happening, continued to lash out with his chaku sticks. Just as he had hoped, he came face to face with the natives who had abused him and Bill. With a savagery totally foreign to him, he lashed out instinctively and, before he knew it, he had killed them both with strikes across their heads.

Bill, John, Marianna, Kimmiko, Manolo and Gwendolyn took sporadic gunfire as they moved quickly toward the clearing. "Where's the boat?" demanded Bill, not sure of who might answer.

"Over there, beyond the trees!" answered Manolo, as he pulled back. He was returning fire at the natives, but once the remaining ones from the trees began coming down, he had to stop. He didn't want to injure anyone with "friendly fire." "Watch out *Capitán* Bill, the good native we met, Mondo is fighting them!"

"How do we know which ones to shoot at?" demanded Bill.

"Quien sabe?" Who knows.

They saw the shadow of the boat and moved quickly toward its safety. Along the way, they passed a low wooded table piled with weapons - their weapons, including Bill's Winchester. Hastily they grabbed them and continued toward the boat.

Jack was out of targets, except for the natives who seemed to be fighting each other. He decided he should follow his friends, before he was shot or stabbed by either the enemy or the natives who were fighting them. Suddenly he screamed. He had not seen Robin sneak up behind him with a long, discarded native spear. He suddenly felt a hot white pain as Robin jabbed out, aiming for his neck, but hitting him in the left shoulder. The point hit his shoulder blade and bounced off the bone with a sickening crunch.

Jack spun madly around, causing the spear to drop to the ground. Jack lashed out with his chaku sticks, but missed, as Robin spun back around and disappeared into the crowd, running for his life. Jack fell forward and began to pass out as the burning pain overpowered his brain.

The dog, who had started all the commotion, was following Bill and the others by instinct. He had not yet caught up with them when they rounded the bend and saw the boat. Suddenly, they heard Jack scream.

"Where's the Doc?" shouted Bill. They all started to turn and go back, but Bill stopped them. "Manolo, get the girls on the boat and start her up. Stay at the helm and prepare to leave with us or without us. Kimmi, get on the starboard gun next to Manolo. If you have to shoot, keep shooting and don't stop. Just fire into the biggest bunch of natives. Don't worry about trying to tell them apart - you can't. Now everybody move!" He looked at Manolo, "Just give me five minutes, little *amigo*," he smiled and patted him on the shoulder. He and John turned and moved back into the clearing looking for their friend.

Splashing through knee-deep water five feet to the boat Manolo, Kimmiko, Gwen and Marianna managed to jump onto the deck of the PT boat. Suddenly, the water was alive with fish churning and boiling, and obviously angry at their missed opportunity. "Mommy!" shouted a joyous Aleta as Gwendolyn fell into her arms. They hugged each other tightly. The girls all went below deck together so that Marianna and Gwendolyn could get shirts on and they could all calm each other down. Up on deck, Manolo started up the engines and Kimmiko took over the starboard machine gun from one of Mondo's guards. There were still four or five friendly natives on board, acting as guards to the young ones on the strict orders of Mondo.

On shore, John and Bill quickly found Jack. He was laying

on the ground moaning in pain as six natives surrounded him with spears and prepared to end his life. John, cursed and started to raise his Uzi, but he didn't even get off a shot as Bill, crouching like the "Rifleman" of the old T.V., series cracked out six shots, literally as fast as an automatic weapon. With the trigger tied back, he only had to move the wide lever of the Winchester up and down, causing it to fire automatically. Six shots - six dead natives. They ran over and grabbed their friend.

Suddenly there were gun shots all around them as Thomas and Robin both opened up with handguns. Fortunately for Bill, John and Jack, at that instant, several natives, both good and bad were fighting around them and separated them from the bullets. At least four of the bad natives died this way. Miraculously, none of Mondo's troops were injured. Bill and John picked up Jack and began dragging him back to the boat.

They made it to the shore, just as the barking dog arrived. Bill recognized the animal as the one who had distracted the Medicine Man and felt he owed it to the poor creature to give it a hand.

Manolo, at the helm saw his friends and gently eased the boat forward to help them avoid the piranhas. They were all around the boat now. In fact, several of Mondo's empty boats had been sunk as the fish had attacked them looking for people to eat. Even Cornelia and her baby, Damien, had had to retreat to the PT boat earlier. The fish had crushed her boat and the natives on board had helped them up before they were eaten alive.

The dog was barking frantically as if it had to get on the boat. Bill grabbed it and tossed it onto the bow which was now only three feet away. With the help of the natives, Bill and John got Jack aboard and then they themselves jumped aboard. The dog took off sniffing frantically and disappeared below as if looking for someone.

Now that they were all aboard, and, as Mondo and his troops kept up the fight, they were free to leave. Bill ran to the bridge, shouted orders to Manolo and fired up the engines of the PT boat. Manolo and John dove into the machine gun turrets, quickly displacing Mondo's troops, who were only too happy to oblige. Kimmiko helped place Jack gently on the deck behind the bridge and in front of the day cabin. She pulled out the first aid kit and began placing a rough field dressing on his wound, which was more ugly and painful than serious.

The natives on board ran to the bow and jumped off onto the water's edge on the jungle side and raced off to join in the struggle. One of them helped Cornelia and her baby off the boat, and took them to hide until the fighting slowed down and she could find Mondo. John and Manolo jacked rounds into the magazines, turned toward the shore and were ready for action.

****

Meanwhile, as Bill fired up the engines and prepared for departure, the Chief, Thomas, Robin and a still dazed, wounded Leon, met in one of the ornate golden buildings roughly five hundred feet from the fighting. Several of the Chief's own elite guards had spirited them away for their own safety. Now there were at least thirty guards outside to protect them.

"*Senior* Reichen," said the Chief, "all may be lost unless you can get them. Even now, their boat will leave us and they will return with the *Federales* to find us. We will then be at their mercy. They know where we are. You must kill them." They could hear the boat even now, engines roaring above the din of the shouts of the still fighting natives. It was backing out and preparing to head downstream.

"How will we catch them?" asked Robin. "That boat will do over 45 knots. I've seen it personally."

"We have a boat ready to go. It is full of armaments. My troops will accompany you and will help you dispose of them. Now I must deal with these former and most evil tribesmen who dare to attack me as though they think they may regain their ancestral home!" With that the Chief ran out into the evening and rallied his troops to the attack.

Two big natives motioned Thomas, Leon and Robin to come with them. They ran a short distance to an ornate, gold shed, which was about sixty feet long and thirty feet wide. It sat next to the river. There was the hum of an engine idling as they entered through a side door. They saw the Riverine Boat, with its guns and missile launcher, manned by three very tough looking natives, all wearing helmets. "Massive Cool, *Mon*!" was all Robin could say, mimicking a Jamaican accent.

****

It was total chaos on shore. The bad natives and the good natives had been fighting savagely, causing casualties on both sides. However, the battle was beginning to turn to Mondo's troops. What Chief Omagua did not know or appreciate, was that many of his own people hated the life they were forced to live here or despised his and Prince Sajava's rule. Many had not attended the evening ritual, preferring to stay home with their families in various huts throughout the jungle. Most of the golden houses and buildings were reserved for the Chief, his war council and various levels of his government. When several natives ran into the jungle to get men for reinforcements, they had come willingly, believing their village was under attack by hostile forces. Once many of them had arrived and started fighting, they began to realize these people were fellow Chibcha Indians. The found themselves among long lost cousins and, in some cases, brothers, fathers and adult children. Their fighting rage vanished and they began hugging and kissing each other. They found they needed to disappear back into the jungle to celebrate, lest they be swept up in the fight again.

One of these men was Chief Omagua's younger son Prince Damien. He too had responded to the call to arms, in spite of his gentle and passive nature. Barely 20 years old, he left his wife and baby girl, secretly named Cornelia after his sister who he had not seen in over fifteen years, back home in their humble hut. Her name was also kept a secret because the Chief had decreed that his sister's name be stricken from use by all in El Dorado. His young wife, not yet eighteen, hugged their baby tight, as they both cried when Daddy left.

Damien raced through the jungle. Ahead of him, he could see the glow by the river through the thick jungle. He knew his father and brother had been holding one of their sick sacrificial rituals. He assumed this one had gotten out of hand and that the angry villagers who were the victims of the sacrifice were now attacking them. He could hear the shouts of angry men and the unmistakable sounds of spears and swords clashing, and even the occasional sound of gunfire, as he knew they had acquired many guns over the years.

He burst through the trees into the clearing and practically fell across his brother Prince Sajava, who had been stabbed through the thigh and was writhing about in pain. "Brother!" Damien shouted, "Who...? How can I help you?"

He tried to pick him up, but was angrily waved off by Sajava. "Get away from me you *gallina,*" he hissed. "I don't need your help!"

Damien stepped back, hurt by his brother's outburst. Sajava then jumped up and, limping badly, returned to the fight. Damien suddenly found himself in his own fight as a native, masked by heavy war paint, swung a pointed spear at his unprotected head. Damien ducked and met the challenge by bringing up his own spear. For over a minute they dueled, their pace growing more frantic with every clash. He found something familiar about this native, even more than the way he fought. The two seemed to anticipate each other's every move. But Damien had not fought this particular way since he was a child.

Suddenly, Damien fell backwards. He tried to over-compensate and pull himself around. The move failed and he overbalanced. He found himself on his back, with his spear several feet away. His challenger leaped on top of him, with his spear raised high in the air, ready to deliver a fatal blow.

Damien, the fight in him suddenly gone at the thought of his imminent death and never seeing his new baby and young wife again, put his hands up to shield his face, as he turned away, expecting a pain beyond measure.

Nothing happened.

He pulled his hands away from his eyes and looked up at the native standing over him. The man was slowly lowering his spear.

"Damien?" he whispered quietly.

Damien, confused, tried to sit up, but the man held him down with one foot. "Who are you?" he asked

"I am Coraz'on," he said happily, "your childhood friend."

"Coraz'on!" exclaimed Damien. "My old friend, why do you run with these natives and attack us?" His joy at meeting his closest friend from childhood was tempered by his near death and also the confusion all around him.

"No, no, Damien. We are here with Mondo and your sister Cornelia. We are helping to rescue friendly Americans from the evils of your father and brother."

"What? Americans, here?" he demanded.

Coraz'on jumped off his friend and helped him to his feet. "Yes, there is no time! Your cousins are here. With your help, we can reunite the village!" He reached up tenderly and touched Damien's face. Suddenly they embraced.

"Let's go at once! We must stop this and reunite our people." said Damien.

"And what of your father?"

"I alone must challenge him and Sajava's evil ways. This fighting must end now! Please help me!" he said with desperation and fear in his voice. Oddly enough, as they ran off together toward the smashed head ceremonial table, Damien felt more courage than he ever had in his life. He hoped it would last. He would need it.

****

Bill, still holding his boat a few feet offshore, was searching for targets. Manolo had told him of the heroics of the natives who had helped them. He held his Winchester at his side and scanned the shore with the searchlight. All he could see was the blur of natives as they fought with each other. John and Manolo were having the same problem. There was no way they could help from the boat. Complicating things was the constant bumping of the boat by the giant piranhas. Several times they were almost knocked over as the fish kept hitting each side of the boat over and over without warning.

It was obvious that they had to get out of there. Reluctantly, and feeling they were deserting the very warriors who had saved them, Bill reversed the engines and began backing out. Manolo jumped out of his turret and, on Bill's command, threw off the line which held them to the beach. They began backing out into the river, all the while being buffeted by the fish. He swung the bow down river and, with a sad look back at the natives, slowly increased the power to the engines. He looked over at John, who sadly nodded his agreement that they had to get themselves away and get medical attention for Jack.

Suddenly tracer bullets from a machine gun lit up the night

from somewhere up river, raking across the stern of the boat. Down below, they heard the women scream.

"What the hell was that?" Bill shouted. More bursts of tracer bullets were all around them.

"Bill," shouted John, "get us out of here!" He spun around and tried to aim at the approaching threat.

Manolo, now back in the gun turret also spun his machinegun around and prepared to return fire. "Manolo!" shouted Bill, "Get below and check on the girls!" Below, they could still here them screaming. He could only imagine what one of those automatic guns would do to a human being. He shoved the throttle forward and the PT boat responded with a roar of its engines.

On the enemy boat, Thomas Reichen and two of the natives were on the machine guns firing at the escaping PT boat. Leon and Robin were hanging onto the bridge.

"They're getting away!" Thomas shouted angrily. The native driving the boat increased their speed until they were almost keeping up with the PT boat. They continued to fire, the tracers splitting the night as the chase continued down the dark river.

On the PT boat, Bill shouted over the roaring engines and gunfire, down below, "Manolo! What's going on down there? Is anybody hurt?"

Manolo poked his head out the hatch in the Bridge, "*Si, Capitán* Bill. The *Senorita*, Marianna was hit in the side, but it passed through her skin only."

"Is she bleeding?"

"*Si*, but it is not too bad. I have bandaged it."

"Good," shouted Bill, "Then get up here and help us!"

Manolo started to go back to the Oerlikon 20mm cannon, but Bill stopped him.

"No little *amigo*," he said affectionately, "You will be too easy to kill. Get in the machinegun.

Manolo looked in Bill's eyes. If he were on the cannon, he could surely hit the speeding boat behind them, but he could just as likely be shot, as there was little armor around the gun. He nodded gratefully at Bill as he climbed into the forward turret and began to return fire.

******

Damien and Coraz'on made it to the smashed head table and the remaining sacrificial altars just as the fight was turning. Mondo and his forces had either wounded or killed most of the very bad natives and had succeeded in convincing many of the other natives under Chief Omagua's command to lay down their weapons and join their long, lost brothers and cousins in peace. Only a few remained fighting in the brightly lit clearing and in the dark jungle.

They searched around the altar for weapons they could use. The spears worked, but they knew they needed guns if the Chief and the Prince showed up.

As if on cue, Chief Omagua saw them and, realizing what they were doing, went insane with rage. He leapt onto one of the altars with a scream on his lips. "You will pay the price for your insolence!" he screamed at his youngest son and his friend, who he recognized as Coraz'on from long ago. He raised his sword and swung it at the two young natives, barely missing his own son in his rage.

They both dived out of the way and, picking up two discarded swords, turned to face him.

The Chief grinned a wicked smile. "I always knew you were one of the *gallinas*," he hissed. "Now you will pay the price demanded by the Law!" He raised his sword high and jumped off the altar, moving swiftly toward Damien.

Damien, retreating quickly, yelled to Coraz'on, "Find Mondo! Bring him here to help me, *amigo!*"

Coraz'on turned without saying anything. He ran toward the water, where he last saw Mondo fighting a group of natives.

******

Bill Treese knew he was in the fight of his life. Nothing since Viet Nam was even close to this. The gunboat behind him, which he could tell from the sound and the pace was a Mark II Riverine gun boat. It was small, but very quick and maneuverable. His PT boat was faster and more heavily armed, but he had too many civilians on board. He knew he had to get away from here, but it would be difficult, especially at night.

His searchlight cut the night ahead of him. He thought he would be reaching the main river soon, which meant that he might be caught up in the thick jungle underbrush the natives had used to hide this tributary.

"Look there!" screamed John, pointing ahead. "Twelve o'clock, dead ahead."

Bill looked, not believing what he was seeing. He hoped

the darkness was playing a trick with his eyes. Ahead of them it looked for all the world like twenty or more giant piranhas, some as long as fifteen feet and over four feet wide splashing in the water five hundred feet ahead. They were blocking the channel.

"Mother of God!" he whispered hoarsely.

Swinging around to look behind him, Bill saw that the enemy was only about two hundred yards behind him. He could not proceed ahead, or they would hit the blockade of fish. This would likely destroy the boat and likely cause their immediate deaths, either by explosion or by breaking up and becoming a midnight snack. Immediately, he made the decision to turn around. He banked to the right and heeled sharply over to his left. "Full turn to port!" he shouted to no one in particular. Kimmiko, who was still on deck behind the bridge and also behind Bill, threw her body across Jack, to keep him from sliding off the boat.

They were so close to the enemy, that they passed by them in less than two seconds after they had made their turn. Both boats gave a full volley of fire to the other as they passed. Because of the suddenness of the maneuver and the fact that no one was a trained gunner's mates, no hits were scored. Now the PT boat was proceeding back up the river toward the City of the El Dorado. Thomas Reichen, disappointed that none of them had hit the escaping PT boat with anything significant, yelled for them to turn the boat around and continue the chase. The native turned in a similar maneuver, although it was somewhat unnecessary, as the Riverine boat was only half as long as the PT boat. Somewhat surprising, the piranhas also moved away from their post and raced upstream after the escaping boats.

******

Coraz'on found Mondo, near the water where he expected. What he didn't expect, was that Mondo was wounded with an arrow in his side and was, even now, being tended to by his wife Cornelia. "Chief Mondo, Chief Mondo," he cried, the Chief is attacking your wife's brother, Damien!"

Cornelia screamed and leaped up. Mondo grabbed her by the ankle. "Stop woman!" he commanded sharply. "We will all go now!"

He pulled himself up painfully with Coraz'on's help and the help of two other natives who were tending to him. "Take us there Coraz'on!" he commanded.

******

Most of the fighting had stopped. The natives, good and bad, were gathered around the two fighters. The chief with his sword, swung madly at his son, Prince Damien. In his rage at his loss of face and the possible loss of his tribe, he was using this as one last desperate attempt to regain his position as the Chief. He was fighting like a man possessed. Perhaps the others could be turned he thought, to the old ways.

Damien, in spite of his youth and his gentle nature, was a fierce fighter. He had learned to fight well and fought to win.

However, once he learned these things, he tucked them away and turned to the gentler pursuits of life. He studied the Bible and read poetry. He also liked love stories, but of course no one knew these things except his wife, and possibly, by instinct, his infant daughter, who he often read aloud to since before she was born. Now he knew one thing was certain: he would not kill his father. He would rather die than do that. If his wife or his child's life were in danger, no man, not even his father would have been safe from his rage, but here and now, he would not take his father's life. Even as he thought this, he had to duck as his father swung his sword, almost hitting him in the neck.

The roar of two war boats, engaged in a fierce battle, split the night. They passed the city at over forty knots, shooting in all directions. Everybody dropped to the ground except Damien and Chief Omagua as though no one, not even the gods themselves, would dare disturb this royal battle. The observers rose to continue to watch the fight. No one would interfere for fear of his life.

******

Jack, still lying under Kimmiko, knew he had to do something. He could hear the frantic yells between Bill, John and Manolo. He thought if he could get to the cannon, he might be able to help turn the tide. One thing was for sure, someone was going to get a direct hit, it was only a matter of time. He pushed up on Kimmiko, squeezing her arm to get her attention.

She looked down on him. "Lie still Uncle Jack. It'll be okay."

He looked up at her, "Kimmi, you have to get off me. I need to get to the back of the boat."

She shook her head sternly. "No, stay there. We are safe here as long as..." she was suddenly bucked off Jack as Bill had to take a sudden maneuver to avoid a large grinning piranha. She flew up toward the steel wall surrounding the bridge and hit her head. She dropped down flat on the deck, unconscious.

"Kimmi!" Jack screamed. She was out cold. He took a brief medical and neurological assessment of her. He could still think and act like a doctor, he marveled, even though he was wounded and in complete fear of his life. He felt her carotid pulse and felt her chest moving up and down a little too quick and her breathing was shallow, but she would make it. He pulled back her eyelid and, in the faint glow of light from the instrument panel, he saw her pupil contract. He grabbed a length of rope and quickly wrapped it around her arms and abdomen until she was securely tied to the bridge. She would be okay unless the boat rolled over or blew up, then they would all be dead, he reasoned.

Quietly and quickly, he began crawling toward the stern cannon. He almost fell off twice while Bill maneuvered wildly trying to escape their pursuers. He passed John in the port, rear turret. He tried to tell him to forget that and take care of Kimmiko, but he could not be heard above the automatic gun fire and the roar of the engine, so he gave up and kept on moving aft. In a matter of seconds, he made it to the cannon. He grabbed the handle and, hoisting himself up to a semi standing position, he took aim at the enemy boat and opened fire. The distinctive "POM! POM! POM!" sound of the

Oerlikon 20mm cannon could be heard above the din of the racing war boats. Tracer bullets streamed out toward the oncoming war boat.

Although the people on both boats were surprised to see the cannon open up, the reactions were completely different. Bill, John and Manolo shouted for joy, encouraging Jack. On the enemy boat, the native skipper juked a hard left, lest they be suddenly blown out of the water. Robin, foolishly stood up near the bow and received and 20mm shell across his chest. He was knocked off the boat and died instantly, never knowing the fate of his body as the piranhas moved in.

Jack and the others kept up the volley, and, as luck would have it, one of the cannon's shells and several of the machine gun's bullets hit the side of the enemy boat as her skipper turned to port. Smoke began pouring from the enemy vessel, but instead of coming about and ceasing fire, they continued their pursuit and gunfire at the PT boat.

Bill had had about enough. He was now over 1,000 yards ahead of the slowing Riverine boat and he swung his boat sharply 180 degrees. He began his run directly at the bow of the enemy vessel. He still had one torpedo left. They were head-to-head and closing fast. He counted out the mark and released his fish when there was a scant three hundred yards between them. He eased off his bow and banked to the right.

Thomas and Leon saw the torpedo leave the approaching PT boat. Thomas knew it would be a direct hit and decided he had about four seconds to make a decision. He just hoped the piranhas had not caught up with them. "Jump!" he shouted to Leon. They both hit the water approximately two seconds before the torpedo made a direct hit on the bow. The riverine boat disintegrated in a tremendous explosion, throwing both Thomas and Leon almost to the shore! Although stunned, the explosion saved their lives, as they madly scrambled onto shore just seconds ahead of the closing jaws of several piranhas. They lay on the shore hyperventilating approximately a quarter of a mile from the El Dorado.

****

Even as the Chief and his son Damien battled, seemingly to the death, his other son, Prince Sajava, was running and dragging his bad leg through the jungle. He had won his last battle with an enemy native, who he had recognized as one called Hannee, who had fought with him fiercely when they were boys. It was clear to him who these natives were. He knew they were led by his father's sworn enemy, Mondo and his *putah* sister Cornelia. Even though he knew he was probably mortally wounded - the blood even now flowed constantly from his wounded leg - he thought he could lead these transgressors down to the fish. He could win, even in death. He was loyal to his father and the old ways. He could see the clearing just up ahead and he could hear the sounds of the battle. Not content with a spear and a blowgun, he was fully armed with a Colt .45 A.C.P. and a Browning 9 mm. He was ready to shoot. And to kill.

****

Bill turned the boat hard down river. He knew he had been wrong to leave the natives who had helped them. "I'm going back to the El Dorado!" he yelled to John above the roar of the engines. "By God, we have to finish this!"

John nodded. He was still in the gun turret, but he was almost played out. His emotions drained by the events of the day. He knew he had to hang on.

A grim-faced Manolo was still in the other turret. He knew that they still had a fight on their hands. Jack, weak from his loss of blood, had managed to crawl back to the bridge, where he found Kimmiko waking up, holding her head crying. Now it was his turn to take care of her. He loosened the rope a little holding her to the deck and, laying her on her back, started working on her neck and head where she had struck the bridge armor plate.

As he neared the city, Bill suddenly cut the power of the boat. The raging engines slowed and the loud roar changed to a soft purr of the diesel engines. He pulled a lever on the bridge which caused the linkages over the six mufflers on the stern of the boat to close down. This diverted the exhaust gases through the mufflers and into the water, allowing them to approach quietly. Bill coasted toward the shore. He could see the light in the clearing and knew the battle was still going on, but at whose advantage he did not know.

"What's your plan?" John asked.

"I'm going in, but I want to surprise them this time. If we have to open up, I don't want them to even know we are there."

John nodded. Bill looked over at Manolo, "Could you please run down again and make sure the girls are squared away. We may still have a fight on our hands and I want to make sure our backup troops are armed and ready."

"*Si, Capitán* Bill."

"Jack," Bill looked down with concern, "are you two going to be okay?"

Jack looked up and nodded. "I just lost some blood, but Kimmi's going to have a heck of a headache tomorrow."

"Right now," Kimmiko groaned. Bill and Jack managed a smile, but John remained grim-faced as he looked down at his daughter.

Manolo went below as Bill nudged the boat into the shore. He had forgotten for the moment about the giant piranha, who even now circled below the boat.

******

The battle raged on. Damien had had several opportunities to win, but each time he had stopped just short of killing his father. He could not do that. He would not cross that line, just as he would never want his child to take her father's life. The arc of his father's sword cut across his brow, opening his forehead, causing blood to spill down his face. he stepped back, temporarily blinded. Out of reflex, Damien brought his sword up just in time to deflect the blow which would have killed him. Dancing back, he then lunged forward, striking Chief Omagua below his tenth rib with the tip of his sword. He immediately pulled it back so that the cut was less than an inch deep. The blow was not mortal, but it caused the Chief to scream and drop his sword. He fell to his knees and Damien brought the flat part of his sword down across the Chief's head knocking him unconscious.

As the Chief fell forward, the good natives let out a shout of triumph. Even the subdued natives, were joyful, knowing the reign of terror was ended. Mondo, who had just arrived with the others, and, in spite of his painful wounds, crawled to the Chief and tossed away his sword. He felt the Chief's carotid pulse and, as Damien held his breath, made a determination. He locked eyes with his long-lost brother-in-law and said, "He'll live." Damien closed his eyes, thankfully.

Cornelia left her husband and, in one swift gesture, grabbed a cloth and held it to her brother's head as she held him tightly.

"Gracias, muy Cornelia, bonito," he said to her sweetly. He had not seen her for over fifteen years, but he knew instinctively it was her. Damien began to relax, finally, after all these years.

Suddenly, Prince Sajava burst into the clearing. Taking aim with one of his guns, he shot one of the natives standing near Mondo through the shoulder. He shot another in the leg and still one more through the side. Pandemonium broke out as the natives, good and bad, dove for cover. Cornelia, who was closest to him as he charged toward Mondo, screamed as she leapt through the air toward her brother. Her fear fed her courage as she attacked him unarmed. He was shocked that a mere woman would dare to assault him. He fell backwards as she struck out with her small fists and feet. Knocking him to the ground, she pummeled him like an animal. Grunting, he pushed her off him as though she was of no more concern than a fallen leaf.

"Putah!" he cried, "Go back to your *pendejo* of a husband!"

He rolled free of her, but could not find his guns, which had been knocked back behind him. Blinded by his rage, he struck out at Cornelia, knocking her out. He leaped onto his brother Damien, who was trying to hold the flap of his skin back over his eyes and began to strike him mercilessly. They rolled over and over again in a fearsome battle. Damien knew he was fighting for his life, but Sajava, older heavier and stronger, was full of rage, in spite of his wounded leg. Other natives yelled words of protest, but did not know what to do.

Thomas Reichen and Leon suddenly burst through the jungle clearing. They headed toward the battle, picking up two rifles as they lay in the arms of dead natives. Thomas took aim at Mondo, who was trying to take care of his wife and fired. He dove out of the way just in time, pushing her behind an altar as the bullet whizzed over their heads. Leon was not as skilled a marksman as Thomas. He began shooting blindly at anything that moved. It was he who John shot first.

Bill and the crew of the PT boat were watching from the boat as the battle raged. When Prince Sajava broke through the clearing, Bill had jumped into the port side, rear gun turret and had tried to shoot him. But everything was moving so fast that he couldn't get a shot off. By the time Thomas and Leon came through, only John had a clear shot at one of them and had taken it. The burst of .50 caliber machine gun fire had only grazed Leon, but had knocked him down and had caused the other natives, as well as Thomas, to drop down and take cover.

Prince Sajava, still battling with Damien, gave a sharp command in his native language to the surface of the water.

They had rolled down next to the shore's edge. Suddenly, the river was boiling with fish. They pushed into the sides of the PT boat and one even managed to jump onto the bow of the deck. Kimmi screamed as Bill spun the machine gun as far as he could, given the barrel restriction imposed by the steel tube around the gun tub, and shot the fifteen foot creature in the head with a five second burst of fire. It slowly rolled off the deck into the water where it was ravaged by the other cannibalistic fish.

Suddenly more fish were jumping onto the boat. Manolo, out of reflex and because no one else was giving orders, began backing the boat rapidly away from the shore. Bill and John were firing continuously as the fish either hit the boat or jumped onto the deck.

Once they had reached the middle of the river, Bill jumped out of the gun turret. He ran to the stern to make preparations for the depth charges. "Manolo!" he screamed, "move out, but keep it slow."

Obediently, Manolo moved the throttle ahead one quarter speed and maintained a heading up river. Bill could see the fish, leaping and jumping in the wake of the boat. Several had overtaken her and were bumping the sides of the boat. Bill set the depth charges to go off almost immediately when they hit the water. "Manolo," he yelled, "prepare to roll depth charges!"

Manolo grabbed the control on the bridge. "Rolling one!" he cried in perfect English.

The depth charge rolled off the port side and landed behind the boat. There was a tremendous explosion and pieces of dead fish rained down everywhere.

"Rolling two!" Manolo cried excitedly, as several more

fish met their doom as a result of the detonation of the high explosives.

"Turn around!" yelled Bill, as Manolo began to head back towards the city. "I think we got most of them! John, keep shooting at anything you see in the water!"

Back on shore, Damien had regained the advantage over Sajava. The latter's loss of blood from his wounded leg was making him weaker and weaker. Lying on his back, he looked up over Damien's shoulder and shouted out to Thomas Reichen. Both he and Leon ran down towards the shore, with Leon holding his side which was bleeding. They reached Damien and knocked him off Sajava into the water!

As though he were hit by an electrical shock, Damien jumped up from the water as a piranha tried to close its jaws around his legs. He leaped free and landed on top of Leon, who screamed as Damien twisted and threw him over his head into the water and into the waiting jaws of the fish. In a moment it was over.

Thomas took aim at Damien with his rifle. Damien had jumped away from the water and spun around just in time to see Thomas' barrel pointing less than a foot from his face. Thomas smiled and pulled the trigger. The trigger fell on an empty chamber with a sharp click. Roaring with rage, Damien leapt toward Thomas who hit him with the barrel of the rifle, knocking him down. He fell over Sajava who was trying to get up in spite of his wounds.

Thomas, suddenly realizing he was alone in this fight, spun around looking for a way out. Just then he saw the PT boat touch the shore. From the angle they were at, those on board could not see him. He ran toward the boat, past the sacrificial altar and grabbed the Medicine Man's ritualistic sword. He jumped toward the boat, and, grabbing a line dangling into the water, started hoisting himself up and over the bow of the boat. He leapt on the deck with a roar of rage and ran up over the bridge and landed in the cockpit, knocking Manolo over. John just missed him with a volley of machinegun fire, the tubular stop around the gun turret, caused the barrels to aim too high up.

Looking around frantically, Thomas spied the Oerlikon cannon mounted on the stern deck He knew that if he reached it, he could blow those on deck apart and still be able to get away in the boat. He looked around. The depression railing which protected those on deck from the cannon taking aim at them had been blown away by the Riverine boat. To make matters worse, John's forward gun had jammed and he couldn't maneuver it to where Thomas was anyway, because of the configuration of the gun railing, which was designed to protect the occupants of the boat from friendly fire. Manolo had been knocked back against the bridge armor and had suffered the same fate as Kimmiko. He was now unconscious. Jack, still protecting Kimmi, tried to grab Thomas' leg, but was mercilessly kicked out of the way.

Thomas came around the starboard side, making his way back to the gun. Suddenly, Bill rose from behind the forward torpedo tube like a Jack-O-Lantern! He was armed with a flat broad sword, the type used by the Caribbean pirates. Their eyes met and, like two ancient warriors of the Amazon, they came together with a grunt and a clash of steel. They fought like two expertly trained men. It was brutal and, to each, exciting. John had leapt out of the turret, but was knocked back over the side by the two fighting men. Fortunately, he fell down parallel to the shore and so he landed on his feet half in and half out of the water. Here it was too shallow for the piranhas, but he leapt back instinctively anyway, quickly touching his feet to make sure they were still there.

Jack quietly moved Kimmiko over next to Manolo, who would also be okay he reasoned. He quietly placed Bill's fallen Winchester rifle in her arms and silenced her with a finger to his lips. He began crawling quietly backwards toward the Oerlikon gun on the side of the boat opposite where Bill and Thomas were fighting. He covered the thirty feet in less than a minute. He pulled himself slowly to his feet and, grabbed the handle and the trigger mechanism. Slowly, he turned the gun around until it faced the two men fighting some twenty feet away. He still had the barrel pointing down toward the deck.

Suddenly, Thomas, with a mighty backhand, knocked Bill back toward the bridge. He ran back towards the cannon, hoping to get off some shots. He would blow away the entire bridge if necessary and steer this barge by hand, he reasoned. He never saw Jack. Just as he reached the gun, Jack brought the barrel up between Reichen's legs and hit him squarely in his groin. He let out a sharp groan and felt his legs and body go limp as the impact made him sick to his stomach. He fell back slightly and the barrel now pointed directly at his manhood. He looked up dizzily and saw Jack smiling at him.

"Oooh nuts!" Jack said happily.

****

Back on shore, both Sajava and Damien were armed again, having grabbed fallen spears. With Damien holding his forehead together, they circled slowly, each looking for an opening. Sajava looked at his younger brother with contempt. "To the end, brother!" he said.

"Not today boys," came Cornelia's voice from behind them. They both turned around to see all of the natives standing and holding a struggling Chief Omagua. He was gagged, tied tightly with rope from head to toe and was furious. Mondo, Cornelia and John, who had joined them, came forward.

"The evil is ended," said Cornelia. "We will now lead our tribe to goodness." She pointed to Sajava. "We will spare you, but you and my father will be sent to the authorities and placed in prison."

The now excommunicated Prince Sajava turned toward the river. He gazed out quietly for a moment. He turned back toward his sister. *"Putah,"* he said contemptuously. "I will still rule the fish. They will not betray me!" Suddenly, he raised his spear and, hurled it at his sister. Instinctively, John shoved her out of the way and the spear flew through the air into the still struggling Chief Omagua. The spear hit him in his belly and he fell over screaming, mortally wounded.

Sajava, horrified at this turn of events turned and ran into the river, seeking sanctuary with the fish. Even as he started swimming toward the center of the river toward a small ceremonial barge which he fed the fish from, he suddenly realized how tired and weak he had become from the incessant bleeding of his leg. He grew more and more tired, even as the giant fish swam around him.

He thought he was safe, he only needed to reach the barge. He was starting to sink and he was having a hard time seeing. He felt as though he were swimming in a warm cocoon. He was within a few feet of the raft when he passed out and began sinking. The smell of dying prey overcame the remaining piranha's senses. They had been trained not to attack this one, but his smell had changed. They hit him from all sides, tearing him apart.

On shore, Prince Damien walked slowly toward his sister and Mondo. As they embraced, Cornelia held him at arm's length. Even though Damien resembled their father, she could now only see the kind face of their deceased mother in him.

"Chief Damien," she said softly. Then she turned toward their now united tribesmen. "Chief Damien!" she shouted as she and Mondo held Damien's arms up triumphantly. The natives let out a cheer of joy as long, lost friends and relatives searched each other out. There was much hugging and cries of joy as discovery after discovery were made. A messenger had been sent to Damien's hut and brought out his young wife and infant daughter. They all hugged each other as he quickly recited the events of the evening to his stunned, but joyous wife. He introduced his daughter to her uncle and aunt. Cornelia cried as she held her baby brother's new infant. "What's her name?" she whispered. "Cornelia, was the reply, which made her cry even harder.

The old native who had been with Cornelia when she had first boarded the PT boat now brought Mondo and Cornelia's son to them. They handed the infant over to Damien. "Our youngest son," Mondo said proudly, "His name is Damien," which caused Damien to also cry softly as he held the baby close to his breast.

Mondo placed his arm around John, "My new friend, we have much to celebrate tonight!"

******

CHAPTER VII

LESSONS LEARNED

EVERYONE SLEPT AND RESTED FOR TWO DAYS. It was a heady experience for all. Jack took over, after tending to his own wounds. He was now the chief medical officer and had set up a triage area. All of his training from chiropractic school came in handy. While he had never performed surgery, he had the same four-year training as a medical doctor, and was competent to care for cuts, burns, bullets, infections and bite wounds from the fish. The women natives helped him and together all were cared for.

Mondo, Cornelia and Damien sat with the old tribal councils and formed a new government. They would have peace and, with their promise to help John explore and do archaeological digs in and around the city - for a fair price of course - they would be able to present their city to the world. They would, all agreed, to limit tourism and control the gold. There was much left to be mined and discovered. This would be shared fairly. They knew they did not have to worry too much about being descended on by gold seekers, as the very location of the place made it almost impossible to reach by land, river or air. Also, anyone who tried to loot the place would be hunted down before they ever got started.

Bill, John, Manolo and the girls happily explored the City of the EL Dorado and took many pictures. John had decided to stay here and begin explorations immediately. There were several caves and mines which held many relics of the past. He would make arrangements with the University to send back samples, photos and some of the gold, all with the approval of the new tribal government, who were eager to make their way into the new century. There would be a lot of money, actually U.S. dollars, heading down to their jungle community.

Kimmiko and Manolo had also decided to stay with her dad. They found that they were very happy with each other and were experiencing the thrill of the young falling in love. This place held many mysteries and the promise of great adventure.

With Damien's help, Marianna found a perfect location for her company's transmission site. She would return with Bill and Jack on the PT boat when they shoved off for civilization in a few days.

Gwendolyn and Aleta asked if they could stay for the time being. They really had nothing to go back to and the people here were very friendly. Also, Gwendolyn and John liked working together. They too seemed to have much in common and found themselves very compatible with each other. Aleta was happy, now that she was reunited with her dog. She thought she had lost to the caiman when their boat sank at the falls.

Thomas Reichen would be taken down river and turned

over to the *Federales* when Bill, Jack and Marianna left. Even now he was in shackles and chains in the hold of the boat. Several of Mondo's fiercest warriors were guarding him around the clock. He had no hope of going anywhere, he knew, except to a Colombian prison. There was a very large price on his head and he was resigned to it. He sighed, perhaps one day he would return and seek out his vengeance, he thought.

Finally, the feasting began. They all ate, drank and danced the night away. Everyone celebrated. They ate tons of giant piranha fish, which, barbecued and rubbed with salt and garlic, tasted for all the world like wild pork. Kimmiko and Manolo danced a lively dance with the natives in a joyous ritual.

John looked over at his friends Jack and Bill, who were laid out next to him, both feeling like stuffed pigs. "Do you think they know that this is the wedding dance?" he asked smiling.

Bill looked over at him and grinned, "Well, I always wanted a son to marry your daughter. I guess we will both be grandparents someday." he smiled at his friend.

John looked at him. "So will the money and the gold we will be paying you, help you keep your boat?"

Bill smiled, relaxed for the first time in over a week, "Yeah, baby! I figure my take to be over $150,000 to start, unless your university lawyers get too greedy and change my contract. Of course, I am the only one who can get them this far up the river to take a peek at their investment. If they mess around, I guess I can introduce them to the rest of the fish we haven't eaten yet!" he laughed, as everyone around them chuckled.

"Jack," said John, "now that it's over, what do you think about a little more adventure in your life?"

Jack smiled, "To tell you the truth, I just want to get back home to my wife and kids. I guess that's what everyone says after a major shocking event. I really, really miss them. I guess my life has changed somewhat, now that I have had to kill to survive. But I am still a healer and I always will be. It was fun to help everyone out at the end. I still like the adventure and the prospect of discovery. But," he paused, "next time, no bullets, no spears and especially *NO FISH!*" They all laughed, as the smoke, rose from the fires and mingled softly with the misty haze over the mighty jungle river.

THE END

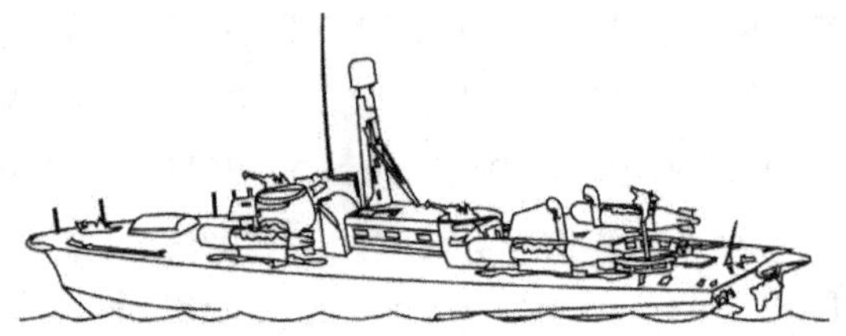

DID YOU ENJOY
THIS NOVEL?

Please feel free to leave a review on Amazon, Goodreads, LibraryThing, Reedsy Discovery, SFBook Reviews, or any of your favorite sources.

You can log onto our website at **www.michaelgazdar.com**, to see the latest books and news.

You can also order the following books in the Lost El Dorado series:

The Return to the Lost El Dorado
The Lost Treasure of the Jamaican Pirate
The Lost Treasure of the Darién Gap
The Lost Treasure of the Nazi Gold Train

Thank you for being an important part of our literary world!

www.ingramcontent.com/pod-product-compliance
Lightning Source LLC
Chambersburg PA
CBHW072100300726
48975CB00003B/646